CROSSING THE LINE

KELLY JAMIESON

To Hannah
Read + dream.
Kelly Jamieson

B

Boldwood

First published in Great Britain in 2025 by Boldwood Books Ltd.

Copyright © Kelly Jamieson, 2025

Cover Design by Head Design Ltd

Cover Images: Shutterstock

Every effort has been made to obtain the necessary permissions with reference to copyright material, both illustrative and quoted. We apologise for any omissions in this respect and will be pleased to make the appropriate acknowledgements in any future edition.

A CIP catalogue record for this book is available from the British Library.

Paperback ISBN 978-1-83633-683-9

Large Print ISBN 978-1-83633-682-2

Hardback ISBN 978-1-83633-681-5

Ebook ISBN 978-1-83633-684-6

Kindle ISBN 978-1-83633-685-3

Audio CD ISBN 978-1-83633-676-1

MP3 CD ISBN 978-1-83633-677-8

Digital audio download ISBN 978-1-83633-679-2

This book is printed on certified sustainable paper. Boldwood Books is dedicated to putting sustainability at the heart of our business. For more information please visit https://www.boldwoodbooks.com/about-us/sustainability/

Boldwood Books Ltd, 23 Bowerdean Street, London, SW6 3TN

www.boldwoodbooks.com

To all the shy, introverted, socially awkward, empathetic peeps out there who are brave enough to push outside your comfort zone and share your gifts with the world.

1

MABEL

"I can't do it."

"Yes, you can," I say.

"I don't know how."

"I'll help you. Here." I take control of the computer mouse. "First, we open Word. Then we click on File... then Blank Document. There."

"Okay." Mrs. Melvin takes a deep breath. "Now what?"

"Just type what you want to say."

I step back to give her privacy to create her document.

"Don't go!" Her head jerks around.

The other library patrons at the rows of computers look up at us.

I smile. "I'm not leaving. I'm right here if you need me."

She nods and faces the monitor again and starts typing.

"Now what?"

I move closer again. "We have to save it. We go to File again..." I point on the monitor and she moves the cursor and clicks. "Then Save As... you need to name it."

"I don't know what to name it."

"Let's call it Melvin letter... good... we'll save it to the desktop."

"I don't see that." She sounds almost ready to cry.

"Click browse..." I gently guide her through the process, then help her access her email online and send the document. This takes longer. I glance at the clock on the bottom of the monitor. I'm scheduled for story time at ten-thirty in the children's section and it's almost that time.

She sends the email, but doesn't attach the document, so we do it again. Then it's done!

"There! You did it!"

The tiny lady beams up at me. "Thank you so much for your help."

"That's what I'm here for."

I delete her document from the computer for her, then quickly return to the desk to get my books for story time as my co-worker Jemal grins. "That took a while. You're so patient."

I smile. "I guess. She's sweet. Okay, I'll be in the children's section."

I trot to the back of the library where a group of kids are gathered. I've never been worried about making a fool of myself, much to my family's dismay, so for the next half hour I make monkey noises and dance like a giraffe and sing off-key.

My day at Sherrinford Public Library is busy and full of helping more people with technology, assisting them with job applications or job search activities, and finding research materials. I also direct a lot of people to the bathrooms.

In between helping people, I push in chairs, pick up slips of paper from the floor, make sure there are no empty chip bags or Starbucks cups left around, and straighten the shelves. Then it's time to go home.

I love my job.

We live close enough to the library that I can walk home. The January air is chilly and my pace is brisk down tree-lined streets, their branches winter-bare. Yesterday's snow has been cleared from the sidewalks and streets and is already melting. I turn at the walk to our house, in a new development here in Sherrinford, Pennsylvania. I prefer older neighborhoods and houses with character, but my boyfriend, Julian, lived in this newbuild when we met, and I moved in with him about a year ago.

My stomach tightens as I near our home.

Julian's a professor of anthropology at Penn State. He's smart and smooth and handsome. When we met, I couldn't believe he was interested in *me*. But lately, I feel like his attraction has turned to annoyance. I don't understand why. He's so critical all the time, even though I've been trying to tone down my quirks so I don't upset him, and trying to be understanding and supportive of his stressors.

Julian arrives home not long after I do. With my music playing, I glue on a smile and dance over to him to kiss him hello, ignoring his head shake. We share how our days went as we make dinner together. But when I tell him about Mrs. Melvin, he shakes his head. "People are idiots."

"She's not an idiot. She just doesn't know how to use technology."

"People need to learn. That's the way the world is now."

"I know, that's why I spent so much time showing her how to do it."

"That shouldn't even be part of your job."

"Well, it is." I smile, but on the inside I'm frowning. "You just said that's the way the world is now. There's a lot more to being a librarian than checking out books. The library is a safe place for people to learn that stuff."

More than a few times, Julian has questioned my career choice. He thinks librarians should be quiet, serious, and orderly. That is not me.

So not me.

I mean, I take my job seriously. I can be professional and quiet when I have to be. But that's not my normal state. I'm the person who misplaces things, who has no control over my social calendar. But I'm better than I used to be!

"Did you know the real name for a hashtag is octothorpe?" I ask Julian as I measure rice.

"No. Is that what you wore to work today?"

I look down at my long flowered skirt and chunky sweater. I've taken off my Doc Marten boots, but I wear those almost every day. "Yeah."

"You need to dress more professionally. Clothes like that make you look unserious. You'll never get promoted if you dress like a hippy."

My laugh is short, since I applied for a promotion a while back and didn't get it. "Maybe I've changed my mind and I don't want to be promoted."

"Of course you do. Everyone wants to move up."

He wants to move up. Promotion to full professor is all he talks about. After that, he has his sights set on department head.

I shrug and turn on the stove.

"Wear something more suitable when we go to Tim's place for dinner this weekend."

My insides twist. *Wear something more suitable.* I nod slowly as I turn on the stove.

Tim is head of the Department of Anthropology and Julian's obsessed with impressing his boss and team at this dinner. Which means I have to dress "suitably." Oof.

"Wait, when is that dinner?" I ask.

"Saturday. I told you weeks ago."

Crappleberries. "I know." I bite my lip. "But that's Bellamy's birthday party."

"That same night?" He turns incredulous eyes on me. "You just realized that now?"

I suck my bottom lip and nod. "I'm sorry. Somehow, I thought your faculty dinner was Friday night."

"Jesus, Mabel. Could you get it together for once?"

"I'm sorry," I say.

He shakes his head. "Well, you'll have to miss her party."

"No. I can't miss it. She's my best friend. We've never missed each other's birthdays in over ten years. And her mom just died." Well, six months ago, but Bell's been having a hard time with it.

His eyebrows jerk together. "You can't miss this dinner. What will people think if you don't come with me?"

"They'll think I had a prior engagement." I attempt a placating smile. "It's not personal. Just tell them that."

"Oh hell, no. You're not missing this dinner."

I roll my lips in and look away. The oil in the pan is smoking. I grab the pieces of chicken I cut up and dump them in. They sizzle and hiss, oil splatters, and a haze of smoke billows into the air.

The smoke detector goes off.

"Mabel!" Julian shouts over the ear-piercing shrieking. "What the hell?"

"I'm sorry! I was distracted. *You* distracted me." I pull the pan off the burner and frantically wave a towel to disperse the smoke.

"Fuck. Now you've ruined our dinner."

"It's not ruined." I stir the chicken, blinking back tears.

"Are you crying?"

"No. The smoke hurt my eyes."

"Don't try to manipulate me with tears to get out of going to that dinner. It won't work."

Impotent anger simmers in my stomach and I focus through a blur on stir-frying the chicken.

"You don't need to go to Bellamy's party," he continues. "She lives too far away. You should make friends here in town."

"I have friends here in town," I say quietly. "But she's my best friend."

He lets out a long-suffering sigh. "If you really love me, Mabel, you'll come to the faculty dinner. You know how important it is to me."

"Let's talk about this later. Is the rice done?" I change the subject.

I don't know when later is going to be because I'm not going to miss my best friend's birthday. But I want to keep the peace. So for the rest of the week, I avoid talking about it. Until Saturday morning.

"Have you decided what you're wearing to dinner tonight?" Julian asks me.

My insides twist painfully because I know what's coming. "I'm not going to the dinner."

"Oh, fuck. Here we go again."

"I promised Bellamy I'd be there. She's been having a rough time. I want to be there for her."

"Mabel. If you don't come to this dinner... we're done."

My head snaps up. I meet his eyes. His are cool and steady.

"That's crazy."

"Oh, I'm the crazy one? I don't think so."

I swallow thickly. My throat burns, my insides feel frozen and empty, and my muscles won't move.

When I met Julian, he was instantly attracted to me. I'd never had much luck with guys; I'm just a bit different. Here was a man – intelligent, handsome, sophisticated, and successful – who was interested in me. It was heady and uplifting. We entered into a whirlwind relationship where he showered me with flowers and gifts and compliments, telling me he'd never met anyone like me, that I was his soul mate, that I understood him so much better than anyone. My family was happy. They like Julian.

Then things started changing. He questioned things about me. I love to dance but he says I'm embarrassing, my clothes are unprofessional, and my friends are boring. But his biggest issue is with me watching hockey. He thinks it's barbaric and boring. But my brother is a professional hockey player. I grew up watching him play and I'll always cheer him on.

When I tried to talk to Julian about these things, he told me he acted like that because he cared about me. When he got controlling, it was because he was afraid to lose me. It didn't make sense, but yet I liked that he cared about me. He'd remind me how good things were when we started dating, and he was right. He told me he'd been in more relationships than I had, and this was how it worked. I started to feel invisible, and yet I still felt lucky to be with him. To be wanted.

Now, I regard him somberly. A flock of sparrows flaps their wings in my midsection. "I'm going to Bellamy's party. And if that means, we're done... then we're done."

He blinks. "You don't mean that."

"I do mean it."

"Mabel. Come on. Aren't I more important to you than her?"

What a question to ask. Asking me to say who's more important in my life. And maybe even a month ago I would have said him. I *should* say him, right? The man I love? But... I can't. "No, Julian. Not when you ask me questions like that. Not when you give me ultimatums. I'm not doing this anymore."

His face reddens. "Mabel, you're being ridiculous."

I hate how he says my name. I try not to punch him in the face. "No. I'm not. I'm doing what's right for me."

"What about me?" he demands. "What about my career?"

"Your career will be fine."

"You would seriously end things between us over this? Come on."

"I seriously would."

"Nobody else will ever love you. You're so flaky."

I wince at the shaft of pain lancing through me. It hurts because... because... I'm afraid it's true. I'm so *fucking* terrified that everything he says about me is true. My insides turn cold and shivery, and for a few seconds, my resolve wavers. Then I lift my chin. "You're trying to change me. And I won't do that. I won't be someone I'm not for a man."

He narrows his eyes at me. "Well, have fun being alone for the rest of your life."

* * *

I stay with Bellamy in Philadelphia that night.

After the party at a trendy restaurant with friends, we go back to her place and I tell her everything that happened this morning. And that has been happening for months. She's not surprised.

"One time I was visiting you and we were going out for dinner and he told you to go change. I hated that." She presses her lips together.

"You told him I looked beautiful. You stuck up for me."

"I tried. It didn't help. And there were other times, too. I hated him."

"You never told me." I regard her sadly over the rim of my wine glass, both of us curled up on her couch, now in our pajamas.

"I tried to hint at it, but you got defensive of him, and it seemed like you really loved him."

"I did love him." My bottom lip pushes sadly out. "I loved how things were at first. But then he changed. Slowly. I told myself he needed me. You know, he didn't have the best upbringing. His dad was really hard on him."

She nods.

"And I always sensed that underneath his confidence was some serious lack of self-esteem. But when I tried to be supportive and understanding, it was never enough. I think I was love-bombed. He was so charming at first. Then it fades away and they start tearing you down."

"Oh, Mabel."

I look up and see her shiny eyes and quivering bottom lip.

"I hate that you went through that. I'm sorry I didn't try harder to make you see what was happening."

One corner of my mouth hitches up. "It probably wouldn't have worked. I probably would have been mad at you. I needed to see it for myself. And no worries about me doing it again. I'm not going to change who I am for a man." I repeat what I told Julian. I've repeated it to myself many times now.

Bellamy nods her approval.

"But what if no man is ever going to accept me for who I am?"

Now she clucks with disapproval. "Not every man is like Julian."

"I know. And I don't need a man to be fulfilled."

Bellamy nods. "I agree with that. But I do think you'll find the right man. The man who'll accept you and worship your crazy questions and love of books and research and your funky wardrobe. Along with your big heart and empathy and energy."

She lifts her wine glass in a toast and my heart expands in my chest at her words. I don't know if I believe that. But I do know that right now, I'm done with men.

2

BEN

"We'd like you to get more involved in the community."

I blink. "Uh. Okay."

I'm sitting in Marc Miller's office. He's the general manager of the New Jersey Storm, the NHL team I play for. He and my coach have called me in for this meeting, and I'm confused.

"We have an opportunity that we think would be perfect for you," he adds.

I swallow and try to tamp down the protest rising inside me. "Okay," I say again. "What is it?"

"The hockey club has been getting more involved with an organization called Keeping Kids Safe," Marc says.

I nod, although I've never heard of the organization.

"Their mission is to help kids affected by abuse. I was talking to Sue Milner, the executive director there, and we think you would be an excellent ambassador."

Why me? But I keep the question to myself. This conversation is getting me flustered.

"Most of the guys have some cause they work for." Marc names a few of my teammates and the charitable organizations they support.

"I donate a thousand dollars for every goal I score to the Fineberg Children's Hospital," I remind him and my coach.

"Yeah, we know that," Coach says. "And that's great. But we're thinking a little more high-profile. It would be great for you to raise awareness of child abuse and draw attention to the group's initiatives."

That sounds… terrifying.

Don't get me wrong. It's not that I don't want to help people, and a group that supports abused kids is fucking admirable. But I'd rather write a check than put myself out there and meet people. And I'd rather play hockey naked, fall on my bare ass, and get frostbite on my balls than do any kind of public speaking.

Again… why me?

"That sounds really… interesting…"

Coach leans forward, his gaze intent on me. "We decided to go with three alternate captains for the rest of the season."

I nod, aware of this. Instead of naming one individual captain when our last one got traded just before Christmas, the team elected to have three alternate captains for the rest of the season. I'm one of them, and proud of it.

Normally a team has two or three alternate captains who support the team captain and fill in for him when needed. The captain is the only player who can discuss things with the refs during games, like questions about penalties and how the rules are interpreted. Officially, captains don't have any real authority, but they're the leader in the dressing room and sometimes take players' concerns to management. They're also the team's representative to the public. Some captains organize social functions, too.

"We want to name one captain and two alternates next season," Coach continues.

Again, I nod. That makes sense.

"You're a good leader for the team," he says. "You're a quiet guy but you lead by example." He pauses. "You're not quiet on the ice."

A half smile hooks up my lips. "True."

"You take in everything and learn," he continues. "You come to play, every day. Your work ethic is strong and that's important. It's something everybody seems to follow."

These words of praise have me tugging at the collar of my shirt. I clear my throat. "Thanks."

"With a little more presence in the community, we think that your leadership-by-example and blue-collar work ethic would allow you to take the next step in your career." He pauses. "Captain."

"Shit, really?" This time the words escape my mouth.

They both laugh.

"Yeah, really," Marc says. "Would you be interested in meeting with Sue? To learn more about what they do and how they help kids?"

It's sad that I actually hesitate.

Our team is playing like shit. We have issues on the ice and in the room. Our last captain, Danny Kosinski, kind of lost the plot. He was more into promoting himself than the team, and more into cliques than team building. I may be quiet, like Coach said, but I see everything that's going on. I know exactly what we need to do to be better.

I could do it.

I just wish I didn't have to do all that other shit outside of hockey to get the job. I hate small talk. I break out in hives in big crowds, and meeting new people makes my hands sweaty. I stay home more than I go out, and I'd rather hang out with a few of my buddies than go partying. Or even dating.

I can smile at the camera in a ceremonial puck drop and shake hands. I've faced the media even though I don't like it. Surely I can organize a few team dinners. Go to management with team concerns? That's a little unnerving. Be the face of a charitable organization? Ugh.

The message is clear, though – if I want to be captain, this is what I have to do.

I love this team. I love my teammates. I'd do anything for these guys and I want us to be winners so bad I can taste it. I played for a championship team once and I know that sweet, sweet taste of success – hoisting the Cup in front of all our fans. I want that again. I want it for this team.

The muscles in my neck and shoulders are hard as hockey pucks. I roll my shoulders, trying to relax. And I say, "Of course."

Ah, fuck. What am I getting myself into?

"Perfect!" Marc beams. "We'll set up a meeting with Sue and you two can talk."

Sure, sure. "Sounds good."

"We have faith in you, Ben." Coach claps a hand on my shoulder. "Prove us right."

I smile and shake hands with them before leaving the office.

Everyone else is gone by now; we had practice this morning and then after lunch in the players' lounge, Coach called me into this meeting. I'm glad there's nobody here to ask what's going on, but I'd kind of like to bounce this off someone. Luckily, I'm staying with my buddy Smitty.

I just bought a condo in his building after the lease on my apartment expired. I found this place in the same building where Smitty and a couple of other guys live, but I have two months with nowhere to live so Smitty offered me his spare bedroom.

I head out to the parking area reserved for players. My new apartment building's not far from the Hargrave Center in Hoboken, where we play games and practice, so it doesn't take long to get there. When I walk in, Smitty's sitting on the couch, talking on the phone. He waves at me and I walk to the fridge for a bottle of water.

"I guess she can stay here," Smitty says unenthusiastically. "But maybe she and Julian should be trying to work things out."

My ears perk up. Someone else is coming to stay here? And it sounds like Smitty's sister, since her boyfriend is a guy named Julian. What's going on?

"Yeah, yeah. I know. But she'll have to sleep on the couch."

Okay, whew. I was a little worried I was getting the boot. I guzzle cold water, leaning against the counter.

"I will. Okay. Bye, Mom."

He ends the call and drops his phone on the coffee table. He shoves both hands into his shaggy, dark reddish hair and mutters, "Hell."

"What's wrong?"

He looks up with a resigned expression. "My sister's coming to stay here for a while." He rolls his eyes. "Sorry."

I saunter over and sit in a chair. "That's okay. It's your place. You want me to move out?"

"No, no, it's fine. You were here first."

I snort. "Okay. But she's your sister."

"I know. And typical Mabel – apparently, she's leaving her boyfriend and moving to New York. Or New Jersey, since she wants to stay here while she finds a new job and an apartment."

"Whoa."

I know Mabel. Smitty and I played hockey together as teenagers, back in Westville, Pennsylvania, so I know his family. His twin sister Mabel was a character. I knew she had a crush on me, but I avoided her because she scared the shit out of me, to be honest. She was so full of life, always surrounded by crowds of girls, and I was awkward and tight-lipped, since everything I said came out wrong. The day she accidentally pulled my pants down in front of the whole school was a clear sign that I should stay miles away from her.

"Yeah. Shit. I thought she was really happy with Julian. I don't know what's gotten into her. Mom's not happy either."

"Maybe she met someone else."

He makes a face. "Eh... I don't know. Mabel's a little kooky, but she's not a cheater."

I nod.

"What a pain in the ass. And it has to happen when you're here. Sorry, man."

"Hey, no worries. If you want, I can totally find somewhere else to stay." I could go to a nice anonymous hotel and hide away by myself for the next six weeks or so. I really hate not having my own space where I can retreat and be alone, but staying in a hotel sounds depressing.

"As long as you don't mind sharing a bathroom and having her sleep on the couch, it's fine. Hopefully it won't be long."

I can't say I'm enthused about another person moving in, and it being Mabel isn't great, mostly because of our history. But it's been ten years since I saw her. She probably doesn't even remember me.

"Crap, I forgot about your meeting with Coach and Mr. Miller," Smitty says. "What was it about?"

I discharge a long breath. "They want me to get involved with some organization that helps abused kids."

"Really? They told you that?"

"Yeah."

"Huh. I mean, we're all kind of expected to do community work, but I've never heard of them telling us exactly which charity to work for."

"They said…" I'm not sure if I should even tell Smitty this. "Don't say anything to anyone else about this, okay?"

His eyebrows lift. "Okay."

"They said if I do this, I might be named captain."

His jaw drops nearly to his lap. "Shut the fuck up."

"No lie." I rub my chin.

"That's fantastic!"

"I'm kinda tripping about it."

"Why? You'd be a great captain."

I'm silent. There aren't many people I'm comfortable enough with to spill my guts to, but Smitty is one of them. I've known him the longest of any of the guys on the team, even though we played on different teams for years. We were good buddies as teenagers, stayed friends as pro players, and hung out and trained together every summer when we went home. But still I hesitate. "I'm not cut out for a bunch of PR stuff. I'd be the face of this organization, and you know what that means. Making speeches, press conferences, ribbon-cutting bullshit." I heave a sigh like I'm about to face a firing squad. "That's not exactly my comfort zone."

He nods slowly. "Yeah. But you can do it."

"I'm not so sure." I give him a wry smile.

"Of course you can. And you want to be captain."

"Yeah. I do. I…" How big-headed is this going to sound? "I think I can help the team." Okay, I tamed that down a bit too much. I need to sound more confident. "I know what the team needs. I saw the crap Danny was pulling. I know how he made the guys feel. I know it really put a damper on morale."

"True."

"I feel like I can turn things around. It's just… the people stuff is hard for me, you know?" I rarely admit that out loud, but Smitty knows me and how much I hate being the center of attention. It's like introversion is a character defect or something. There've definitely been times I've felt ashamed of it. Obviously, people know I'm kind of reserved and I don't say much, but admitting how hard and exhausting it is for me to do normal people shit is embarrassing.

"I know." He makes a duck-lips face. "But I think you can do it."

"Yeah?"

"Hell, yeah. You're a great player. You work your ass off. You *show* us how to do it."

Something heats behind my breastbone. "Thanks." His confidence in me makes me want to do it even more. "But the outside stuff... ugh. I don't wanna."

He laughs. "It won't be so bad."

"Easy for you to say." Smitty may not be a wild child like his twin sister, but he's friendly and sociable and has no trouble finding women. Unlike me. I mean, I have no trouble finding them either. For one night. More than that, though, and they bail.

"Yeah, I know, but seriously, you got this. You have to do this. You have to take this opportunity."

I nod slowly. "I know."

"Okay, that's settled. Let's go out to celebrate tonight."

"We can't tell anyone else."

"I know, I know. But I'm sure Dilly and Crusher are in for tacos and tequila."

Our teammates: Dillon Landry and Nash Wilson. We hockey players gotta have our nicknames. Smitty is actually Marek Smits and I'm Benny to my teammates.

Smitty grabs his phone and starts texting. "They don't need a reason for tequila."

"True that." I grin.

* * *

When my buddies ask me if I got in trouble when I got called to Coach's office, my mind goes blank. I can't think of anything to bullshit them with, and I can't tell them the truth. I stare vacantly at them. Then Smitty bails me out by saying, "They talked about possible line changes."

They frown at Smitty.

"What?" Crusher says. "Why was Mr. Miller there?"

"I don't know," I manage to say with a shrug. We've got guacamole and chips in front of us along with flights of tequilas. I pick up my glass and sip my Extra Añejo.

"What's your most embarrassing sex story?" Smitty asks all of us.

Jesus. Way to change the subject. He couldn't talk about the weather?

"It has to be the time a woman was trying to deep throat me and threw up on me." Crusher picks up a chip. "That was bad."

We all groan in sympathy.

"Was she drunk or just disgusted?" Dilly asks with an evil smirk.

"Asshole," Crusher says. "She was wasted."

"Mine are all about whiskey dick," Dilly says sadly. "It doesn't matter how hot she is, sometimes the big boy just won't cooperate."

We all make sympathetic noises.

"Big boy." Crusher lifts an eyebrow.

"Let's not go there," Smitty says. "How about you, Benny? Got an embarrassing sex story?"

I think. "I do not," I finally say. Like I'm going to tell them about the first time I had sex. I told the girl I loved her and then never saw her again. I know better than that now. My sexcapades have not been plentiful, but they've been uneventful in terms of embarrassment, thank God.

"Okay, this one's good," Smitty says. "I was going out with this girl in Binghamton when I played for the farm team. She kept getting itchy... down there. We weren't using condoms. We were afraid she was allergic to my semen. So she went to her doctor and he told her to tell me to stop eating peanuts. She had a peanut allergy."

"Shut up." Crusher stares at him.

"Truth." Smitty holds up a hand, grinning. "When I stopped eating peanuts, the problem was fixed."

"Or you could have used condoms," I say.

He gives me a look. "I'd rather give up peanuts."

The guys all laugh and I grin.

"Okay, this didn't happen to me," Crusher says. "But a guy I knew got bit on the schlong, she was going down on him and when he came, she accidentally bit down, hard. He was spurting blood and had to be rushed to the hospital."

"Yeah, there's a big artery there," Smitty says. "Wow."

"Okay, that's embarrassing," Dilly says. "At least I was the only one who knew about Carrie vomiting on me."

"Until now," I point out, scooping guacamole with a chip.

"He passed out and came to in the ambulance with a tourniquet on his dick. *That's* embarrassing."

"Oh, hell yeah." Dilly nods.

"He could never have another blow job. He had blow job PTSD."

"That sucks. I love blow jobs," Smitty says.

We all grunt our agreement.

The waitress arrives with our meals, ending our bizarre conversation. I'm used to that with these guys.

We talk hockey during dinner, although we try not to talk shop all the time. Trying to eat light, I ordered a pan-seared chicken breast with a sauce made of pumpkin seeds and tomatoes. I'm all about healthy eating during the season. The chips and tequila are a treat. You have to treat yourself once in a while, and I did get sort of good news today.

I could be the next team captain. It still has me tripping.

After dinner, we walk home from the restaurant along the Hudson River walkway. The view of Manhattan across the river is stunning, all glittering skyscrapers reflecting on the water, lights turning the clouds above into a moody oil painting. A frigid wind blows off the river and a few icy flakes of snow pelt us as we near home. It's a really nice building with tons of amenities, like a gym and valet parking, even a coffee station. I also like that the apartments have fireplaces, and I can't wait to stretch out in front of it with the book I'm reading.

The elevator stops on fifteen to let out Crusher and Dilly, who room together, then continues to seventeen where Smitty's condo is. He walks in ahead of me and stops short.

Music blasts from speakers. Music we did not leave on when we left for dinner. We walk in to see a woman dancing in the middle of the living room, throwing her long hair around, who then screams along to the music, "Who's afraid of little old me!"

We both freeze in place, staring.

"Aaaaah! You're home!" she cries as she spots us, then throws herself into Smitty's arms. "Hiiiiii!"

It's Mabel.

"Hey. I thought you weren't coming until tomorrow." He hugs her back. He rags on Mabel, but he really loves her and they're pretty tight.

"I know, I thought so too, but I was all packed and..." Her voice hitches, barely perceptibly. "And I wanted to come!"

I take note of the tightness at the corners of her eyes and the fake brightness of her smile.

She steps back and taps her phone, ending Taylor's song. Silence falls around us. When she looks up, her gaze lands on me over Smitty's shoulder. "Oh. Ben." She blinks eyelashes long enough to give off a breeze, her tone noticeably cooling. "Hi."

She seems surprised to see me. I thought Smitty told his family I was staying with him temporarily.

I feel the tops of my ears burning and I shove my hands into the pockets of my jacket. I resist the urge to disappear into my room. "Hi, Mabel." *Say something. Some kind of small talk. Anything. Fuck. I got nothin'.*

As usual, awkward silence fills the void.

3

MABEL

"Didn't Mom tell you Ben's staying here?" Marek asks me, heading to the couch. "That's why you have to sleep on the couch."

"No, she did not tell me that." I frown. I did not expect this. I thought I'd have a room of my own where I could wallow in my misery and shame and spend hours listening to T. Swift and doomscrolling on my phone between crying jags and eating boxes of Cheez-Its.

I look around. I can handle sleeping on the couch, I guess, although living with two guys and not having a room of my own is... not ideal. What if they spy on me when I'm asleep and I drool on my pillow? What if my boob falls out of my tank top while I'm sleeping? It happens!

And one of the guys I'm living with is Ben Antonov.

The guy I had a crush on at age seventeen. The guy I followed everywhere. The guy I watched at every hockey game. And lusted for. Okay, I was more stan than fan.

He was also the guy who avoided me at every turn. That still stings. In my mind, I called him stuck-up, stupid, rude. He rejected me and that hurt, therefore he was a jerk.

Now here we are. Fantastic.

I knew Ben plays for the same team as Marek now, but I didn't anticipate actually seeing him, never mind living with him.

"Is this a permanent roomie situation?" I attempt a smile but I'm just showing my top teeth, no doubt looking like a grouchy poodle.

"No. I'm only staying a couple of months," Ben says, not meeting my eyes. "I'm moving into a condo in this building, but I don't take possession of it until 1 March."

Great. He still hates me.

"Okay, then!" I flash another smile and grab a suitcase. "I'll put my things over here."

Floor-to-ceiling windows offer a spectacular view of the Manhattan skyline across the river, but how the hell am I going to sleep like this?

I park my suitcases in a corner.

"Did you have dinner?" Marek asks. "We just ate."

"No. But it's okay, I'm not hungry."

"If you need something, help yourself." He gestures at the kitchen.

"I'm sure you're well-stocked with junk food."

"Uh..."

"I'm kidding. Don't worry, I can look after myself."

"I'm gonna, uh... hit the hay," Ben says. Without looking at me, he disappears down the hall.

I meet Marek's eyes. "Sorry. This is weird."

"It's fine."

"Do you have any beer?"

His lips twitch. "There might be a couple in the fridge."

I stalk over to the fridge and open the door. As expected, it's full of yogurt, greens, and a lot of chocolate milk. However, I spot a few cans of ale at the back. I grab one, pull the tab, and take a gulp.

"I think that's Ben's beer."

I choke and nearly spew beer, the bubbles stinging my nose. "Shit."

Marek laughs. "It's fine. I'm sure he won't mind."

I'm sure he will. Too late now. I drop down onto the couch with my beverage.

"So, what happened?"

I eye him. "You mean with Julian?"

"Yeah."

I purse my lips and inspect the pull tab on my beer. "It wasn't working out."

"That's pretty vague."

Yes. Yes, it is. I'm still too ashamed to tell my brother what I let happen. "It wasn't any one thing. And it was mutual."

"Are you sure? Because he texted me about a week ago and asked if I knew where you were. He said he was worried about you."

My head snaps up. "What? What did you say?"

"Well, I *didn't* know where you were, so I told him that." He studies my face. "When did you move out?"

"A few weeks ago. I stayed with some friends."

"You quit your job?"

"Yeah. I had to work my two weeks' notice. And now I'm here! I'm excited to move to the big city."

Unfortunately, my twin brother has always been perceptive when it comes to how I'm feeling and he frowns at my dissembling. "I thought you two were good. I thought you'd get married."

Jesus. I swallow, my stomach frothing. Maybe it's the beer. I take another swig. "I did too, for a while. Oh, well! Thank you, next!"

After a long moment of prickly silence he says, "Mom and Dad are worried about you."

"I've talked to them. I told them I'm fine." I roll my eyes.

He still seems dubious. "Okay. Well. We have our morning skate tomorrow, but when I get home, I'll take you out and show you around the neighborhood."

"You don't have to do that. I've been here before. I'll figure it out. I don't want to be any trouble."

"Ha. Mabel, you're *always* trouble." He says it affectionately but still, I wince a little inside. My reputation is going to follow me for the rest of my life. He stands. "I'll get some bedding for you."

"Just show me where it is."

He leads me to a closet in the hall and pulls out sheets and pillows. Then he shows me how to lower the shades on all the windows with the touch of a button – fancy! – and he, too, heads to his room.

"Marek."

He stops and turns. "Yeah?"

"If Julian contacts you again... please don't tell him I'm here. Tell him I'm okay. But don't tell him where I am."

He frowns and gives me another long look. "Okay. Sure. Good night."

I turn the couch into a bed, luckily finding the big soft throw blanket I gave Marek for Christmas last year. Then I hike to the bathroom to wash my face and change into my nightie. I take in the men's products in the shower, and the hair-styling cream on the vanity. Ben's. His brown hair is thick and kind of long on top and for some reason it tickles me that unassuming Ben uses styling cream to get that perfect tousled look. The products are all the same brand, one I don't recognize. I pick up the beard oil sitting on the counter. He has a beard now. Not a Brent Burns beard, one of those close-cropped ones that's barely more than stubble. It outlines the strong oblong shape of his jaw and frames his smile. Though I didn't see him smile much tonight. I do remember that he has a great smile though; wide and white.

I huff out a laugh, remembering my adolescent crush. Poor Ben.

Poor me, for suffering all that rejection.

I set my toiletry bag at one end of the long vanity and scrub off my makeup. I slip my nightie over my head and scrunch up my travel clothes. I think Marek has a washer and dryer here. I desperately need to do laundry.

With one lamp on beside the couch, I snuggle in with another beer and my phone.

I blocked Julian's phone number, and I blocked him on Messenger, Facebook, and Snapchat. I didn't expect it, but after the night I stayed at Bellamy's he blew up my phone – first demanding I come home, then apologizing, then begging for us to talk. Not gonna lie, it was hard to resist him begging. I cried. I stayed strong. And I blocked. *After* I replied a few times, telling him it was over.

I send Mom a text, telling her I'm here and I'm fine. I've already asked her to not share my whereabouts with Julian, which she thankfully agreed to even though she's disappointed we've broken up.

I look up at the ceiling and expel a long breath. "God, I wish I had some Cheez-Its."

Yes, my self-soothing techniques have included copious amounts of alcohol and junk food. Yes, I'm aware that's not the healthiest approach.

I'm so tired.

I've tried to keep myself angry at Julian. Anger will keep me strong. It'll keep me from dissolving into an ocean of tears. It'll keep me from caving and running back to him. I'm not even going to listen to him.

But that anger is exhausting. Even my bones are tired.

And even though I'm trying to stay angry, those thoughts creep in – that Julian was the way he was because I'm not good enough. And then I feel sad, and scared, and I run with that sadness like an NFL running back on cocaine. Nobody will ever love me. I will live the rest of my life alone, like Julian said. I'll probably get several cats and turn into the stereotypical librarian – I'll yell at the kids who make noise and scowl at patrons disapprovingly over my reading glasses when they ask for materials on birth control. I'll be a spinster who enjoys bingo and jigsaw puzzles. Maybe I'll take up knitting.

This all makes me even more tired.

* * *

I awake to soft rustling noises. My eyes pop open and I listen. What is that? Wait, where am I?

I lift my head and peer towards the sounds. Right. Marek's place.

The apartment is dark with all the blinds closed but light slices across the room as the refrigerator door opens. Then closes.

I push the covers down and sit up. "Hey."

The shadowy figure startles. "Oh. Hey. I was trying not to wake you."

Ben. I thought it was Marek.

"That's okay. What time is it?"

"Eight thirty-four."

I smile at the precise answer and slide my legs over the side of the couch. "I would kill for coffee. You don't happen to have coffee over there, do you?"

"Yeah, there's a Keurig."

"Perfect." I stand and pad to the kitchen in my bare feet. "You can turn the light on."

Ben nods and hits the switch for the kitchen lights.

I pause at the counter, yawn, and raise my arms above my head in a full-body stretch. "Why do they call it beauty sleep when you wake up looking like a hot mess?" I fluff my tangled hair and open my eyes and... I'm pretty sure I catch Ben looking at my thighs. I tug the hem of my nightshirt down, heat running up my throat.

It's a good-sized kitchen, basically galley-shaped with the stove and cupboards on one side and the open counter with a sink on the other. I spy the coffee machine and squeeze by Ben to get to it.

Christ on a bike, he smells good.

Is that the body wash I spied in the shower last night? The one described as white pepper, dark amber, and black oak? It's enough to make my knees weak.

Wait. This is the guy who snubbed me. Repeatedly. Never mind how good he smells.

Ignoring my strangely shaky legs and spinning head, I open a cupboard to look for coffee pods. Jackpot. I fumble one out of the carton and manage to successfully start a cup brewing.

"You need a mug," Ben says.

"Ack! Shit!"

He hands me one and I shove it under the spout just as the magical elixir flows out.

"Thank you." I slap my forehead. "This is why I need coffee." I take a breath. "I'll go get dressed while my coffee's brewing."

I squeeze past him again, sucking in like I'm trying to fit into my high-school jeans, and zip over to my suitcases. I paw through the clothes, searching for something clean and appropriate, finally grabbing a pair of leggings and a sweater. And a bra and panties.

As I straighten, I'm aware that my long T-shirt again rode up while I was bending over. I close my eyes. *Please baby Jesus and the baby donkey, don't let Ben have seen my ass cheeks.*

Without looking at him, I march to the bathroom and get dressed. My face in the mirror is crimson, with an attractive pillow crease on one cheek. I rub at it and sigh. Oh, well.

Ben has set my coffee on the counter where he's sitting on one of the stools eating a bowl of something. I pick up my coffee and lean across to peer at his breakfast. "What is that?"

"Overnight oats."

I frown. "What are the black things?"

"Chia seeds."

"Ah. That sounds healthy." He also has strawberries on top of it. "Is it good?"

"Yeah." He pauses. "Want to try some?"

"Oh, that's okay! I'll pick up some Pop-Tarts. That's my favorite breakfast. Along with a good cup of Joe." I lift my mug and smile brightly.

"Pop-Tarts."

"Yeah. My favorite are the frosted confetti ones. They taste like birthday cake, which I love. I also like the Eggo ones. But they taste like an Eggo, so you might as well eat an Eggo. I should pick up some of those too. I like waffles." I sip my coffee. "Do you like Pop-Tarts?"

"I haven't had one since I was twelve."

"Oh. Right. You must be into nutrition like Marek is. I get it. You're pro athletes. Your body is your tool." I stop. "That didn't come out right."

He bites his lip.

"I mean you need to worship your body," I say hastily. "Oh, fuck. Shut up, Mabel."

His lips spread into an actual smile. "I know what you mean."

"Where's Marek? Is he up yet?"

"Yeah, he went out to get some fruit."

"Well, damn. I could have asked him to pick up Pop-Tarts." I sigh heavily. "But I have all day and you guys have to go to work!"

"Right."

"What time is your morning skate?"

"We like to get there around nine." He glances at his phone, sitting on the counter. "Lots of time."

"Do you guys drive together?"

"Yeah. And sometimes our buddies Crusher and Dilly. They live in this building, too."

"Carpooling is good. Better for the environment. Saves on gas. Not that you guys need to worry about money." Jesus, I have to stop babbling.

The door opens and Marek breezes in. "Oh, hey, you're awake. Did you sleep okay on the couch?"

"I actually did. Crashed like a log." I pause, that simile not quite working, then shrug. "Hey, can I do laundry today?"

"Sure. The washer and dryer are behind the doors next to the closet in the hall."

"Great."

Marek starts throwing things into a blender – the frozen berries he just bought, a scoop of protein powder, a squeeze of honey, and milk.

"Did I tell you last night you need a haircut?" I ask him.

Ben snorts softly and scoops up his oats.

"No. And I don't need a haircut." Marek runs a hand through his shaggy curls. His dark coppery hair's about the same color as mine, minus the balayage highlights. "I like it like this."

"Okay." I shrug and drink my coffee.

I move out of the kitchen and find the remote, then open the blinds on the windows. The sky is overcast, with pewter clouds making the light dull and cold. With my coffee, I stroll over to a window to take in the view. The steel-colored Hudson River stretches out in front of Manhattan, the buildings a jumble of block shapes, the spire of the Empire State Building reaching to the clouds.

I'm going to live here now.

Not right here, as in this apartment. I'll find my own place, as soon as I can, although I hear that's a challenge in New York. I pull air into my lungs and let it out slowly.

Who am I, even?

I'm no longer Julian's partner. I'm no longer a librarian. I'm no longer a member of the Sherrinford and Penn State community. I'm pissed about all that. I've lost all that, and what has Julian lost? Other than me, who he manipulated for his own purposes. It's not fair.

My jaw and temples ache and I realize I'm grinding my molars together. I force myself to relax my jaw and take another sip of coffee.

Julian manipulated me into depending on his approval and now I don't have that and... and I was trying so hard to please him and be someone else, I'm not sure who I really am anymore. I'm hollowed out. Cold and empty. Scared.

"Hey."

I start and turn at the low voice behind me. It's Ben, his thick eyebrows drawn together, his mouth a straight line. He shoves his hands into the pockets of his jeans, raising broad shoulders. His body is hard and fit, long, and lean.

I glance to the kitchen, but Marek has disappeared.

I blink at Ben. The intensity of his expression sends hot sparks sizzling over my skin, yet the softness of his voice confuses me. A tremor flutters in my middle. Seconds tick by.

Then he says quietly, "Are you okay?"

4

BEN

I've never seen Mabel look like this – her brown eyes are big and shadowy, like she's in pain, and her mouth is soft, the bottom lip extra full as if she's super sad. Since she woke up and came into the kitchen, I tried to ignore her bare thighs in the long T-shirt she was wearing. I resolutely refused to look at her chest, and I only let myself eyeball the backs of her legs as her shirt rode higher when she bent over for one second. Maybe two. When she squeezed past me, I steeled myself against the brush of her arm against mine and didn't even breathe until she was gone, but the warm, flowery scent of her lingered in the air.

But now I forget the hot feelings she stirred in me and I'm kind of worried.

She gazes back at me for a long moment, then smiles. Her eyes crinkle up at the corners appealingly and that smile has always been magnetic, even when she was a teenager.

Yeah, I'd rather not remember those days.

Being around Mabel back then was excruciating. When she looked at me, I got even more tongue-tied and awkward than I normally was. She was pretty and fun and on fire, and I was a doofster who played hockey. Sure, the girls liked the guys who played hockey, but after a couple of hours with me painfully trying to make conversation, I was usually curbed pretty quick. So I focused my time and attention on hockey, not girls.

I'm pretty sure Mabel had a crush on me back then. She persisted more than other girls in trying to get to know me, but like I said, I was even more awkweird than usual with her so I tried to avoid her. Then there was that incident at school when she accidentally pantsed me. Jesus. I still break out in a hot sweat remembering that.

"I'm fine." She beams up at me. "All good."

But I can see the cheerfulness is forced. I search her face until the silence becomes excruciating.

"Okay." I nod. "Good."

"I need more coffee!" She holds up her mug and moves around me to the kitchen.

Now she's fully dressed in a pair of black leggings and a loose fuzzy white sweater, but I still can't stop myself from watching her.

"Okay, ready Freddy?" Smitty calls, emerging from his room with phone and wallet in hand. "Who's driving?"

"Freddy?" Leaning on the counter, Mabel turns an amused glance on me.

I shake my head. "He has all sorts of weird expressions." I start toward the door. "I'm ready."

Smitty grins. "See you later, alligator."

Mabel groans. "That's so old. You need to do better than that."

"Gotta go, buffalo."

She rolls her eyes and I follow Smitty out of the apartment.

"Crusher said he's driving today," I tell my teammate, pushing the button for the fifteenth floor in the elevator.

We make a quick stop to pick up Crusher and Dilly, then continue down to the underground parking.

On the way to the arena, we stop for coffees. We have our game day meeting at nine-thirty and talk about what we need to focus on tonight playing against the Charleston Cyclones. After that we hit the ice for about an hour. Reporters in the stands watch as we do our line rushes.

Today I'm thinking about what Coach and Marc Miller said to me yesterday. It makes me more aware of what I'm doing on the ice, more conscious of the fact that they're probably watching me, more mindful of how I participate and interact with the other guys.

They really think I could be captain.

It adds a little speed to my feet and a little power to my shot. I observe the other guys a bit more critically than I usually do, although I'm always paying attention to what everyone else is doing. I don't always do anything about it, but today when I see Noah Lawson, one of our young D-men, really dialed in, I skate over to him as we wind up. "Good focus," I tell him. "You look ready for tonight."

He doesn't smile. He never smiles. It's a running joke. "Thanks."

Well. I tried.

I'm pretty set in my game-day routine. After the morning skate, I go stretch and spend some quality time with a foam roller. I fucking hate it but also kind of love it. I've never been very flexible and lately I've been feeling really tight in my shoulders and upper back. I work my way down to my hamstrings and quads. When I find a painful spot, I pause there. "Fuuuuu-uck," I breathe out as the pain rises to a peak. "Jesus."

It feels so good when I stop.

Then I eat lunch with the guys in the player lounge, today taking chicken, broccoli, and quinoa, and head home for my nap. As Crusher drives us home, I remember Mabel being there. Shit. It's bad enough I'm staying with someone else and not in my own place, now we have a chatty roommate sleeping on our couch. Which makes me feel guilty, because *I* should be the one sleeping on the couch. Or staying in a hotel. Maybe I should do that. Hotels suck, though.

So, when I follow Smitty into his place, I mumble a greeting to Mabel and head straight to my room. I can't mess with the routine. I always lie down at one-thirty, scroll through TikTok for twenty minutes, then sleep until three-thirty. Although, it does take a little longer to get to sleep than usual, with the faint voices floating down the hall from the living room as Smitty and his sister talk. Smitty's not locked into a nap on game days. He sleeps if he feels like it, sometimes an hour, sometimes two if he's tired, or not at all. We've always been different that way.

When the apartment goes quiet and my eyes are closed in the dim room I can pretend I'm alone and go to sleep. I love my game-day naps.

I also love my post-nap snack – beef jerky, pretzels, and an apple.

This all might sound anal, but I used to be even stricter about my routines. I didn't like how messed up I felt when something went wrong, though. Because shit does go wrong – like one day they didn't have Cool Blue Gatorade – and you have to be able to roll with it.

I pick out a suit and get dressed. I only have a few suits and they're all pretty old. The social media team is always taking "walk in" photos of us before games and posting them online, and things have gotten competitive between some of the guys. Crusher spends a fortune on custom suits, and Dilly has a selection of hats he always wears. Archie dresses as outlandishly as usual. They never take pictures of me, but I'm totally fine with that.

I pause at the door of my room, bracing myself to encounter Mabel, then stride out to the living room. Which is empty.

Okay.

That's fine. Good. I find my beef jerky. But when I look for my pretzels, they're gone. What the hell?

Marek emerges from his room, also dressed in a suit and tie.

"Did you eat my pretzels?" I ask him, peering into a cupboard.

"No."

"I can't find them."

He makes a face. "I hope Mabel didn't eat them."

"Oh hell, no." I whip my head around to stare at him. "She wouldn't do that. Would she?"

"It's possible." He grabs a protein bar.

"Didn't you ever teach her not to touch your snacks? Especially on game day."

He laughs. "I don't care about my snacks as much as you do. And the last time she and I lived together, we were seventeen."

Well. This is why I try to relax about my routine. Shit happens.

The door of the condo opens and Mabel bursts in, arms laden with shopping bags. "Hi!" She heads straight toward us and deposits her load on the counter. "Whew!" She shoves her long hair back and smiles at us. "I went shopping."

Smitty nods, one eyebrow lifted. "Yeah, you did. Hey, did you eat Benny's pretzels?"

I frown. I was just going to let it go.

"I did!" She throws her hands up. "But I bought you more!" She rummages through reusable bags and pulls out a bag of the exact kind I like. "Here you go!"

"Thanks." I take them, annoyed about how relieved I feel.

"I'm sorry." She gives me a contrite look that's fucking adorable. My annoyance fades. "I was desperate for junk food. I need crunchy things to relieve my stress." She snaps her teeth together.

I blink.

"Your stress," Smitty repeats.

"Actually, I was bored." She shrugs. "I don't really like pretzels." She begins unpacking things and I take note of Cheez-Its, rice crackers, and popcorn. "I mean, I like them, but they're not my favorite. I'm glad you have an air fryer, because I can make my carrot chips." She pulls out a big bag of carrots, then a huge jar of almonds, followed by taco chips.

I don't know what to make of all this.

"Time to go." Smitty opens the dishwasher to deposit his glass. "Are you sure you don't want to come to the game tonight?"

Mabel purses her lips and sighs. "Maybe the next one? I kind of want to hole up here with my Cheez-Its."

I meet Smitty's eyes. That is not like Mabel. She loved coming to our games when we were kids. She also hated staying home alone. A feeling of unease pulses in my gut.

Smitty hesitates, then shrugs. "Okay. Maybe the next one."

"Yeah."

We head out and I'm glad I'm driving tonight since it takes my mind off Mabel and her abundance of junk food and sad eyes.

Back at the arena, I go in the cold tub, cut a stick, change my skate laces, and listen to music. I have a game-day playlist I always listen to – but I do change it every season. Having the playlist makes it easy so I can focus on the game. Right now, it's upbeat stuff like Daft Punk, Kygo, and the Weeknd.

I don't talk much, but now I wonder if I should. The captain of the team should be more involved. The idea makes me tired. I'm trying to conserve my energy for the game. How the fuck can I ever be captain of this team? I shake my head as I tape a stick.

But now I'm noticing I'm not the only one who doesn't talk much. I glance around the room as everyone does their own thing. Shit. I remember what it was like playing for the Chicago Aces. With coach Brad Wendell and captain Marc Dupuis, the team was a unit. Brad was a great communicator who knew how to get the best out of all his players. Marc "Super Duper" Dupuis was a role model for everyone. They developed a culture that valued collaboration, accountability, respect, and rewarded effort before results. And they got results, winning three Stanley Cups in a row.

Tonight's game against the Cyclones is a big game. We have a history. Last season they beat us out for the last wildcard playoff spot, eliminating our playoff hopes. This is the first time we've played them this season and I think we're all remembering our humiliation at their hands.

And they're in our division, so every game against them is a four-point game in the race to the playoffs. Both teams have been playing less than great. Right now, we're ahead of them in the standings, but a win for them could jump them above us.

"We need to redeem ourselves," Dilly says in the room after the warmup. "We can't let them do that to us again."

We all nod. I feel like I should say something, too. But I don't know what.

Coach reminds us not to let our emotions get the better of us. Yeah, we hate this team, but we need to stick to our game.

He's right, too.

It's time to hit the ice. Our goalie, Archie, is always first on, and he's dialed in, with the weird feral look in his eyes he has when he's in the zone. He's an odd guy – bizarre habits, strong opinions, doesn't give a fuck what people think – but he's a good goalie and this year he's been playing fantastic.

I jump onto the ice. The lights are flashing, the crowd is cheering, and I do a few quick laps around our own end. Energy flows through me, making me feel big and powerful. Fuck, yeah. I love this game.

Now we just have to win.

5

MABEL

Popcorn is the perfect snack for hockey. It's not just a tradition; it's perfect because you can mindlessly scoop it into your mouth over and over while watching the game and never really get full because it's all air. But it is crunchy. And salty. My favorite things.

I settle on Marek's couch with a big bag of popcorn I bought earlier to watch the Storm game. I don't always get to watch Marek's games; there are too many during the season, geez, they play eighty-two games which is insane. But I like to watch when I can.

The team is coming onto the ice for the anthems and the camera zooms in on Ben as he enters. I'm startled at the intense look on his face – eyes focused, jaw set, mouth firm. He's such a quiet guy off the ice, friendly enough but reserved. Seeing that fierceness on his face is... hot.

He's one of the starting players so he lines up on the blue line as the anthem plays. He's the biggest player out there. I watch him drop his head forward, his feet sliding back and forth on his blades. Then he puts on his helmet and lines up at the faceoff circle.

Ah, shit.

This is all bringing back high school – going to Marek's games, watching Ben, getting all worked up. My friends all loved the hockey players and I loved that I had an in with the team because of my brother. I also loved that I had an "in" with Ben.

I blow out a long sigh. That crush never worked out for me. I tried so hard that last year of high school to get him to notice me, and oh yeah, he noticed me, but not in the way I wanted.

My friends and I got invited to parties where hockey players were. Ben drank water and stood in the corner despite our best efforts to flirt with him. I wasn't the only girl interested in him; his standoffishness and brooding expression intrigued all of us. My friend Jenny went out with him once. I was so jealous, but after, she told us not to bother. According to her, Ben had no rizz and was the most boring date ever. That didn't deter me; he fascinated me, with his aloof demeanor, his impressive hockey skills, his rare smile that was surprisingly sweet with an intriguing hint of shyness.

But Ben avoided me like I had Ebola, especially after that unfortunate incident where I exposed his dinosaur boxer shorts. It kind of hurt.

On his first shift, Ben lays a crushing hit on a Cyclone player that has the crowd cheering.

Holy crappleberries.

That seems to set the tone for the game, with a lot of fast action and physical play.

The Storm get possession of the puck and with some slick passes, take it out of their zone, through the neutral zone, and in on the Cyclone's net. The first shot is kicked away by the goalie but Ben gets the rebound and quickly snaps it into the net.

"Yeah!" I throw my arms in the air. "Wooooo!"

I feel unreasonably proud of him as I watch the replays.

He's a good player. I knew that in high school. He and Marek were both scouted by NHL teams and expected to be drafted. Then they went away to different colleges, got drafted by different teams, and my passionate crush faded.

This is bringing it all back.

Which is bonkers because I'm broken-hearted and depressed. My boyfriend, who I loved, turned out to be an abusive, raging narcissist. My whole life has been blown up. I should not be thinking horny thoughts about anyone, let alone Marek's friend. Who avoided me in high school. Who lives here right now.

Awkward.

Shocker. Me making things awkward.

I'm just lonely. I miss Julian. Sort of. There's no way I'm getting involved with anyone ever again. Or at least not for a long time. I need to get my life back in order and sort my shit out.

Marek's been kind of down about how they've been playing this year, but this is a pretty good game. Surprisingly intense. There are also a lot of turnovers that make me cringe and a lot of passing instead of shooting at the net. Ben gets an amazing chance to score when he and Carson Alford get a two-on-one, but when he passes it to Carson, the center misses it – oh my God! And there goes that chance to go ahead. But Carson redeems himself by chasing the puck, battling hard for it along the boards and finally getting it out to Hakim at the blue line, who one-times it into the net, tying it three-all.

Near the end of the third period, the score still tied, a Cyclone player hits a Storm player from behind into the boards, knocking his helmet right off and dropping him to the ice. The crowd shouts with outrage and within two seconds, Ben has barreled up to the Cyclone player and dropped his gloves. The other guy drops his mitts too, and they go.

"Oh my God!" I cover my mouth as I watch the fight.

They dance around and throw hands until Ben decisively takes the guy to the ice. He kneels closer and says something in the guy's ear I'd love to hear as the linesmen swoop in and pull him off.

The crowd is cheering for Ben as he skates to the penalty box.

I have to smile. That was badass.

The player who took that ugly hit – number eighty-six – seems okay, thankfully, and the Storm appear energized by this after the next faceoff. They have a power play, yay, and they quickly go on the attack, scoring a beautiful power play goal with less than two minutes to go in the game.

"Yessss!" I beam as I watch them celebrate. "That's it, baby. That's the game. Pull your goalie," I advise the Cyclone. "That's it... okay, boys..." I'm kicking my feet on the floor, eyes fixed on the action as the Cyclone control the puck in our end, passing, passing, and then Ben intercepts a pass and quickly shoots the puck down the ice where it smoothly glides into the empty net. "Yeah!"

I fall back into the couch cushions, smiling. "Go Storm!"

This is the happiest I've felt in weeks. It just took a hockey game. Weird.

Ben is one of the players the media talks to after the game. I suck on my bottom lip as I watch him stand in front of the Storm backdrop.

"Ben, it felt like you came to play tonight," one of the reporters says. "Did you as a team have something to prove tonight against the Cyclone?"

Ben tugs at the brim of his ball cap and looks down. "Uh, yeah, I guess."

There's an awkward pause. Is that all he's going to say?

As if he realizes that's not enough, he says, still not looking up and kind of mumbling, "For sure we remember them beating us last year and that maybe gave us a little extra boost, but there were some things we could definitely have done better."

There's another pause, as if the reporters are waiting for him to elaborate, and then one guy says, "That fight with Horák seemed to fire your team up. Was that what you were thinking?"

"I was thinking that was a dirty hit," Ben mumbles.

I hear the reporters all chuckle.

"We're a team," Ben adds. "We've got each other's backs."

I nod in agreement.

"What things do you think you could have done better tonight?" a reporter asks.

This time Ben is more forthcoming, listing some of the Storm's problems. But then he kind of regroups and says, "We did some good things too, though. I really liked our power play tonight."

I purse my lips and nod again. He's right. I like how he gives his teammates credit. And he sounds more confident. Despite my past crush on him, I can admit he's not really the best at public speaking.

He's always been like that – quiet, reserved. Never liked being the center of attention. I bet he hates having to be interviewed on camera.

I'm still awake but in bed – in bed, meaning on the couch with my pillow and blankets – when Marek and Ben get home.

"Hey." Marek strides to the kitchen and fills a glass of water from the dispenser on the fridge.

"Hey." I push myself up, setting down my book. "Congrats on the win."

"Thanks."

Ben walks to the kitchen, too, wearing his game-day suit and tie. He opens the fridge and pulls out a bottle of chocolate milk, which he cracks open and drinks.

I take in his suit and try to keep my expression neutral at the long baggy pants and loose jacket. "Two goals, Ben. You played great."

"Thanks."

His usual chatty self. I smile. "And a fight."

"Yeah." He shakes his head.

"We needed that win," Marek says. "Especially against the Cyclone."

"Right?" Ben leans against the counter. "Everyone really brought the energy tonight. I liked it." He rubs his chin. "We gotta fix those sloppy passes. If I'd made that pass cleaner Alfie would've scored."

"He was a step behind the play," Marek argues. "It wasn't your pass that was the problem."

"He's right," I speak up.

They both look at me.

"I watched the replays." I smile. "But you're right, Ben, there was a lot of sloppy passing."

He lifts an eyebrow in a way that sets off some heat in my lower belly. God, he's still handsome. More handsome, even.

"Thanks for your analysis," Marek says with affectionate sarcasm.

I roll my eyes. "Goodnight." I pull the covers up over my head and slide down into my makeshift bed.

I don't go to sleep, though, because I'm hyper aware of Ben here, my ears attuned to the noises of the guys turning off lights and heading to their rooms.

I imagine Ben behind his closed door taking his suit off, first the jacket, then the too-long and too-loose pants and... *God, stop this, you idiot!*

There can be none of that while I'm staying here. I can't be developing another crush on Ben so quickly. It's some kind of rebound thing. I have way more important things to focus on right now.

* * *

I spend the next few days with my laptop, updating my resume, contacting people for references, and searching out job postings. New York Public Library – oh hell, yeah. School librarian – okay, sure. Law librarian? Yeah, I'm qualified, but that's not my experience. Brooklyn Library? I nibble my lip. I guess Brooklyn could be okay. More law librarian postings. Wow. There are a lot of those. There are university jobs for project managers in data collection. Um... maybe?

My first responses come back and they're positive. Yay! I schedule screening interviews and start preparing myself, thinking of possible questions and answers, going through my old performance reviews, which were always stellar. That makes me a little wistful for the job I gave up, but after a moment of submersing myself in pity I rally and straighten my shoulders and focus on now. Change is good. It'll all be fine.

Marek and Ben are away on a road trip to Canada, so I have the place to myself for a few days. The first day is awkward because Marek's cleaning lady comes, who's actually a girl my age. Her name is Mariya. She's gorgeous and has an accent. I feel guilty for sitting around while she cleans, so I help her and hear all about her family in Ukraine, in between her telling me to sit down and not do her job.

Then I'm alone. I kind of like the energy the guys bring when they're around, although I have to admit it's been a bit distracting running into Ben wearing nothing but a towel around his waist or shirtless in the kitchen making his breakfast. Doing laundry in nothing but a pair of athletic shorts. Holy Roman Empire, he is high-key hot. Somehow my hurt feelings from his rejection in high school have been overtaken by thirst.

I'm in the middle of a Zoom interview when they get home. My eyes widen in panic, afraid they'll start yammering about hockey or something. Out of camera view, I lift a hand and frantically wave it at them without turning away from the screen.

Luckily, they get my message, but they have to walk behind me to get to the kitchen. I bite back a smile when Marek gets down on the floor and army crawls from the door to the kitchen.

"How well can you perform under pressure?" the interviewer asks.

"Well." I pause. "I'm not sure I know all the lyrics, but I can try my best."

There's a beat of silence then a shocked grunt from the kitchen behind me and choking laughter. I blink, but ignore them.

Then the recruiter bursts out laughing. Whew.

"I'm kidding," I say lightly. "A little joke to break the tension. In fact, that is how I deal with pressure. I believe in being mentally flexible. One thing I do is mentally distance myself from my thoughts, because the things we think under pressure are often not true, thinking things like 'I can't do this.' Libraries are being tasked with providing more services for their communities with continually shrinking budgets, and librarians are being asked to take on responsibilities that go far beyond their job description. In my previous position, we had a significant number of patrons who needed social services for issues like homelessness, unemployment... drug dependency. There were medical emergencies, fights, sexual harassment. These situations required me to respond promptly and professionally, while trying to help the person in front of me.

"What I try to do is be aware of my emotions in the situation and recognize if I'm nervous or afraid or frustrated. I try not to get overwhelmed by my emotions by changing my self-talk and remembering my values so that I can say and do things consistent with my values and not my emotions."

The interviewer nods and segues into the next question. "Tell us about one of those incidents. What was the outcome and how did you resolve the problem?"

I tell the story of the day I'd noticed that a man who seemed to be sleeping in a chair was actually unresponsive, his lips turning blue. "We'd been provided with naloxone and the training on how to use it, so I quickly told one of my colleagues to call 911 and I got one of the kits and injected it into his leg and then his arm." I pause, the memory still a bit emotional. "He kind of fluttered his eyes and gurgled, so he was alive. I was glad we had the Narcan to deal with it. Unfortunately, the same things that make libraries ideal places for reading and studying also make them appealing places for consuming drugs."

We wrap up the interview shortly after. She promises to be in touch, and I guess I have to keep my fingers crossed that it will be for a second interview. Once my camera and mic are off, I jump and face Marek and Ben. "Geez, you guys! They could have heard you laughing at me!"

Marek grins. "I can't believe you said that in a job interview. Under pressure. Ha."

"It was pretty funny," Ben says.

I catch my lower lip between my teeth. "Thanks."

"You aren't going to get the job making jokes like that," Marek says.

I frown and walk around the couch toward them. "Why not?"

Their gazes drop from my suit jacket and blouse to the baggy sweats I'm wearing on my bottom half.

"Nice outfit." Marek grins again.

"Whatever. It was a Zoom interview. They couldn't see my pants." I take off the jacket.

"Okay. As long as you know not to dress like that when you go meet with them. And don't make bad jokes."

"I'll make all the jokes I want. What do you know about job interviews? You've never had a real job in your life."

"We had to interview with teams when we were getting drafted," Ben says. "Worst days of my life."

"Bah. Those were nothing." Marek waves a hand.

"Maybe for you." Ben grimaces. "I felt like I was being waterboarded the whole time."

"They ask the same things over and over – our background, our family, who influenced us growing up."

Ben's eyebrows shoot up. "Once they asked me what I wanted people to say at my funeral. I didn't practice for that one. I went completely blank."

"Good thing you can play hockey." Marek smirks.

"Tell me about it." Ben shakes his head. "Another team asked, 'What would you do if you could go back in time and learn something sooner, and how would it change things?'" He makes a sound of disgust. "I hate being put on the spot."

I watch him with interest, fascinated with his aversion to these questions. I plant my butt on a stool, prop my chin on my fist, and ask, "What did you say?"

He rubs his forehead. "After a few long painful minutes of silence, I told them that after my dad passed away I realized how short life is. I realized I should have told him how much I loved him and appreciated everything he did for me so I could play hockey. We should never take anything for granted because tomorrow's not guaranteed."

"Oh." Emotion swells up inside me, like a wave of water. I blink at the sting of unexpected tears. I didn't know his dad had passed away.

"They were probably looking for something hockey related. Instead I got all heavy on them." He rolls his eyes.

"I think that probably told them a lot about you as a person," I say softly. "Is that the team that drafted you?"

"Yeah."

I nod. "They're looking for character, not just hockey skills."

"That's true," Marek confirms. "One team asked my Uber score."

Ben and I burst out laughing.

"That could tell them something about your character," I chortle.

He grins. "Okay, I have to change and go meet Patrick." His agent. "You're coming out tonight, right?" he says to Ben.

"Uh. Maybe."

Marek gives him a look. "I'll talk to you later." He disappears into his bedroom.

"Where are you going tonight?" I ask.

"Eh, some of the guys want to go play pool at a bar."

"You don't like pool?"

"I don't like people."

I actually burst out laughing. Then I see he's not joking. "Oh." I tip my head. "Really?"

"Eh... I like some people. I mostly don't like a lot of people together."

"It's called a party."

His lips twitch. "Some call it that, yeah. Others call it torture."

I remember those high school parties. I thought everyone loved parties. Who wouldn't? Friends, fun, flirting. Usually some (at that time illegal) beverages and cannabis. Dancing. What's not to like?

"I'm not very outgoing," he adds unnecessarily.

I nod. "Yeah. But they're your friends."

"Which is the only reason I might go. I don't like strangers."

"Strangers are friends you haven't met yet."

He barks out a laugh, startling me. "Jesus."

"I didn't make that up. William Butler Yeats said that."

"I don't care who said it, they obviously never met an introvert."

I smile. "So you don't like making friends."

"It's a lot of work."

I laugh. "I never thought of it like that. I could come with you."

He frowns. "Why?"

"I can be... like, your wingman."

"I'm not looking for a date."

"I mean a friends wingman. Not for romantic connections. Just friends. I do it for people all the time. I never even realized it until my college friend Sage told me she couldn't go to a party without me because she'd end up hiding in the bathroom all night."

He eyes me. "I usually find the dog and hang out with them."

I crack up. "You know, I sort of understand that. Dogs are better than people."

"Oh, yeah. And thanks, but I don't think I'll go tonight. We have a practice in the morning."

"But the other guys are going out."

"It's an optional practice."

"Ah. Okay. Well, I better get back to job hunting." I slide off the stool.

As I sit down at my laptop again, Ben says, "What you said in that interview... about dealing with pressure..."

"My bad joke?"

"No, no. The part about mentally distancing yourself from your emotions..."

I turn to face him. "Yeah?"

"I thought that was really good."

I smile. "Oh. Thanks."

"Also... you saved a guy's life."

I bite my lip and nod.

"That's impressive." He walks away.

Crappleberries. Back in high school I thought he was stuck-up and rude, but now... I'm not so sure.

6

BEN

"You're gonna have to be better with the media."

I try not to wince.

I'm in another meeting with Coach and Mr. Miller. I guess they saw my media stuff after the game last night. I'm never good at that and I always hope I'm not one of the ones the media wants to talk to.

"You've had the media training we give everyone," Mr. Miller says.

"Yes." I've also listened to hockey players being interviewed pretty much my whole life. I thought I had it down – the monotonous tone, diverting questions about me individually to comment about the team ("Full credit to my linemates"), giving credit to the opposing team ("They're well coached and they work hard") and even props to the venue and fans ("This is a tough barn to play in"). I know it's better to say nothing than to say something dumb and sound like a shmucknut. The worst thing you want to do is provide motivation for the other team, using your words against you.

Mr. Miller nods thoughtfully. "What about going to Toastmasters?"

My eyes widen. Fuck no! I'd rather eat my hockey socks than do that. Standing up in front of strangers to talk? My worst nightmare.

Of course, that's what talking to the media is. But at least I'm talking about something I know about. "I don't think that's necessary," I say quickly. "I can do better."

"You need to come across more confident," Coach says. "The captain is the leader."

"Right." I swallow a sigh. When it comes to hockey, I am confident. I guess I don't sound that way.

"You also need to be more than the loner in the dressing room," Coach says. "You tend to keep to yourself."

"I know." I nod. "That's deliberate. It's my game-day routine."

"Yeah." Coach's eyes squint a little. "You might have to change that up."

"I was aware of it yesterday," I say, hoping to score a point or two here. "But a lot of the other guys are quiet, too."

"Like I said, the captain is the leader."

"Right." Again.

"Look, you don't have to change your whole personality. We like who you are. We see you lead by example, especially once you're on the ice. We want to see more of it off the ice. You're smart about the game. I know you have things to say about it. Go ahead and say them."

I keep my face neutral. I do have things to say. But as usual, I just... don't. "Okay. I get it."

"Good."

We just had an optional practice, which of course I attended because I always do. I came to the arena myself today since Marek is doing a photo shoot for an endorsement deal he has with New Balance.

When I get home, I'm starving. At first, I think Mabel is out, too, as the apartment is quiet and I don't see her, but she could be sleeping so I close the door quietly and head straight to the kitchen to make a sandwich.

I find bread, mayo, ham, and a tomato and set to work. As I slice the tomato, I think about overhearing Mabel's interview yesterday. When she made that joke, I was sure she'd blown the whole thing. Who does that?

Mabel does that. She made the interviewer laugh. And then she showed surprising insight into how she manages emotions and *then* she told a story about saving a homeless guy's life. I always thought of Mabel as fun-loving and chatty and, well, persistent, and yeah, her bright presence intrigued me, but I never realized there was more to her. She has a master's degree. And impressive experience.

I'm focused on slathering mayo on the bread when I hear footsteps and look up. "Aaaaaaah!" My heart literally stops then lurches in a painful arrhythmia as I see the creature approaching me, all white, with a white animal head topped with white fur and small pinkish ears. "What the fuck!"

It lifts its arms and removes the head and of course it's Mabel.

Laughing.

"Oh my God, that scream. I'm dead." She staggers to the counter and sets the head down, chortling so hard she apparently can't stand. "It's just me."

"Fuck." I press hand to my chest. "I didn't know it was you. I mean I did right away, who else could it be, but... fuck." My heart is still hammering. And now heat runs from my chest up into my face. "What are you doing?"

"It's my llama costume. Some of my boxes arrived from Sherrinford. This was a Halloween costume." She pets the fur head. "Don't you love it?"

Amusement tugs at my lips. "Sure."

"My ex hated it." She frowns. "He wasn't into Halloween at all."

I don't know what to say to that.

"She's my drama llama."

"Uh huh." I exhale sharply one more time and resume my meal prep. "Cute." The face actually *is* kind of cute, now it's not coming at me, with a non-threatening snout, pinkish nose, and smiling lips.

I was just thinking about how surprisingly impressed I was with Mabel and her job interview, and she does this.

Well. She's not boring, I'll say that. And while it was a little kooky, at least she's wearing clothes. There've been too many times I've walked into the kitchen in the morning to see her long, bare legs kicked out from under the blankets, or I've come out of my bedroom to see her darting down the hall from the bathroom in her underwear. Living with her is getting hard on my... well, let's just say it's getting hard.

"What are you making?" She peers over at my food.

"A sandwich." I pause. "Want one?"

"Sure!" She climbs onto a stool. "How was your practice?"

"It was... okay." I slice two more pieces of the hearty wholegrain bread I like, trying to act normal. "It was optional, so we didn't do much. I helped one of the young guys work on his faceoffs."

"That's nice of you."

"Eh..."

"Can't take a compliment, huh?"

Nailed it. Much as I want to be complimented for my hockey skills, or anything really, when it happens I feel all awkward.

"All you have to do is say, 'thanks,'" she advises quietly. "It's easy. Try it."

I pause, then mumble, "Thanks."

"Almost there. Say it with a smile. And eye contact."

"What the fuck?"

She laughs, and it's an amazing sound... light and bubbly and somehow warm. "Just do it."

I meet her eyes, which is easy but also hard because I could stare at her forfuckingever and that would make things *really* awkward. Her attention focused on me makes my dick respond, dammit. Somehow, though, my smile comes involuntarily, in response to hers. "Thanks."

"Excellent!" She claps. "Great job. I like cheddar cheese." She nods at the sandwiches I'm making. She's so matter of fact about it, I don't feel judged or demeaned. Also, she has no idea I'm turned on just looking at her.

"Okay." I soon slide a plate toward her. I pour myself a glass of chocolate milk and glance at a stool. Should I sit? Or go into my room? Does she want me around? Probably not.

"Have a seat." She nudges the stool, apparently sensing my thoughts. "You really *don't* like people, do you?"

I sit and pick up my sandwich. "Why do you say that?"

"Because you were going to leave me to eat all alone. Oh, wait – maybe it's *me* you don't like." She smacks her forehead. "Oh my God, I'm such an idiot. Look, I understand if that's the case. Maybe we should talk about—"

"It's not you." Well, not the way she thinks. "I just figured you'd prefer that."

"What? Why?"

"Because... I *always* figure people would rather be left alone."

"Because *you* would."

"Yeah. Or because I'm not exactly a, uh, brilliant conversationalist." I pause. "I wasn't being rude or antisocial. I just thought that's what you'd want."

She nods slowly, chewing her sandwich. "I see." She appears to ponder that. "Good to know."

Okay. I guess.

"This is really good." She holds up her sandwich. "Thanks for making me one. I need to go buy a few more things."

"Did you run out of Cheez-Its?"

She laughs. "Yeah. I've been bingeing on them since I broke up with Julian. I should probably stop drowning my sorrows in junk food and beer."

She chatters on, and my brain wanders aimlessly for a moment. She's so goddamn attractive. Apart from her lush mouth, spankable ass, and perky tits, she's also friendly and outgoing, making her interviewer laugh, then answering the questions with impressive competence. I'd hire her.

I'm struck with an idea.

A crazy idea.

I *could* hire her – to help me learn how to be more extroverted.

I wrinkle my nose. Hire her... how much would I pay her? I have no clue.

"What's wrong?"

I blink over at her, brought back to reality. "Wrong?"

"You're scowling. Did I say something that offended you?"

"I don't know what you said. I... sorry, I kind of zoned out."

She purses her lips. "Oh. I was just saying..." She points at the fruit bowl on the counter. "If an orange is the color orange, why isn't a lemon called a yellow? Or a lime called a green?"

I stare at her. "I have no idea."

She shrugs. "I'll have to research that."

"Do you have crazy ideas going through your head all the time?"

She laughs. "Pretty much, yeah."

I nod slowly. "So, uh... I also just had a wild idea."

"Ooookay." One perfect eyebrow arches. "Tell me."

I chomp my bottom lip briefly, considering what to say. "We don't have a captain right now."

She nods slowly.

"My coach and the GM of the team talked to me. They think I could be captain. They want me to get involved with a charity and represent the Storm. I have a meeting with the director of the organization next week."

Her head slides up and down again, listening.

"I'm not good at shit like that. I'll have to do public speaking and interviews. Last night I did the media availability after the game and as usual I was a mumbling idiot."

She smiles. "I watched. You weren't that bad."

"Yes, I was. They mentioned it this morning. They want me to go to Toastmasters, for fuck's sake."

"Ohhhh."

"It's not that I'm stupid."

Her smile, still gentle, deepens. "No, you're not."

I like that she says that so confidently.

"I've never been good at..." I wave my hands. "Expressing myself. Verbally. But that's part of being captain. It's communicating with the players. That part's okay; I can talk to the guys. Talking to the refs. I can do that, too. But communicating with management... and the media. Ugh."

"Hmmm."

"So my idea is that maybe you could help me."

Her chin drops and she looks up at me. "Help you?"

"Yeah. I heard you in that interview yesterday. You're so confident. Well-spoken. How do you do that?"

"Uh..." For a confident, well-spoken woman, she seems flummoxed. "I just... do it?"

"You must have some tips and tricks."

She laughs and tucks some hair behind her ear. "Mostly I just fake it."

"Oh." I pause. Really? She doesn't seem like she's faking it. She's a little quirky, but she comes across as supremely confident. "Could you think about it? I'll pay you. I don't expect you to do it for nothing."

She blinks a few times. "Pay me."

"Yeah. Like... you'd be a coach. An extrovert coach."

She grins. "Seriously?"

"Yeah." My gut tightens. Is she laughing at me?

"I don't really think you need help," she says slowly. "Talking's not that hard."

I wish that were true. "Maybe for you. It is for me."

"It's flattering." She gives me that warm smile again. She's charming and flirty and talkative, but I never feel like she's not sincere. "But I really need to focus on finding a job. And my own place to live."

I've already made myself vulnerable enough. I'm not going to beg. Disappointment and rejection settle in my gut like a bowling ball. "Yeah, I get it. It was a crazy idea. Never mind." I look down at the last bit of my sandwich. I'm done. I stand and walk over to the sink to toss the remains and rinse my plate and glass. "Well. I have… stuff to do. I know you're busy, too."

And I escape to my room.

* * *

Smitty and I are at Uncle Ernie's Café and Pizza, a couple of blocks from the apartment. This neighborhood is hip and vibrant, with lots of little shops and restaurants, and Uncle Ernie's has loads of character and great pizza. Also, Uncle Ernie is a huge Storm fan and gives us free beer, so we hang out here a lot. Don't worry; we leave giant tips. Ernie's granddaughter Ayla usually works here as a bartender. She's married to one of my team-mates, Carson Alford, who we call Alfie, but she's on maternity leave since they just had a baby a few months ago.

Some of the other guys are meeting us but they're not here yet and I'm glad because I can talk to Smitty alone.

"So," I say.

"So."

"I kind of got shit from Coach this morning about my interview after the game last night."

He frowns. "What did you say? Did you pull a Serena Williams and tell them you didn't want to be there?"

I grin. "No, but I could have because that's true."

"Did you pull a Torts and tell them to fuck off?"

My grin widens. "No."

"Did you say you aren't telling them squat?"

I laugh out loud. "Not in those words. You know I'm not that guy. It was because I didn't say enough." My amusement fades. "Didn't look confident. I need to do that if I wanna be captain."

"Ah. Right."

"Yeah." I pick up my draft beer and take a swig. "So I had this idea. I guess it was bonkers, but I thought it was good at the time. I asked Mabel to teach me how to be more confident and outgoing."

His jaw falls open wide enough to drive a Zamboni in. "What?"

"And she said no." I give him a glum smile.

He frowns and snaps his mouth shut. "Whoa." He sips his beer. "Huh."

I shrug. "Dumb idea."

"No. I was surprised at first, but I think it's good. She's the perfect one to teach that, right?"

"That's what I thought. But she's going through a rough time right now. Breaking up with her boyfriend, moving away. I get the feeling she's pretty down in the dumps about it."

He purses his lips. "She seems fine."

I don't push it. Yeah, she seems fine. She's putting on a good act. But she's not fooling me.

"I think she should help you," Smitty says. "Why not?"

"She has her own shit to worry about. Job interviews, finding a place." Getting over a broken heart.

"Yeah, but that doesn't take every minute of her day. And maybe it would be good to take her mind off things."

"She said no."

"Oh."

Just then, Archie, our goaltender, arrives. Real name, Ford Archibald. He, too, lives not far from here. He's wearing a cream polo shirt with orange and green stripes that almost look like hockey sticks and an orange and green circle that could be a puck. This fit is relatively tame for him. "Hey, Archie."

"Hey, what's shakin', bacon?" Smitty greets him.

Archie pulls out a chair at our table. "Bacon. Now I want a bacon pizza."

Ernie comes over to take Archie's order.

"Large bacon pizza with jalapeños and a Zen Vibe, please, my good man."

Smitty and I wince at his choice of beer. He likes weird shit. This one's ale brewed with rice and lemongrass.

Ernie grins. "You got it."

Goalies are weird. You have to be, to stand in a net and let people shoot pucks at you at a hundred miles an hour. On a scale of one to psycho, Archie is up there.

"How's the roommate situation going?" he asks us. "Any fights break out?"

"Nah. We're good. I'm easy to live with." I grin.

"I hardly see him," Smitty says with an eye roll. "He hides in his room all the time."

"I'm trying not to bother you. Plus your sister's here now, so I don't want to get in her way."

"What? Your sister?" Archie looks at Smitty. "Is she hot?"

"Phhht." Smitty makes a face. "She's my twin sister. Bleh."

"I'll ask you, then." Archie turns to me with a smirk. "Is she hot?"

Oh, hell, yeah. I can't say that out loud. But can I deny it? "She's okay," I finally mumble.

Archie hoists his eyebrows. "Okay. Does she look like Smitty?"

"Yeah, sort of."

"That's the problem." Archie nods. "Poor girl."

Smitty rolls his eyes. "She does not look like me."

"But you're twins," Archie says.

"Not identical twins." Smitty shakes his head. "You can't be identical if one's a boy and one's a girl. We came from two eggs, not one."

"Right. Who's older?"

"Don't even ask that question."

Archie grins. "She is, right? And probably holds it over you."

Smitty sighs. "Yeah."

"So she's staying with you? For how long?"

"Until she finds a place, I guess. She and her boyfriend split up."

"Ah. Why didn't you bring her tonight? I should meet her."

"You're not meeting her."

Archie frowns. "Why not?"

"You're too weird."

Archie shrugs. "Fair."

Despite his eccentricities – or maybe because of them? Who knows? – he has no trouble finding women. He's had a lot of hook-ups, but, like me, never had a steady girlfriend in the time I've known him. I don't know if they realize how odd he is, or he doesn't want to settle down.

Ernie brings Archie's Zen beer and another for Smitty and me.

Archie reaches for his beer. "Okay, you guys, I'm worried about my hair."

We gaze at him, taking in his hair – brown with lighter gold pieces, thick, longish, wavy, kind of a mess.

"What's wrong with your hair?" I ask.

"I think it's falling out."

I snort. "I don't think so."

"Why do you say that?" Smitty studies Archie's shiny locks.

"Because of the creatine. Apparently it makes your hair fall out." He runs a hand through his curls.

"Ah." Smitty shakes his head.

A lot of us take creatine for increased strength and better performance on the ice.

"That's a myth," I say.

"Is it?" Archie messes with his hair again. "Everyone thinks creatine causes hair loss."

"There's been more research. It doesn't."

Smitty nods in agreement. "That's true."

"It's all from one study years ago," I add. "But it was never actually proven that creatine causes hair loss."

"It's because guys are paranoid about losing their hair," Smitty adds.

"Some more than others." I give Archie a pointed look.

"Shut up," he says mildly. "My hair is important to me."

"Because chicks love it when you pour water on it and then fling it back."

He grins. "I don't do that for the chicks."

"You sure as fuck do," I reply with a grin.

"I have good hair." He pats his mop. "I try to take care of it."

He definitely does. We all bug him that his suitcase when we travel is full of hair products. One time we managed to get into his room and added glue to his hair gel. Unfortunately, it ended in a trip to the hospital.

"Hair loss is genetic," Smitty says. "Blame your parents."

"I heard it comes from the mom's side of the family," I say.

"No, that's not true either." Smitty shakes his head. "It can be from both."

"My dad's hair is still good," Archie says.

"Maybe you should start using that stuff... what's it called... minoxidil." I stick my tongue in my cheek.

"I might." He shrugs.

Hey. I'm not going to judge him.

His pizza arrives and Smitty and I help ourselves to a piece even though we already ate at home. The jalapeños with the bacon are surprisingly tasty.

Which is why I don't judge his weird food choices.

7

MABEL

"Why won't you help Benny?"

I'm back on Marek's couch in yoga pants and a silk blouse, preparing for another screening interview on Zoom. "In case you haven't noticed, I have my own problems to worry about."

He exhales a dramatic sigh. "Yeah, yeah."

I jerk my head up and around to give him a sharp look. "That doesn't sound very sympathetic."

"Things are always complicated in your life."

I frown. "I'm not sure that's entirely fair." I've had some light turbulence in my life, but not lately. Until now. Okay, he's right.

"In high school you faked appendicitis to get out of school so well, you were actually in the OR before you confessed."

I smile. I got in huge trouble for that, but I was kind of proud of myself.

"When we were juniors, at the end of the school year you got everyone to wear a balaclava and aviator sunglasses to school. All day. Every teacher cracked up coming into the classroom."

"But I didn't get in trouble for that," I point out. "It was harmless. But hilarious," I add with more pride. "I haven't done stuff like that for a long time."

"Yeah."

When Marek says nothing for a moment, I look up at him. "What?"

"You *haven't* done stuff like that for a long time," he says slowly. "You've been... different."

I swallow. He noticed that?

"You sort of lost your..."

I lift an eyebrow.

"Your spark," he finishes. "Your individuality."

I study his face, emotion simmering behind my breastbone. I'm tempted to spill my guts and tell him why that is. Tell him what a shit Julian is. But I'm still embarrassed about how I was bamboozled by good looks and charm and steadiness (I thought). "That's how I felt, too," I manage to say.

He nods as we share a moment of wordless communication. "I've got your back," he says quietly.

Heat builds behind my eyelids. "Thank you."

He clears his throat. "Anyway. Back to Benny. You don't spend every minute of the day job hunting," he continues. "And you're staying in my condo..."

"What does that mean?"

"I'm just saying..." He drags a hand down his face. "I'm doing something for you. You could do something for me in return. This is important to Benny."

I purse my lips.

Ben's his best friend. Marek wants to help him. Goddammit, I like that.

Also, I could see how important it was to Ben. Being made captain of the team is a big deal. I could also see how hard it was for him to admit he's not good at the schmoozing part of the job and ask for help. I thought it was a bit off the wall but then I saw how crestfallen he was when I said no, and I actually felt like crap. "I don't think he needs help."

Marek frowns. "He thinks he does."

"I know, but he's a smart guy. He'll figure it out."

"Then it should be easy for you. Just help my friend out. It'll take your mind off your own problems. Benny thinks you're broken-hearted or something." He eyes me searchingly. "Are you?"

Whoa. My throat thickens. Is Ben worried about me, too? *Am* I broken-hearted? I think back to the moment when Julian gave me that ultimatum – that we were done if I didn't go to his faculty party with him. What I felt in that moment was anger. Fury. Even... gah, hatred. I think my heart had been slowly breaking for months before that, every time he hurt me, manipulated me, or blamed me. So yeah, I *was* heartbroken. But now... I'm mad.

"I'm okay," I finally reply. "It's complicated." Then I wince, remembering his earlier comment that my life is always complicated. "I'm... you know, shook. I just broke up with my boyfriend and quit my job and moved out of our home to another city."

"I know." His eyes narrow a bit. "Are you going to tell me why you did that?"

Emotion squeezes my larynx and I drop my gaze. "I don't want to."

"I see that," he says dryly. He pauses, then adds, "Well, I'm here when you're ready to talk about it."

I blink at the rush of warmth in my chest, then nod.

And... he's right. I do kind of owe him for letting me stay here. "Fine. I'll help him."

He grins. "Hey, that's great! Thank you."

"Are you going to tell him?"

"Uh..." He casts his eyes to the ceiling, thinking. "No. I don't want him to know I, uh—"

"Butted in?" I hoist an eyebrow.

"Okay, yeah. You can say you had second thoughts."

Ben is out doing errands.

"I have an interview in fifteen minutes. Which is probably when he'll be home."

Then the door opens and closes and Ben walks in, carrying a couple of shopping bags and a dry-cleaning bag.

"Hey," he says on seeing us.

"Hi."

"Hey." Marek bounds up. "I gotta finish packing." He bolts out of the living room.

Ben drapes his dry-cleaning over the back of a chair and carries his other bags to the kitchen.

I stand and press my palms to my thighs as I stroll casually toward him. "So I was thinking about what you said last night. When you asked me to, uh, be your extrovert coach."

His shoulders stiffen as he pulls things out of the shopping bags. "Yeah?"

"Yeah. I decided I *would* like to help." I give him a bright smile. "It'll be fun."

He sets a jar of Trader Joe's peanut butter on the counter. "Fun."

"Sure! I'll do some research." My mind leaps around. "I love doing research. And I'll come up with a plan. A goal. A list of things to do to accomplish the goal."

He gives me a look. "Oookay."

"And a timeframe. Do we have a timeframe?"

"This sounds very organized."

"I *am* very organized." I may have been a little chaotic as a kid, but I'm an adult now, with a master's degree and a successful career as a librarian. I lift my chin and flash a smile. "Ignore the messy clothes over there." I wave a hand toward my suitcases in the corner.

"I have a meeting with the executive director of Keeping Kids Safe next week."

I suck my bottom lip briefly, nodding. "Okay. You want to be prepared for that."

He shrugs but looks hopeful.

Goddammit. Hopeful Ben is very, very appealing.

"What's that name again? I'll research them, too." I grab a pen and paper and make a note of it. "So we'll schedule our first coaching session for Monday afternoon."

He slowly lowers and raises his chin in agreement. "I'll put it on my calendar."

Is he mocking me?

One corner of his mouth twitches.

Okay, teasing. He's teasing me. I scrunch up my face. "You may think I'm an airhead, but I do actually have a brain and some skills."

His eyes widen and his mouth drops open. "I don't think that!"

I lift one shoulder. "Yeah, you do. Julian did. He was always telling me to do better."

"What the fuck." He stares at me. "I've never thought you were stupid, Mabel."

I gaze back at him, something pinching in my chest. I know he's never been impressed with me. He avoided me for months before he left for college. So him saying that feels... real. I resist the urge to babble a protest and remind him of all that, but I keep my mouth sealed shut and nod.

"We need to discuss pay," he says. "I don't know how much—"

"No. You don't need to pay me. I'm doing this out of the goodness of my heart." I lay my hand on my chest.

He gives me a look.

"And I'm actually excited about it! Oh. I have to go. I have an interview right now."

"Good luck."

"Thanks."

I head back to my makeshift Zoom studio and get ready to blow the recruiter away.

8

BEN

Since it's the All-Star Break and we don't have a game until next week, it feels okay to indulge in booze, a little junk food, and a few hands of poker, which all turns into a late night at Dilly's place. In the morning, I wake up around ten, and when I roll out of bed, my sore muscles and bruised hip protest.

Our last game was physical and I'm still sore.

For me, anyway. I was trying to show the guys how we should play and I'm the worse for wear because of it. But that's okay. It was worth it to get them fired up and we ended up winning by one goal late in the third period, avoiding OT.

I need Advil. I drag my sore ass to the bathroom, rubbing my eyes. My head's a little fuzzy and I need coffee, too. As I walk into the bathroom, I'm greeted with the sight of Mabel standing in front of the mirror, bent over at the waist wearing... not much, her hands under her tits.

She bolts up straight, eyes nearly flying out of their sockets, and crosses her arms over her front, letting out a wake-the-dead screech.

I freeze, my eyes popping as wide as hers. My mouth falls open and about a million thoughts race through my head in the space of two seconds. The first one being, holy fuck, she's hot. The second being, her bra is see-through. Then I back out and slam the bathroom door shut.

Fuck! What the fuck?

I rub my face, and yell, "Sorry!" through the door.

Oh, Christ. That image will be imbedded on my retinas for the rest of my life. Mabel Smits naked except for sheer pale pink bra and panties, her tits plumped up in her hands, ass sticking up in the air in a perfect curve.

What the fuck was she doing?

I swipe my now sweaty forehead. Is it too early for bourbon?

I glance down the hall, waiting for Smitty to come running to the rescue of his sister, possibly with a weapon, but all is silent. He must still be asleep. Thank Christ.

The door yanks open and Mabel glares at me. "What was that?" she demands. She's now wearing clothes over her underwear. "Why did you walk in on me?"

"Sorry," I say again. "I didn't know you were in there."

"The door was closed!"

"I know, I know." I hold up my hands, palms facing her. "I was still half asleep and hurting and I needed Advil and I wasn't thinking."

Her gaze wanders down my body. Because I, too, am barely dressed, wearing only my boxer briefs. The air around us goes heavy. She blinks a few times then says, "You need Advil? What's wrong?"

"Nothing. I'm fine. A few bruises."

"I see that." Her eyes linger on my hip where color is spreading from beneath the shorts. My purple boxers with eggplants all over them, almost the same color as my bruises. And in response to her scrutiny, my actual, er, eggplant stirs. "What happened?"

"Just a check into the boards." I will her to stop looking at my crotch.

She rolls her lips inward and presses them together. "I'm done. Go in and get your Advil."

She advances out of the bathroom and I take a hasty step back to give her room. "Thanks," I choke out, and hustle inside to close the door.

Goddammit. I wasn't even thinking. For a moment, I brace my hands on the vanity and drop my head forward.

Smooth, pale skin. Long legs. Luscious curves...

Fuck me.

I take care of business then wince as I open the door. All clear. I hike back to my room to get dressed, pulling on a pair of sweats and a long-sleeved Henley. Okay, this is where I can hole up and recover from the sight of her in barely-there lingerie. Not a problem. So what if I'm a little hungry? And need caffeine. My mouth waters just thinking about it.

I can handle a little deprivation. I throw myself down on my bed again with my phone and settle in to scroll social media all day to distract me from thoughts of nearly bare Mabel.

I make it an hour, and then a soft knock sounds on my door. "Yeah?" I call.

"It's me." Mabel's soft voices floats into the room. "Are you okay?"

No. I am not okay. I am scarred for life by the image of her nakedness. That makes it sound like it was bad. It was not bad. It was very, very good. And I know the first time I lay eyes on her I'm going to remember it. And probably every time after that. I have to leave. I have to move out. Right now. "I'm fine."

"Are you sure? Do you need any more drugs? Water?"

I sigh and throw my legs over the side of the bed. I cross the rug on the floor and steel myself to open the door. She stands there looking at me with soft brown eyes, her bright hair flowing over her shoulders.

"I'm fine," I say again. "I took some Advil." Then I sigh. "I wouldn't mind a coffee, though."

"Do you want me to make you one?"

I eye her. "Why are you being nice to me when I just embarrassed you?"

She lifts one shoulder. "It was an accident."

"Yeah."

"And I was worried about you."

Yeah. She should be worried... about the filthy thoughts I'm having.

"You're hurt," she adds.

Oh. Right. "It's just a bruise."

"I'll go make your coffee." She turns and heads off.

I follow her. "I can make it myself. I'm not that injured."

But she walks straight to the machine and gets to work.

I slide onto a stool at the counter.

"Those were cute boxers," she says, watching the coffee brew, the corners of her mouth slightly lifted.

I rub my jaw. "Thanks?"

Now she outright smiles. "Sorry. I should be pretending I didn't see them."

"Do you want me to pretend I didn't see *your* underwear?"

The atmosphere in the room goes thick and sticky.

Jesus. What am I saying?

She looks up at me and our eyes meet. The air around us shifts and heats. Her lips part. We both saw everything. We know we saw it. We can't unsee it. "Only if it was horrifying for you."

Of its own volition, my head moves slowly side to side. "Definitely not horrifying."

My groin tightens again. I swallow, our eyes still locked.

"Well, at least there's that," she says lightly, her cheeks a little pinker than usual. "I was worried that I'd traumatized you."

"Not the way you think," I mutter, resisting the urge to adjust myself. "Uh... what were you doing, anyway?"

Her cheeks get even rosier. "I was adjusting... the girls. In the bra cups."

"Oh." Why did I ask that?

"Just making sure everything was perky and in place!"

I swallow a groan. "Tell me about your plan."

"Right." She flashes a bright smile and hands me my coffee. "I've been working on it and we're all set to start tomorrow. Unless you want to start today? I have a lot of ideas and some questions for you. Or maybe you're busy today. If you are, that's okay, we can stick to our plan."

I almost think she feels the same attraction I do. But we both know that can't go anywhere. "I have no plans today." I take the coffee.

"Okay! Good."

Do I want to start this earlier than expected? I haven't prepared myself for it. I don't like it when plans change, unless they're canceled. Then I love it. But I'll go along with this.

My stomach rumbles.

Her eyebrows shoot up. "You need breakfast."

I grimace. "I do."

"I'm hungry too. I can make us something. Do you like eggs?"

"Sure."

"Denver sandwich?"

"Okay. I can help."

"You can toast the bread."

We set about cooking, her getting eggs and ham and an onion out of the fridge, me toasting multi-grain bread.

"Did you work on your plan all day yesterday?" I ask her.

"Mostly. Then I went out."

"Oh yeah? Where'd you go?"

"I went to a full moon circle."

"A full moon what now?" I pause with two slices of bread in my hands.

She smiles. "A full moon circle. For women. I found it online when I was looking for something to do. It was..." She pauses. "Interesting. There's a full moon, so a bunch of women get together in a circle and connect with the energy and power of it."

"That sounds... woo-woo."

"It was definitely woo-woo." She nods and chops the onion. "But kind of cool. We did some meditation and set an intention. Then we let go of something or someone we want to get rid of in our life. Mine was Julian," she adds matter-of-factly. "I cut the cord with an axe."

Uh... I gaze at her, speechless.

"In my imagination," she adds hastily. "Then we danced and howled at the moon. It was very freeing. The full moon is a good time to reflect and make change in our life, and to manifest our goals."

I'm hesitant to ask. "What is your goal?"

"Well." She pauses, her expression earnest. "I need to find myself."

"Oookay."

"I know it sounds dumb." She rolls her eyes. "It's so trite. What I mean is..." She pauses, her gaze going distant. "I was trying so hard to please Julian that I lost sight of who I am. And I was pretty great."

I have to smile at that.

"So it's not really finding myself. It's going back to who I was."

"Do you think you can really go back?"

She focuses on me and blinks, tilting her head. "Oh. That's a good question. I guess you really can't. I'll never be exactly the same person I was before."

This motherfucker seems to have really messed her up. How bad was it? I get a rigid feeling in my gut.

She drops her eyes to the cutting board. "Maybe it's not exactly finding myself... maybe it's *creating* myself. Who I want to be."

"I guess we're all doing that."

The look on her face is mesmerizing. Her lips curve in a small smile of wonder, her eyes reflective. "That's true."

The softness of her lower lip tugs at something in my chest. I want to know more. It's not my nature to ask questions, but she fascinates me and the words slip out. "Who do you want to be?"

"That's what I need to figure out." She gives me a self-conscious smile.

"Did he hurt you?"

She blinks rapidly at my abrupt question. "Not... physically."

Shit. That's good... but not good. "Okay." I exhale. "Well. I'm a good listener if you want to talk about it."

She meets my eyes. "Thank you. You *are* a good listener."

I like that. "So where did this moon circle take place?"

"A place called Zen Haven. They have yoga and a spa and some other stuff."

Butter sizzles in the pan.

"Okay. Wow. That's... interesting."

She bites her lip on a smile. "You think I'm cuckoo, don't you."

"No."

"Yeah, you do. It's okay." She shrugs. "The best part of the whole thing was when I imagined Julian's reaction to me dancing and howling at the moon." She cackles and stirs the diced onion. "He would *die*. And it was hilarious."

I always admired how she did her own thing and didn't care what people thought. This full moon thing is a little out there for me, but she just goes with it.

"And I even made some new friends," she says. "We went out together after. It was fun."

Friends. Huh. "Girlfriends?" I ask before I can stop myself.

She smiles. "Yeah."

As we eat breakfast, she talks about some of the research she did to help me and then we move to Smitty's dining table where she has her laptop open.

"I have questions," she begins. "Let's start with this meeting you have this week. What is it exactly that you're worried about?"

"Are you sure I can't pay you for this? I can definitely pay you."

"No, it's fine. Now... what are you worried about?"

Hmmm. "I feel kind of pressured," I confess. "I'll be representing the team, so if I say something stupid, it'll reflect badly on them."

"Are you worried about embarrassing yourself?"

"Oh hell, yeah."

She tilts her head.

"I never know what to say," I go on. "My head goes empty. I'm not good at small talk. And I know a lot about hockey, but I don't know much about kids who've been abused or how they help them and I'll either go blank or say something dumb."

She nods, totally not judging me, and it feels like a relief to say this stuff out loud. "Okay, that's good to know. What other situations are difficult for you?"

"I hate going to parties."

"Right. You told me that."

"Well, not all the time. If I know people there, it's okay for a while. But if there are people there I don't know, it's the same thing – hard to talk to them. I end up saying things like, 'Hi. I'm Ben. I see you're wearing a shirt.'"

She covers her mouth, eyes dancing with mirth.

"And charity events that we have to do – every year there's one to raise money for some organization. We have to dress up and schmooze with a bunch of people we don't know."

"Okay. You don't like dressing up?"

"Eh... It's okay. I just like to be comfortable. The schmoozing is harder. Anyway, there's a big fundraising event Keeping Kids Safe is throwing that I have to go to and probably speak at. Ugh."

She purses her lips thoughtfully. "This helps me. I got some ideas yesterday about things we can try. I learned a lot about introversion and extroversion. Have you ever done personality tests about that?"

"Yeah, with my old team. The sports psychologist wanted us to do that so he could understand us better."

"What did you learn about yourself?"

"Introvert. Big shock." I make a face. "Which means I get energy from being alone."

"Yes, exactly." She pauses. "Spoons."

"Huh?"

"Spoons. That's your energy."

"Mmmkay. It shouldn't be that big a deal," I say. "But everything is set up in this world for extroverts. Being someone who likes to be alone gets you labeled a hermit. Or stuck-up or boring."

She squeezes her eyes shut briefly.

"What?"

"Nothing." She shakes her head. "It's so true that this is a world for extroverts."

"I'm not stuck-up. I like my friends. And my family." Humor ripples in my chest. "I'm actually a nice guy – once you get through the cynicism, reclusiveness, distrust, and disappointment in humanity."

She bursts out laughing, falling back in her chair. "You have good self-insight," she finally wheezes.

Nobody can accuse me of not knowing myself. I've thought about it a lot. When I'm home alone all those hours, ha. I'm a freak and I know it.

"So in terms of goals – you'd like to be able to meet strangers more easily, make a little small talk, maybe have a deeper conversation...?"

I nod.

"What else?"

"Public speaking. When the media interviews me. If I'm captain, I'll have to do more of that. And working with Keeping Kids Safe, I'll have to speak to groups."

She makes more notes. "Anything else?"

"I just want to be normal."

"Oh." Her mouth softens and she blinks a few times. "Here's the thing. We can't change who you are. But we can practice doing extroverted things to make them easier for you."

"Right. I get that."

"What about women?"

I freeze. "What about women?"

"Do you want help talking to women? Dating?"

My eyes widen. "Uh..."

She waits.

"Not from you," I finally mumble.

She frowns. "Why not?"

I swipe my forehead. "I don't know. That's too weird. Anyway, I don't have trouble getting a date."

Her eyes flicker. "Well, that's good." She doesn't sound impressed.

I want to laugh. "I'm not bragging."

"Uh huh."

Now I do laugh. "Seriously. I go out with women all the time." It's not a lie.

"But you don't have a girlfriend." She frowns. "Or do you?"

"No." I shrug. "Not right now. The women I've met haven't been interested in long-term relationships."

"Really." Her frown deepens.

Actually, I'm pretty sure they didn't want long-term relationships with *me*. But I don't say that.

Mabel bites her lip and gazes at me for long seconds. I can see she wants to say something but she bows her head to her notes. "Well. You might find some of the things we work on help you with girls, too."

"Whatever. That's not my goal right now."

"Fair." She moves to her laptop and uses the track pad. "So, here's what I think we should do."

9

MABEL

Some of the players went away to warm locations for the All-Star break, but Marek and Ben are still here. It's different having them around all the time. I like having company. I'm not so sure they feel the same about me. But it's good that Ben and I have time to work on his extroversion plan.

"The problem with all of these things is..." Ben rubs his chin. "I don't want to do them."

I blink, then burst out laughing.

"I don't want to put my phone away," he says. "It gives me something to do. And I'm not going to stand by myself in the middle of a room. Jesus."

I bite my lip.

"Insert myself into a conversation with strangers? Fuck, no."

"Okay. What about this – fake it till you make it. Acting like an extrovert can actually help you be more outgoing. So... acting confident, smiling, making eye contact."

He nods. "Okay, yeah."

"In conversation, it's good to try for 50 per cent talking, 50 per cent listening. If you can be genuinely interested in what they're saying, that helps. And don't hold back – say what you're thinking."

He grimaces. "Okay."

"Here's a question you can always ask – how is your day going? It's good because it's not like 'how are you?' where they say 'fine,' it makes them tell you more."

"I like that."

"And it's always good to have a couple of topics that are in the news that you can bring up. Like, have you heard they recently discovered dinosaurs might be even bigger than we thought?"

"Really?" His eyes light up.

"Well, yes." I grin. "You get the idea." I pause. "I don't think I have to tell you not to argue with people. Or to be respectful."

"I'm introverted, not an asshole."

"I know. That's why I said I don't have to tell you. Oh! We could do a role play!" I perk up at the idea.

"Christ." He covers his eyes.

Disappointed, I purse my lips. "Or you could practice in front of a mirror."

"That doesn't sound psycho at all."

"It's not psycho. It's part of a plan. Come on, you have to participate."

He sighs. "Fine. Let's role play."

"Okay! I'll be a fan."

He nods with a wary expression.

"Ben Antonov! Oh my God! I can't believe it's you!"

He closes his eyes and rubs his forehead.

"I'm such a big fan!" I gush, then wait for him.

He forces a smile. "Hi."

"You're gonna need to look like you're actually happy to see me," I say dryly.

"I'm trying."

I arch an eyebrow.

"Uh... so you're a Storm fan?"

"I am! I love hockey!"

"Great. Me too." He rolls his eyes. "Obviously."

I nod encouragingly.

"Do you come to our games?" he asks.

"Um, I went to a couple last year."

He nods. "Well, hopefully you get to one this year."

"You guys are playing great."

"No, we're not."

I lower my chin and give him a look.

"Okay. Uh. Thanks. We always want to do better."

I nod approvingly. "Can we get a selfie?"

"Sure."

I grab my phone and move over next to him, holding my phone up in front of us. I lean into him and damn, I get a whiff of that peppery, woodsy scent that makes my knees weak. I have to gather my wits. "Smile!"

I take a picture of us for real, because why not. Then I take a few more, making a face, leaning in closer, slinging an arm around his shoulders. He politely keeps a smile in place. I, meanwhile, am fighting temptation – the temptation of being so close to him, wanting to lean in and press my nose to his neck to breathe in more of his scent, wanting to sit on his lap, touch his face, taste his mouth...

"How long have you been a hockey fan?" he asks.

I know he's talking but the only thing I can think about is riding his beard. "Oh... a while." I move away from him, resisting the urge to wave a hand in front of my face.

"What do you like about it?"

I roll my lips in, then say, "I like the touchdowns."

His eyes shoot wide, then he cracks up. "Mabel."

"Come on, I'm trying to be a puck bunny! Can I get your autograph?"

"Sure."

"Here." I hand him a pen lying on the table. Then I unbutton the top button of my shirt and tug it open. "Right here." I lower my chin to indicate he should sign there. *Dangerous game, Mabel.*

He closes his eyes. "I'm not signing your boob."

I give him a reproving look. "Is that what you'd say to a fan?"

"Yes."

I narrow my eyes. "For real?"

"I don't sign boobs. Okay, I'd say... sorry, I don't autograph skin."

I pout. "Why not?"

He gives me a surprisingly charming smile and says, "It's one of my boundaries."

Huh. I tilt my head. "Okay. You can sign this, then." I shove a notebook toward him and he scrawls his name, adding a small number twenty-three under it. I take it back and clutch it to my chest. "Thanks!"

He looks up and his gaze snags on my unbuttoned shirt and the lacy edge of my bralette showing. Color rises into his face. And probably mine, too, judging from the heat I feel.

I didn't mistake the way he looked at me earlier. Like he, too, wants me to ride his beard.

My whole body is sizzling hot and excitement twists in my lower belly.

The problem is, I like him looking there. I like affecting him that way. Oh, hell. I flip my hair back. "You're so hot," I say, trying for fake-flirty. I reach out and squeeze his biceps. "So strong."

Okay, this is a mistake. I'm taking it too far. Because I'm kind of real-flirting.

"Thanks." His voice is low and gruff and sexy as fuck.

"I like your shirt." I let my gaze wander over his hoodie like the... I stop myself. I never liked the term puck bunny because it seems kind of slut-shamey. Women are allowed to be attracted to whoever they want, even hockey players. I may have defended myself as a teenager when I had that crush on Ben, telling myself I was attracted to him despite the fact he was a hockey player, not because of it.

I'm not sure if that's true, though, because it's really hard to separate Ben from hockey. It's who he is. And honestly, as a teenager, I didn't even know him. Not like I'm getting to know him now. Now I know he's not stuck-up or stupid. He's shy. And smart. And yeah, still hot.

Heat runs through my veins.

"Thanks," he says, again in that low, craggy tone. He's watching me.

Our eyes meet. My hand is still on his arm. I rub his solid, rounded biceps and blink. "You should probably tell me to take my hands off you."

The corners of his mouth lift. "Maybe I don't want to."

Gulp. Mesmerized, I stare at him, at his eyes, his mouth. "You let fans grope you?"

"No."

"Oh. Just me, then."

One corner of his mouth quirks higher.

Heat floods my body, nearly melting my panties. "I'm sorry about pulling your pants down," I blurt.

Now he rolls his lips inward, fighting a bigger smile. "I was traumatized by that."

"I know." My eyebrows slope down and the corners of my eyes tighten up. "It was an accident. I didn't mean to embarrass you."

"What were you trying to do?"

"I wanted to talk to you. You kept avoiding me." I bite my lip and peer up through my eyelashes. "I had a little crush on you back then."

"Oh, wow. Breaking news."

I stare at him and then, despite my mortification, I bust out laughing. I thunk my forehead on the table. "Oh my God. I am dead."

"Sorry."

"It's okay. I figured everyone knew." I sigh. "Just me embarrassing myself chasing someone who didn't want me."

"I didn't get it," he says quietly. "Why would someone like you have a crush on me?" Inexplicably, he reaches out and lifts my hair back over my shoulder.

My bottom lip pushes out as a tingle runs down my spine. "Someone like me? A puck bunny stalker?"

"No. Someone fun and bubbly and... shining."

My forehead tightens and I lift my head. "Shining?"

"Yeah." His eyes move over my face. "Bright. Glowing. Like a light." He shakes his head. "I sound like an idiot."

"No." I pull my bottom lip between my teeth, not hating his description of me.

"You were lively." He pauses, clearly searching for words. "Spirited. You were always with a bunch of people and you were always having fun. Or involved in something. You literally danced on a table at a party once."

I grin. "I did."

"I remember you at school cleaning up after an event and you were singing into the mop handle while you washed the floor."

I nod. That sounds like me.

"You organized a protest against anti-LGBTQ policies."

"I did. You're not anti-LGBTQ, are you?"

He huffs. "No. I admired you for that. You were fun and fearless and the total opposite of me. That's what I meant."

I'm still hanging on his gaze, connected by some kind of invisible tie. "Yeah." I slowly lower and raise my chin. "I got that a lot. I had lots of friends, but guys always thought I was too much. Unpredictable. Weird."

"Maybe you're a *little* weird," he says, smiling again.

"Yeah. I know."

He pulls in a breath. "Don't take this the wrong way... but I was kind of scared of you."

"Is there a good way to take that?" My teenage mortification returns, and I dip my chin as heat sweeps from my chest into my face.

He touches my hair again, so gently. "I mean, I was scared of everyone." He flashes a wry grin. "I was so shy. I know I still am, but I've gotten better than I was back then."

Yeah. He was shy.

"You were a hockey player. All the girls wanted to get with you."

He rolls his eyes. "Because I was a hockey player. Lots of guys loved that kind of attention. I just felt awkward."

I remember his teenage image as quiet and brooding. I remember when Jenny managed to score a date with him and I was so jealous, but afterwards she dismissed him and said he had no rizz. I'm not going to tell Ben that, but it lends truth to his teenage discomfort. And makes me feel uncomfortable with how I misjudged him.

My hand has slid down his arm and my fingers are curled around his wrist. We've completely forgotten the role play. But Ben is talking to me – openly, honestly, holding eye contact. Progress?

"I guess we were sort of going through the same thing." My voice comes out husky. I look at my fingers as they move to his hand and gently squeeze.

"That is really weird."

I huff out a small laugh. "It really is."

The apartment door opens.

We both jerk apart, hands releasing. I shove my chair away from Ben as Marek walks in.

"Hey," he says, looking at some mail. "What's new, kangaroos?"

I laugh. "Kangaroos, huh? We're making progress."

My eyes meet Ben's in a brief, hot exchange that communicates... something. Guilt? Regret?

Why guilt? I glance at Marek as he tosses the mail onto the counter and heads to the fridge. Would it be wrong for Ben and me to... I don't know... hook up?

My chest squeezes tight. Why am I even thinking that? Now I can't meet Ben's eyes.

"Dilly wants to go to an escape room tonight," Marek says.

"That could be fun," Ben replies.

"Someone also suggested axe throwing."

Oh, hey. "Axe throwing would be super fun!" I say. "I'd love to throw axes." It makes me think of chopping that cord between me and Julian. I could envision Julian's face on the wall instead of a bullseye when I aim my axe.

They both look at me.

"Oh. I wasn't invited, was I." I sigh.

"You can come with us," Ben says.

Marek lifts his eyebrows. "Sure. I guess."

"Okay!"

Marek clears his throat and looks at his phone. "Okay, looks like axe throwing it is. The group chat says yes. It's BYOB so we can pick up some beer, and then get something to eat after."

"Fun!" I haven't had much of a social life here although I am going out with Cami and Tala on Saturday night to a mixology class. We'll be learning how to make cocktails! "What time?"

Marek frowns at his phone. "We have a reservation for six. It's a two-hour session."

"Okay! I better get ready." I hop up and scoot over to my suitcases in the corner.

"You need to tidy that up," Marek says.

I pause and look at the open suitcase with all kinds of clothing spilling out of it. "Sorry. I'll do that tomorrow."

It's really getting old living out of suitcases and having no privacy. But I'm working on it.

I dig out a pair of flare-leg jeans and a crocheted sweater in shades of cream, peach, and green. The white lace bralette I'm wearing will work under it. Then I head to the bathroom to change and fix my hair.

When I come back, both guys look at me. Ben's eyes move over me in a way that's... hot. My body goes all twitchy and tingly.

Marek says, "That sweater looks like the blankets Granny Smits makes."

"I know!" I look down at myself. "Isn't it cool?"

Marek grunts.

I catch Ben's eye. He gives his head a tiny shake and makes a face that tells me he thinks I look nice.

Thank you, Ben.

10

BEN

"This can be practice for you. A social event for you to practice being outgoing."

We're on our way to the axe throwing place. "I think I've created a monster," I say.

Mabel laughs and tosses her coppery hair back. "I do like helping people. And I'm having fun."

"Okay."

"Aren't *you* having fun?"

I don't answer because as usual, all the things I want to say get lost between my brain and my mouth. The truth is, I am having fun, but it's not because I enjoy dwelling on all my faults, but rather because of spending time with Mabel.

Earlier we had that... moment. Where we were holding hands and gazing into each other's eyes and the air around us was sort of sizzling and... I could have kissed her.

But that's not what this is supposed to be. She's my teammate's sister. She's the girl who tormented me as a teenager.

I realize that neither of those things is actually a reason that I couldn't kiss her. Except for that text message Smitty sent to the group chat:

SMITTY

My sister is coming with us tonight and all you ballbags don't get any ideas, she is off limits.

And that one time in the morning, I kept looking over at her sleeping on the couch, the blankets down around her waist, her soft tits outlined by a thin tank top, and he punched my arm and told me to stop looking at her.

She's still waiting for an answer, so I say, "Sure."

She laughs again. "That sounded enthusiastic."

"Being reminded of all my flaws is tons of fun."

She bumps me with her shoulder. "That's not what it is."

"Okay."

Smitty leads the way into the building where we meet up with the others. He introduces Mabel to Crusher, Dilly, and Archie. There are six of us, so we make two teams of three to compete. We spend about fifteen minutes getting some instructions and signing waivers, which is only a little scary, then head to a wall. There are targets painted on the walls with point numbers in each circle like darts.

We brought drinks, so we all grab a beer.

"I'm going to be so good at this!" Mabel handles her hatchet while bouncing on her toes.

She and I and Archie are a team. I'm screwed, I think. Archie's kind of an oddball and Mabel is acting way too enthusiastic about throwing a sharp weapon. Ah, well.

We let Mabel go first. She stands with the axe in two hands, lifts it over her head, and throws it. It looks like a good throw but holy shit, the axe bounces off the wall and comes back at her. I'm standing to the side but I lunge at her and tackle her to the floor. The axe lands harmlessly on the floor behind us.

"What the fuck!" Smitty yells and runs over. "What are you doing?"

I managed to get myself under Mabel so I didn't crush her into the concrete floor and she's lying on top of me, all soft curves and sweet flower scent, her hair in my face.

"Oh my God," she mumbles, her lips near my ear. "Oh my God."

I grip her hips and lift her as I sit up.

She stares at me with big eyes. "I nearly died."

Honestly, the adrenaline racing through my veins agrees with that. "Holy shit," I say.

She plops her ass on the floor.

"What happened?" Smitty demands.

"I didn't throw it very well," Mabel says, her voice weak. "It bounced back and nearly hit me."

Smitty turns his displeasure on me.

"Hey, I saved her! Don't look at me like I tackled her for funsies. Jesus."

He lets out a breath. "Yeah. Okay. Maybe you'd better just watch, Mabel."

"No." She pouts. "I want to throw axes."

"Let's go over the form again," I say. "Remember, you don't need to crank it that hard. These aren't regular axes. They're not as heavy."

"Right." She pulls in a breath and exhales a long stream. "Okay."

I pull her to her feet and Archie hands her the axe.

"I was picturing Julian's face," she mutters as I move behind her. "I may have overdone it."

I want to laugh. "We should have brought photos. Then we could all aim at him."

She giggles and looks at me over her shoulder. "Damn, why didn't I think of that."

I reach around to her front to get her hands in the right grip – sort of like a golf club. "Not too tight." I guide her hands up.

Big mistake. Huge.

I breathe in her scent. Fuck, she smells good. Her ass brushes against my thighs and all my blood runs south. Lust wraps around my cock and squeezes.

I swallow thickly and move her hands forward. "And release right in front of you. Here."

"How do you know this?" she asks, still sounding out of breath.

"I just listened to the guy. You want to try again, or wait and watch us?"

"I'll watch you guys first."

"Archie?" I look over at him.

"Okay, I'll go." He swings his axe and steps forward.

This time there is no unfortunate boomerang and his axe embeds nicely into the wall. Not on the target, but on the wall.

"Shit." He frowns as he moves forward to retrieve the axe.

I grin and take my own turn. Three points! I punch my fists in the air. "Yeah!"

Mabel grins. "Okay. This time I got it."

She throws again and sinks the blade into the wood, neatly scoring one point.

"Good job!" I put up my hands and she beams as she moves toward me to slap them.

We do five axes each, alternating with the team next to us, cheering and jeering. I'm not failing to notice the way the guys all watch Mabel when it's her turn, and it's not because they're worried about getting axed. They're checking her out. Her ass does look bangin' in those jeans.

Smitty notices too, and scowls. He misses his next shot. I have to grin.

"Focus!" I call to him.

He gives me a dirty look.

We win the first round, although only by a couple of points.

"This is fun!" Mabel's cheeks are pink, her eyes sparkling. "After that first little mishap."

"Thank God nobody got hurt," I reply.

"No kidding. Whew. I need another beer."

I actually can't believe they let people drink booze and throw sharp objects, but I, too, accept another beverage.

In the end, our team loses the next two rounds and we're done.

"It was close, though," Mabel insists as we get our jackets on and leave. "I'm sorry you had to have me on your team. I think I dragged us down."

"Not at all," Archie says courteously, with a flirty smile. "You did great."

I level a warning look on him. He ignores me.

"I can't believe you've never done it before," he goes on, pairing up with Mabel on the sidewalk.

"Ah. You're just being nice." She touches his chest.

I narrow my eyes.

"Where are we going now?" Dilly asks. "I'm starving."

"How about Uncle Ernie's?" Smitty says.

"Yeah. Good idea."

We call an Uber that'll fit six of us and are chauffeured over to 12th Street, not far from home. Uncle Ernie greets us when we walk in with a wave and a big smile. "My favorite hockey players! How is your All-Star break going? Why aren't you on a beach in the Caribbean somewhere?"

"Can't afford it," Smitty says.

Uncle Ernie scoffs. Then he spies Mabel. "And who is this lovely lady? A new girlfriend?"

"No!" Smitty barks. Then more calmly, "This is my sister. Mabel. Mabel, this is Uncle Ernie."

"Pleased to meet you." She gives him a charming smile and shakes his hand.

Like everyone else, he's smitten. "Likewise. I had no idea Smitty had such a beautiful sister."

"Ah, thank you."

"I have a table for you over here." He leads us to a bigger table that all six of us fit around. "You need menus?"

The guys all shake their heads, but Mabel says, "I do."

He swiftly retrieves a menu and gallantly hands it to her. She begins to look it over as the rest of us order beers.

"Something to drink, Mabel?" Uncle Ernie asks.

"I'll have a Diet Coke."

"We don't have Diet Coke," he says apologetically.

Mabel ponders that. I expect her to ask for a regular Coke, but she says, "Okay, then, I'll have a margarita."

I blink at that leap.

Uncle Ernie disappears to get our drinks.

"Mozzarella sticks. Wings. Fried ravioli." Dilly looks around the table. "Yeah?"

"Two orders of wings," Smitty says.

"Just one with buffalo sauce," Dilly replies. "I know you don't like the hot stuff." His gaze moves to Mabel. "Do you like hot stuff, Mabel?"

She lifts her eyes from the menu and gives him a smirk. "I definitely do."

"She's got bigger balls than you, Smitty."

Smitty scowls again. I think he regrets bringing Mabel. "Watch it."

Mabel elbows him. "I can handle it."

"Christ. Don't encourage them. You have no idea…"

He's right.

Uncle Ernie arrives with our drinks and takes the order for the appetizers we're going to share, plus several large pizzas.

"This black truffle burrata toast looks good," Mabel says. "Anyone want to share that?"

"No," we all say.

"Okay, fine. I'll share what you're having."

"So, Mabel. Can I get a woman's opinion on something?" Crusher smiles at her.

"Sure."

Smitty and I exchange wary glances.

"What do women think of uncircumcised men?"

"Oh, fuck, no. We are not talking about circumcision," Smitty growls.

Mabel rolls her lips in but otherwise appears unfazed.

She opens her mouth and Smitty holds up a hand. "No."

She shrugs.

"Okay, what about bald guys?" Dilly asks. "Do chicks like bald guys?"

She blinks. "Why do you ask?"

"I'm asking for a friend. Actually for Archie. He's losing his hair."

"I am not losing my hair!"

"You told us you were," Dilly says.

"I was worried about it." Archie runs a hand through his thick waves. "But I don't think I am."

"You have great hair," Mabel tells him.

"Thanks."

"Don't encourage him," Dilly mutters. "He's obsessed with his hair."

"I'm not obsessed."

We all snort.

"Bald guys can be very attractive," Mabel offers.

"Jeff Bezos," Smitty says.

Mabel winces. "Not who I was thinking of. More like… Shemar Moore." She smiles.

"He's hot," agrees Crusher. "What?" He looks at all of us. "He is."

"Prince William," Archie suggests.

"Er... maybe for some," Mabel replies. "I also like Stanley Tucci."

"I don't know who that is," I say.

"Oh! Let me show you." She reaches for her phone.

I hold up a hand. "That's okay."

"I want to see," Archie says.

So Mabel spends a moment finding a pic of the guy and poring over it with Archie.

She and Archie seem to hit it off.

I don't like that.

I take a long pull of my beer.

"Maybe I should shave my head," Archie says.

We all go dead silent and stare at him.

"Kidding!" He lifts his beer.

Our chicken wings arrive, one platter of buffalo, one of garlic parmesan. We all dig in and they're gone before the mozza sticks and fried ravioli arrive.

"It's like we're trying to clog our arteries on the break." Crusher dips a mozza stick into tomato sauce.

"Back to healthy eating next week," I say.

"When's your next game?" Mabel asks.

"Tuesday," I reply.

"That's a nice long break. Over a week."

"Yeah."

"We should have gone to Aruba," Smitty says.

"I have a meeting," I remind him. "With Keeping Kids Safe."

"Oh yeah, right. You could have postponed that, though."

"Maybe. I didn't want to book a trip because I thought I was getting into my new place 1 February, but now it's March."

"You're staying with Marek until 1 March?" Mabel asks.

I meet her eyes. "Yeah. Sorry."

"No, no, don't apologize. That's not what I mean."

"You're not making her sleep on the couch, are you?" Crusher says.

I cringe. "Um... yeah?"

"You asswipe." He punches my shoulder.

"No, I fit on the couch easier than he would," Mabel says. "It's fine. Also, he was here first."

"How long do you think you'll be staying?" Smitty asks his sister.

"I don't know. I need to find a job first."

"What do you do for a living, Mabel?" Archie asks.

"I'm a librarian."

I see they're all taken aback by that.

Mabel laughs. "I love being a librarian."

"Hmm. Okay." Crusher nods. "Sexy librarian."

Smitty makes a noise in his throat.

"That's just another stereotype," Mabel says. "Trying to subvert the typical matriarchal image."

We all say nothing.

"But you *are* the guardian of the books," Crusher says.

"Yes, but I use power, not sex appeal."

"Jesus." Smitty shakes his head. "I knew this was a bad idea."

I grin. Mabel is definitely a handful.

I'd like a handful of her...

No. Stop. I can't be thinking about her that way, no matter how smoking hot that moment earlier was.

But then our eyes meet across the table and she smiles and I smile back and that heat blasts through me again like my blood is on fire.

"Your friends are fun," Mabel says lightly to Smitty, then looks at me again.

On our walk home, Mabel moves beside me and says quietly, "You did great socializing tonight."

"Yeah. I was with my friends. I'm comfortable with them. That's not hard. It's people I don't know. Even the rest of the team I don't know as well."

She nods. "Okay. Pretend those people are your friends when you talk to them."

I glance down at her as we walk. "Sure. Easy."

She smiles. "Come on. It's not that hard. Let's talk about homework for you."

11

BEN

"Nice day, isn't it?"

I'm in line at Starbucks the next day and this is my homework assignment: start a conversation with someone I don't know and try to pretend they're a friend. The man behind me is older than me, maybe forty-ish? Not intimidating at all, wearing a navy jacket, a neat golf shirt, and khakis. He gazes back at me from behind round glasses. "I guess."

I smile, nod, and search for something else to say. "The weather, I mean."

"That's what I meant, too. Since it's actually a shitty day."

"Oh." Not what I expected to hear. I blink and my head goes blank. Now what do I say? Sorry? Or do I turn around and pretend I didn't hear that? That would be a failure. So, I say, "Why is it shitty?"

"My mom died this morning."

Fuck me. I swallow. "Uh..." What do I say? What do I say? "Sorry."

The guy pushes a finger up under his glasses to rub his eye.

Oh, shit. Is he crying? I stare at him in horror.

"She was only sixty," he says in a choked voice.

I blow out a breath. "Oh, wow. I'm sorry." Okay, I already said that. The line moves a bit and I take a step forward. I could turn my back on him. But... "Are you okay?"

"No," he sobs. "It's so unfair! She didn't have to die."

My chest tightens like a giant rubber band is wrapped around it. "I'm sorry."

Jesus. Stop saying that.

He's literally disintegrating in front of me. I glance around and see others watching us. It's awkward as fuck. I don't know what to say. "What killed her?"

Nooooooo.

"A vending machine." He takes off his glasses and wipes his eyes, his face now radish red.

My mouth falls open. I gape at him.

"She put her money in and her Almond Joy wouldn't come out. She was banging on the machine and then she and her friend tried to shake the machine and it tipped over and fell on them."

I can't... I just can't.

He's now full out sobbing. It's my turn at the counter and I step forward and order my Americano. I turn to the man. "What would you like? Let me get it."

"Oh. Uh." He sniffles. "A vintage caramel mariachi. And a sausage McMuffin."

I squint. Um... what? I turn and repeat it to the barista, cringing at how she's going to react. But she just nods and asks for our names. "Ben and..." I turn to the guy.

He shakes his head and weeps into his hands.

The girl waves at me. "I got it."

We step aside to wait for our orders. I grab some napkins and hand them to him. "Uh... here..."

"Sorry," he sobs. "It was just so sudden."

"Yeah. That is... unexpected."

He's crying loud enough to attract attention from others in the place. My worst nightmare. Everyone thinks we're together and keeps looking at me. I don't know how to tell them I don't even know this guy. But this is all my fault for asking him about his shitty day. *This* is what happens when you talk to people! This is why I don't do it!

Now I'm pissed at Mabel for making me do this. It's fucking stupid and I'm trapped with a guy having a breakdown in Starbucks. Now I've started this conversation, I have to stick with him and make sure he's okay.

"Ben!" My name is called and I step over to grab my coffee. I turn back to my new friend. He's crying into a wad of napkins. "Uh, hey, are you gonna be okay?"

He shakes his head and blows his nose with a loud honk.

I hover beside him, not knowing what to say or do. I desperately want to high-tail it out of here. "Can I... call someone for you?"

He shakes his head again. "I don't have any other family."

Shit. "Did you live with your mom?"

"Yeah."

"Oh. That's... gonna be hard." Fuck! I grind my back molars.

"Ben's friend!"

It doesn't sink in that that's my buddy's order until they've called it three times. Then I jump to the counter to get his drink and sandwich. I hand them to him, the cup labeled "Ben's friend." "Here you go, man."

"Thanks. How much do I owe you?" He stuffs the soggy napkins in his jacket pocket.

"Don't worry about it." I take a breath. "I... look, I hope..." I never know what to say. Even when it's something benign like "have a nice day." What do I say to a man whose mom just died? I search for something and eventually come up with, "I'm sorry about your mom." Again. "I hope she rests in peace." Heat slides up into my face at my weak response.

He nods, his mouth turned down at the corners, but says, "Thanks. I appreciate that."

What would I say if he was a teammate having a bad day? "You got this." I sound confident. "You're gonna be okay. It's tough right now, yeah. But I have faith in you." I give him a clap on the shoulder then leave the coffee shop. Outside, I hike down the sidewalk as if I'm being chased by all the people in that shop who witnessed my shame. I'm sweating and my skin is tingling under my arms and at the back of my neck.

Shit, shit, shit. All I had to do was make a little conversation with a stranger and I ended up causing him to completely melt down.

I turn into a parking lot and jump into my vehicle. I slam the door shut and sit there panting like I just did a bag skate. I barely walked a block but I guess it's more from agitation than cardiovascular effort. I bang my head back against the headrest and close my eyes.

Is every attempt I make to hold a conversation with someone going to be a disaster like this? I want to blame Mabel, but that's unreasonable. I asked her to help me. And I'm the one who pooched it.

Okay, okay. It can only get better, right? And I'm determined to do this. I need to treat this like I do when I fuck shit up on the ice. You can't let that mess with your head, you have to let it go and move on. I can do that.

I get home and walk in on more drama.

"Why don't you talk to him?" Smitty asks Mabel. They're sitting in the living room, Mabel with her laptop in front of her.

"I don't want to talk to him."

I close the door and they both look up at me.

"Hey," Mabel says.

Talk to who?

"He's worried about you," Smitty says to her, ignoring me.

"If he calls again, tell him I'm fine. That's all he needs to know."

"You two could have gone for counseling," Smitty says. "Tried to work things out."

Ah. They're talking about her ex.

She purses her lips. "I don't think so."

Marek's forehead creases. "Did he cheat on you?"

Her mouth drops open. "No!" Then she snaps it closed. "At least, I don't think so."

"Okay, good."

I hate the way Mabel's face is tight with discomfort. I know Marek's trying to help, but I also know she's not ready to talk about whatever happened. Weirdly, I want to go over to her and hold her.

"I had my reasons for leaving," she says quietly. "Can we leave it at that for now?"

Marek frowns. "I just want you to be happy," he finally says.

"I'm happier now than I was with Julian."

It's none of my business, but I find I really hate this Julian asshole. I turn to go down the hall to my room.

"Did you do your homework?" Mabel calls to me.

I stop, tensing. Slowly, I face her. "Oh, yeah. I did. And it was an epic clusterfuck."

She gives me a wide-eyed look. "How could it be a disaster? All you had to do is talk to someone."

I heave a sigh. "You're dealing with me, remember? The king of awkward?"

She lets out a little laugh. "Oh, come on."

"What did you do?" Smitty asks, not clued in about the assignment.

"I don't even want to talk about it. Maybe later after a six pack of beer." I'm only partly kidding.

I see the dismay on Mabel's face.

In my room, I'm now distracted from my conversational fiasco by the discussion I walked in on. Mabel says Julian didn't hurt her physically, but obviously something bad happened between them. That makes me want to put a fist through a wall. I replay our conversation the other day when she talked about cutting the connection and finding herself.

A soft knock on the door has my head turning. "Yeah?"

"Can we talk?" It's Mabel.

"Sure." I stride to the door and open it.

In front of me stands a cute white llama.

I can't help it – I crack up, falling against the door frame.

Mabel lifts the llama head off and grins at me. "It worked."

"You're a nut."

"I know." She sighs, and her eyes flicker, but her smile beams again. "Come on. Tell me what happened. We'll work on it."

I nod with glum acceptance. "Okay."

We go out and sit at the dining table and I relate what happened at Starbucks.

Mabel listens without judgment. Then she says, "So what was bad about that?"

I gape at her. "I made a man cry in Starbucks."

Her forehead creases. "You didn't make him cry. He cried because his mom died."

I shake my head. "Because I asked him about his shitty day."

She sits back in her chair, regarding me thoughtfully. "I don't see it. Yes, he got upset. He didn't have to say anything. And when he got upset, you ordered his coffee for him, stayed with him until he got control, and tried to encourage him."

I open my mouth to protest. Then close it. Then open it again. "Well. When you put it that way..."

"See?"

"I felt like an idiot. Everyone in Starbucks was staring at us."

She tilts her head and leans forward. "Is it possible they were more concerned about the other guy?"

I picture a light bulb over my head illuminating. I was worried about myself, about feeling stupid. I should have been concerned about the other guy. "Probably. Yeah."

"You need to get out of your own head," she says. "I know that's easier said than done, but instead of worrying about how people are judging you, think of the person you're talking to. And actually, I think you did. You wanted to make him feel better. You felt badly for upsetting him. You have a lot of empathy." She smiles encouragingly.

"I think I get it," I say slowly.

"It's not bad," she insists. "It's something to work on. Instead of turning inward when you talk to someone, pay attention to the person you're talking to."

This makes sense in an uncomfortable way.

She beams at me. "I'm so proud of you."

I stare at her. What just happened?

"Also, vending machines are twice as likely to kill you as a shark." She nods wisely.

I stare at her for a beat, then burst out laughing. "Jesus, Mabel."

"It's true!" She laughs, too.

"Okay. I believe you."

She grins. "Also, don't think *I've* never said anything dumb. Being impulsive means I say whatever I think and that's not always a good thing. I could use some of your restraint and keep my mouth shut sometimes."

She does say some wacky shit.

"So, what we'll work on next is preparing for your meeting at Keeping Kids Safe."

"Okay."

"It seems like it would be a good idea to think about what you want to say ahead of time."

I nod. "Yeah. I'm not good at thinking on the spot."

"So, let's have a look at their website." She slides her laptop over and turns it.

I shift my chair closer to hers so I can see the screen also.

Close enough to smell her unique scent. I've noticed it before, soft, warm, like summer flowers. She smells really good. I want to lean in and take a deep breath.

That would be creepy.

I want to do a lot more than sniff her. Her scent arouses me and makes me remember what she looks like in a sheer bra and panties. Makes me imagine taking her underwear off. Makes me wonder what her sleek ass cheeks would feel like in my hands.

I watch her fingers on her keyboard and track pad as she brings up the Keeping Kids Safe website. Her fingers are slender, her nails short with a pale pink glossy shine. She wears thin gold rings stacked on her ring and middle fingers of her right hand, and on her left hand a thicker gold twist on her index finger. Even her fingers are sexy.

Jesus. What is wrong with me?

I am becoming obsessed with thoughts of her, even when she's not close enough for her scent to fire up my fantasies. I know I shouldn't be thinking about her like this, but it's impossible to resist her bright star quality, her soft mouth, her sweet charisma. She's fucking beautiful.

Now I'm sitting here with a stiffy when I'm supposed to be focused on business.

"Why do you want to work with them?" she asks me about Keeping Kids Safe.

I flail around for an answer, trying to get my mind out of her panties and onto the task at hand. "Because management says I have to."

She laughs. "Okay, you're going to have to come up with something better than that."

"Yeah, I know. I was kidding. Sort of. I like that they give kids who need it a voice. It seems like kids who are abused are afraid to speak up about it. And sometimes they aren't heard when they do." I read a terrible story about a girl whose father sexually assaulted her and when she tried to tell her mom, the mom didn't believe her.

Mabel nods, her eyes downcast. Then she clears her throat. "Right. That's good."

"So maybe I can be a voice for them, too," I say. "Maybe I have some influence. Maybe kids will listen to me. And adults, too."

She nods again, then says, her voice low, "That's perfect."

She gives me a little pop quiz on the non-profit's history and mission, then moves on.

"Small talk," she says. "Let's come up with some harmless things you can talk about before you get to the business stuff. If they ask about you, do you have a canned bio you give people?"

"Um... maybe?" I never thought of it that way, but yeah, I've been asked about myself in lots of interviews for various purposes. We polish that up a bit – where I grew up, where I played hockey, how I got into the NHL.

"What about family? If someone asks about your family."

"I have two younger siblings," I tell her. "My brother Owen and my sister Kerrigan."

"How old are they?"

"Owen's twenty, Kerrigan's eighteen."

"You're quite a bit older than them."

"Yeah."

"And your parents? Did they support your hockey?"

"Yeah. My dad passed away when I was nineteen. He got to see me get drafted."

"I'm sorry," she says slowly. "You mentioned that he had passed away. I didn't know that."

I nod. "Thanks. It was a tough time." I still miss him. "My mom's supportive, too. Owen and Kerry both play hockey. Owen's in college at Quinnipiac and Kerry's a freshman at Princeton."

"Wow. Elite hockey family."

"It won't be a professional thing for them. Well. You never know, I guess. But they're pretty good. They're actually coming to visit me on Friday."

"Oh, cool. Okay. What are some questions you could ask other people to make conversation?"

"Oh, Jesus." I shove a hand into my hair. "Uh..."

"You could ask how long they've been working there. At Keeping Kids Safe."

"Yeah! That's good."

"And how they got into that kind of work."

I nod.

"If they're from New York originally. If not, when did they move here and why."

"Those are good." I don't know why I don't think of stuff like that.

"And as they answer you might have other questions, like where they went to college, or their family. When you end the meeting, you can ask about weekend plans, or their evening."

We talk about other small talk ideas and I try to file away all these things in my brain.

"Remember." She meets my eyes, smiling. "It's not about you."

Her smile and gentle tone take any offense out of the words. In fact, her smile is so captivating I have a hard time looking away.

"Right." I never want it to be about me. So why is it about me and my comfort level in my head? Something to think about.

* * *

I arrive at Keeping Kids Safe in Jersey City a little early. It's not really that far from the condo, about a twenty-five-minute drive. I park on the street and study the narrow, three-story row house that is apparently their office. This street is somewhat run-down, but the Keeping Kids Safe building is neat and tidy, painted a dark blue with a bright white door with a bare tree in front.

I pull out my phone and quickly review the notes I made with Mabel. I know more about this organization now, including its history and structure and mission statement: to restore the health and wellbeing of those affected by child abuse through a coordinated community response.

I like it.

Child abuse is not something I want to think about. In fact, it makes me a little sick, but at least I'm doing something to help.

I open the door and walk in. Two women look up and smile at me.

"Hi!" the older one greets me, her smile bright white against dark brown skin. Her box braids are twisted into a bun on top of her head. She straightens and moves toward me with her hand extended. "You're Ben Antonov. I'm Sue Milner. It's so nice to meet you!"

I shake her hand, smiling back. "Nice to meet you, too."

"This is Maya Pérez, our Manager of Communications. She's joining us today and will be working with the communications team at the Storm on messaging and social media."

"Great." I shake Maya's hand, too. "Nice to meet you."

"Come on into my office. Can I get you a coffee? Water?"

"No thanks, I'm good."

She leads me to the back of the obviously remodeled house to what was at one time a bedroom. The office furniture isn't modern and high-end like at the Storm offices; her desk an old wooden one, the chairs well worn. I take this as a good sign that the money they raise goes more to helping kids than decorating their office.

"How is your day going?" I ask her, proud of myself for remembering Mabel's tip.

We make small talk and for once I'm prepared. I feel a little like I'm in a job interview, but I've already thought about these things and manage to put words together. "All kids need a voice. I have a lot to learn about your organization and what some of these kids are going through, but I hope that my voice can be one that resonates for them. I think what you're doing here is very important and I'm eager to help how I can."

Sue and Maya talk about a plan for announcing that I'll be an ambassador for the organization, someone to raise awareness about the prevalence of child abuse in New Jersey and draw attention to their initiatives.

They tell me about the new Keeping Kids Safe Center they'll be moving to this summer and how they'd like me to be part of that. "With huge thanks to the New Jersey Storm organization for their financial support," she adds.

When Sue talks about the kids and helping them, I'm struck by her passion. "When children experience abuse, they become involved in a lot of different systems – the justice system, child protection services, possibly the healthcare system, and prosecutions. Those can all be very difficult for kids to deal with. And those systems are important. But systems don't heal kids or families. When a child has been hurt, our first priority should be restoring what has been taken from them so they can thrive."

Her dedication is infectious, and I find myself motivated and eager to get involved.

"Let's take a tour of the offices and I'll introduce you around," Sue says.

The first employee I meet is Rocky. He's blond and handsome and has four legs. I crouch down to greet him and rub his head.

"Rocky's our helping hound," Sue says. "He helps comfort children and families who come here. It's really good for their stress levels to pet a dog. Sometimes he joins in meetings or stays with kids during interviews."

"I love that." I rub his ears. "You must be a good boy, Rocky."

"He's the best boy. He also comforts *us*." Sue smiles wryly. "I'm sure you can imagine that it's stressful for us, at times, too."

"Oh, yeah." I grin at Rocky, who smiles a big golden lab smile back at me.

They show me around their offices and introduce me to a lot of people whose names I won't remember – a couple of other managers, and a few case navigators and forensic interviewers.

"Most of our case workers and interviewers are out," Sue explains. "They often meet with kids where they are: at home, school, sometimes hospital."

Ugh. I don't like that. And I can't imagine interviewing kids who've been hurt.

"But you'll probably get to know some of them as you work more with us. And you'll meet some of our team who aren't here every day, like Dr. Saleem, who is an instructor at Princeton."

"My sister goes to Princeton," I say with a smile and not a little pride.

"Oh, wow, good for her." Sue smiles. "Well, should we schedule another meeting and talk more about your role?"

"Yeah." I nod emphatically. "I'd like that."

When I leave their offices and climb into my vehicle, I sit there for a minute. Okay, that went better than I expected. Thanks to Mabel, I was prepared with the ideas that we brainstormed together, ready for Sue's questions, and I even managed a little casual conversation. And I'm surprisingly enthusiastic about my next meeting.

12

MABEL

I can't wait to get home and hear how Ben's meeting went.

I wasn't enthused about doing this coaching gig, but now I'm invested. I want him to do well. I want to see him happy and confident.

My heart got all soft and squishy when he was telling me about his encounter at Starbucks. I know he honestly felt he'd screwed up, but I saw it differently. And that was an eye-opener for me. We're all hardest on ourselves. Yeah, even me. Probably. But I hate it that Ben was down on himself when what I took away from his account was a guy horrified he'd hurt someone and desperate to make it right. He just needs to see that about himself. And if I can help him do that, I'm in. All in.

Then I remember how our talk got away from "coaching" and became more personal, talking about high school and how we were sort of going through the same thing. Maybe that's why I feel a connection with him. Every time I talk to him, we share more, and also... we look at each other. He looks at me like he wants to lick me. And I definitely want to lick him. Everywhere.

I pull in a deep breath and let it out.

I had a job interview this afternoon at a private all-girls middle school on the Upper East Side in Manhattan. It sounds like a lovely school, although I'm not sure if school librarian is what I want to do. I do enjoy working with kids. But I'm applying for anything and everything. The interview went well, I think.

Ben's already home when I get there, he and Marek in the living room with their phones.

I bounce over to the couch and plop down, looking expectantly at Ben. "How was your meeting?"

"Good." He smiles back. "It went well. We set up another meeting for next week to get into more specifics about my role there."

"Excellent!" I clap my hands with genuine delight.

"How about your job interview?" he asks. "How did it go?"

"Good, I think. It's really a cool school, very posh Upper East Side, they seem very progressive. We'll see, I guess."

Our eyes meet and we share a moment of happy pride in ourselves and each other. I want to grab his hand and squeeze it. Or hug him.

And breathe in his scent, and kiss his mouth, and feel his arms around me, too.

Whoa. That's inappropriate.

"You probably wouldn't have to inject someone with naloxone working there," Ben says.

"Probably not! Although..." My forehead tightens. "Rich kids do a lot of drugs, I hear."

Marek clears his throat. I look up and see him watching us with a crimp between his eyebrows, looking back and forth between us. Is he picking up the tug of attraction between us?

I've leaned in close to Ben while we talked, so I shift back.

"When do your brother and sister get here?" Marek asks Ben.

"Should be soon. Kerry's coming by train, but Owen is driving."

"And you're going out for dinner," Marek says. "The three of you?"

"Yep."

"I'm going out, too," Marek replies.

"A date?" I ask immediately.

"As a matter of fact, yeah."

"Oooh." I bounce on the couch. "Who is she? Where did you meet her?"

"Never mind. I'll tell you if it turns into a second date."

"Phhht." I frown at him. "At least tell me her name."

"Nope."

I make another irritated sound. "Fine. I'm probably cramping your style by being here. I'm going to change." I find a pair of leggings and a sweater and use the bathroom to change and tie up my hair into a loose, messy bun. I hear noises and voices as I do my hair and when I return to the living room, Ben's brother and sister have arrived.

"Hi!"

Ben introduces us. Marek has apparently met them before but a long time ago when they were kids. They're quite a bit younger than us so I don't think I ever met them. They're young adults now, and there's definitely a family resemblance. Ben's brother is clean-shaven but has the same square jaw and thick hair as Ben. All three of them have the same eyes – that rich honey brown – and similar shade of brown hair. Owen's about an inch taller than Ben, and Kerry's tall, too, with a slender, fit build.

"I hear you both play hockey," I say. "That's so great."

"They're both at school on hockey scholarships," Ben says with obvious pride. "Both great players."

"What position do you play, Kerry?" I ask.

"I'm a left winger."

"Like your brother." I smile. "How about you, Owen?"

"I play defense."

"Cool. I guess that means you can skate backward."

They all laugh, thankfully.

"Would you like something to drink?" I ask them, playing hostess since Marek isn't. "We have beer, wine, juice, and I think there might be a couple of kombucha left if you prefer non-alcoholic."

"Kerry's not old enough to drink," Ben says.

"Oh my God." Kerry rolls her eyes. "Are you going to tell Mom on me?"

He laughs. "Nah, have a drink if you want."

"I'd love a glass of wine," she says, looking at me.

"Great. Owen?"

"Sure, I'll have a beer."

"I'll have a beer, too, thanks," Ben says.

I stop in my tracks and give him a look.

He laughs. "Kidding. I'm coming." He rises off the couch and strolls toward me, all long and lean and athletic. And hot. God, he's hot.

He made a joke. An easy, teasing joke. With me. I like it.

Marek heads out as we're getting drinks, and I put together a small charcuterie plate with what I can find in the fridge and set it on the coffee table. And I watch Ben with his siblings.

"How's school?" he asks Owen. "Not hockey, your grades."

Owen makes a face. "Eh... Okay."

Ben lifts an eyebrow. "Passing?"

"Yeah. Of course."

Ben questions him about specific courses, seemingly very dialed in to Owen's schedule, then gives Kerry the same treatment. But he comes across as interested and caring, not meddling. Kerry mentions some of her high-school friends who are bugging her to go away with them for spring break. "But I kind of want to stay and train. It'll be playoff time."

"Yeah," Ben says. "Your high-school friends who aren't playing sports anymore don't understand what it's like. College athletics is demanding, and sometimes you have to sacrifice breaks."

She nods. "Yeah. They don't get it. But I don't want to lose my old friends."

I remember she's a freshman. I'm about to open my mouth and offer advice, but Ben speaks first. "Yeah, I know. It's hard. Old friends are important. But college is a chance to make new friends. And they understand the kind of sacrifices you have to make."

I nod in agreement. I'm getting the feeling that Ben is a father figure for his siblings, that he takes care of them and that they count on him for support.

Then Owen speaks up, too. "Yeah, I felt like that my freshman year, too," he says. "It's hard leaving high-school friends behind. But you do make new friends."

"Well. We should get ready for dinner," Ben says. "I made a reservation at that place you wanted to go to in Manhattan."

"Ooooh!" Kerry seems excited. "Amazing."

Ben looks over at me. "Would you like to join us?"

I would. I really would. But this is their time to hang out with family. I smile. "That's okay. I have another interview tomorrow I'm going to prep for."

"You sure?" Ben meets my eyes. I think he wants me to join them. That makes it harder to say no.

I make myself nod and give him a reassuring smile. "Absolutely. You all have fun, though. Where are you going?"

"Rupert's," Kerry announces with excitement.

"Oooh, I've heard of it!" It's a new and trendy steakhouse overlooking Central Park. "Sounds great."

"We couldn't afford to go there if Ben wasn't footing the bill," Owen says with a grin. "I'm gonna have the Wagyu strip loin, it's like, a hundred and fifty bucks."

"Jesus," Ben says, covering his eyes. "What have I gotten into?"

"We love steak," Kerry says.

He knows exactly what he's gotten into and he's taking them there because that's where they want to go, and my heart does a little flip-flop in my chest.

Soon I'm alone in the apartment. It's okay.

I've never been one who likes spending time alone. I get energy from being around other people and I hate the loneliness that starts creeping in. But lately I've been channeling Ben, trying to enjoy alone time. It really is good to have time without distractions to focus on my thoughts and feelings. To think about my goals and dreams; the things that Julian took away from me. I can have those back now – I just have to think about them. Decide what I want. Who I want to be. What's important to me. I feel like I'm getting to know myself in a way that I haven't when I'm always in a whirlwind of activity and socializing. Which, now that I think of it, may have been a way to distract myself from thinking about all those things. From feeling all those feelings.

I hope Marek's having fun on his date, with whoever she is. I hope Ben's having fun with his siblings, who seem like great kids. I'm seeing Ben differently lately – his openness and how funny and smart he is when he's relaxed. With his friends last night, axe throwing and hanging out. With his siblings, all easy and open and protective. Even with me. And I'm seeing there's more to him than I realized.

And I like him.

* * *

On Saturday, Marek and Ben invite me to go to a sports bar to watch the All-Star game with them, Archie, Crusher, and Dilly. We walk a few blocks to the place on 10th Street and settle in with beers and snacks. The place is packed, with tons of televisions and, for a while at least, nobody pays any attention to the hockey players.

The guys are fun to hang out with, even if they do try to talk about circumcision. Today I turn the tables. "What do you guys want women to know about men?"

"Like, sexually?" Archie asks.

"Anything."

They all appear to search for an answer.

"That crease in my pants isn't a boner," Crusher finally says. "My pants just do that."

I roll my lips in. "Good to know."

"Jesus." Marek rubs his forehead.

"If you're interested in a guy, don't expect him to pick up on subtle hints," Dilly says. "We're idiots. You have to tell us outright."

I nod. "Fascinating. What else?"

"I, for one, would like longer hugs," Crusher says. "Hugs are nice."

"Long hugs turn into sex," Dilly says.

Crusher grins. "Yeah."

"We want to play with your boobs," Archie says.

My mouth opens and closes. Then I laugh.

Ben glares at him.

"Asshat!" Marek snaps. "That's my sister."

"No!" Archie shakes his head. "I didn't mean *her* boobs!"

I make a face. "Okay, then."

"You have nice boobs!" Archie assures me. "But I just meant, generally."

"Oh, look, there's Alfie." Ben points at a TV where their teammate who's at the All-Star game is on the ice. His jaw flexes.

"Hey!" Crusher shouts.

The guys all turn to watch. The distraction worked.

I catch Ben's eye. I mouth the words "it's okay" and grin at him, and he gives his head a tiny shake, his face changing from annoyed to reluctantly amused.

I end up leaving before the guys do, so I can go meet Tala and Cami for our mixology class. As I gather my jacket and purse, Crusher says, "Your sister's cool, Smitty."

Marek shrugs and says, "I guess she's okay," but I take in the curve of his lips and warmth in his eyes. My brother can be a pain in my ass, but he's okay, too. Mostly.

And I catch Ben watching me, his expression hot and hungry.

Oh.

13

BEN

Sunday morning I head into the bathroom and stop on seeing a lacy bra draped over the towel rack.

I sigh.

This isn't the first time I've encountered Mabel's underwear. Why does she have to leave her lingerie lying around? It annoys me.

Okay, it annoys me because... it's hot. Sexy. Feminine. Sometimes it's a pair of gray cotton panties, or a tank top. This particular garment is purple, mostly sheer and trimmed with lace. I stare at it for a moment, picturing it on Mabel.

I don't need any more encouragement to fantasize about Mabel.

I scrub a rough hand over my face. I have to stop this.

Does she have matching panties?

Fuck! Stop it, you perv.

I have to keep twisted thoughts about my friend's sister out of my goddamn head.

Feeling guilty, I trudge to the kitchen to get something to eat. To my surprise, Mabel's up and dressed. I've learned she's not an early riser.

"Morning," I say, heading straight to the Keurig. "Why're you up so early?"

"I don't know. I just woke up." She sits at the counter with her phone and a pop tart on a plate. "That was fun yesterday."

"Yeah. It was." I lean on the counter waiting for my coffee, trying not to think about purple lace.

"I noticed you were out of chocolate milk," she says. "So I picked some up for you."

"Oh. Thank you."

She smiles and nods.

"How was your bartending class?"

"It was fun!" She looks up from her phone. "We learned how to make Whiskey Sours, Daiquiris, Mojitos, and Cosmopolitans. They all have different mixology techniques."

"Like what?"

"Like, muddling, which you do with the mint for the mojito. Also double-straining, and using essential oils from fruit peels. Some time I'll make mojitos for you guys."

"Cool."

"Then we stayed at the bar for a couple more drinks. It was fun."

"It's good that you're making friends so fast." It's a good thing I have a team full of buddies, because if I moved to a city where I knew no one, I'd be alone forever. But of course, Mabel is making friends without even trying.

"What are you up to today?" she asks.

"Hmm. I dunno. I was thinking about going to buy some stools."

"Stools?"

"Yeah. Like those." I nod at the five stools lined up along the counter. "My condo's the same layout as this and I don't have stools."

"Oh. Cool. I'll come with you."

I don't say anything. In my head I have many comments.

Why?

Also, *Okay, great!*

And, *You don't have to do that.*

"Oh." She purses her lips. "Sorry. Maybe you have other plans. I was just..." She shrugs. "Sundays are hard."

I frown. "Why?"

"Because I don't like being alone and I don't have a job or interviews or anything to keep me busy." She lets out a small sigh. "But it's fine, I'll find something to do."

"Maybe another full moon circle." I poke my tongue into my cheek.

"There's no full moon... ohhh, you're joking." She laughs.

"You can come with me if you want. I don't think shopping for stools is very exciting, though."

"We'll make it exciting!"

She seems so genuinely thrilled to be coming furniture shopping. It makes something funny happen in my chest region.

So a couple of hours later we're in my SUV headed to Target. Mabel is wearing Doc Martens, baggy jeans, and a fake fur coat in a shade of tan that reminds me of a teddy bear. It's ridiculous.

"Target?" She turns big eyes on me. "You're going shopping at Target?"

"Yeah. Why not?"

"Well. I'm surprised. I thought you hockey players with lots of money would shop at high-end designer stores."

"I looked online and they have these leather stools – well, I guess they're not real leather – that match my other furniture."

"Okay."

"I guess I could spend a little more."

She pulls out her phone and starts swiping. "We could *look* at the Target ones, at least. Then you have something to compare to."

I wasn't prepared for the Target trip to turn into a major shopping expedition. Mabel ends up with a cart and loads it up with a bunch of shit like make-up and shampoo and candles. She has to look at everything in the goddamn store.

But I don't even mind, because she's kind of cute as she admires a set of dishes and then cushions that she ends up buying for Smitty.

They only have two of the stools I looked at, and I want five. That's how many fit at Smitty's counter.

"How about Pottery Barn?" Mabel suggests, looking at her phone.

"Sure."

So we head into Manhattan to find that store.

Again, Mabel wanders around like she's in heaven, exclaiming over bed displays loaded up with puffy comforters and pillows, brushing her fingers over upholstered chairs, sighing at a room display that she loves.

"I need my own place," she says with a wistful smile.

"I know the feeling."

She glances at me. "Yeah. You do. You need your space, too." She slips her arm through mine in a gesture of camaraderie that startles me, and we walk through the store.

I find the exact stools I want. They're almost like the ones at Target but real leather, and I admit they feel sturdier, which is probably good when my friends all weigh close to two hundred pounds. They have to order me five, but that's okay because I don't need them for a few weeks, and I arrange for delivery to my new place.

"Okay, you were right," I say to Mabel as we leave.

She bounces with satisfaction. "I usually am."

I laugh. It's an arrogant thing to say but she's so funny and cute it doesn't come across that way.

"What should we do now?"

"Um... go home?"

"Oh, come on! It's your second last day of vacation. Also, I'm hungry. Let's get food."

"Okay. I'm hungry, too. Any ideas?"

"No. It's New York. Let's just walk."

I frown. "Like, just randomly?"

She laughs. "Yeah. There's a pub on every block. We'll find something."

"But it might not be good."

"It'll be fine."

We set out down Fifth Avenue and when Mabel spies a place called Carrigan Ale House, she points. "There."

I shake my head but we go in. It's a dark little place, long and narrow, with a busy bar and most tables full. There's a big, long table down the middle with two empty seats, so Mabel pauses next to them and smiles at the guys sitting there. "Are these seats taken?"

"Nope." They smile back at her. Of course they smile back at her. Everyone smiles back at her.

I go around the table to sit on the other side. We hang up our jackets and settle onto wooden stools. The guy next to me slides a menu over the dark wood table toward me.

"Thanks."

"We can share a pitcher of beer," Mabel says. "How about a Belgian white?"

"Okay." I look over the food selections.

"Oooh, fish tacos," Mabel says.

"They're really good," says the man beside her with a smile.

I frown.

"Yeah? Okay then." She slaps down her menu.

I order a French dip.

"You guys have accents," Mabel says to them. "Australian, right?"

"Right." The guy grins. "I'm Scott. This is Jeff and Oliver."

"Nice to meet you! I'm Mabel, and this is Ben."

They all shake hands with us.

"Are you on vacation?" Mabel asks them.

"Yeah. Big trip to the USA. It's our last day." He lifts his beer.

"Where have you been? What have you done?" Mabel fixes an interested gaze on them, and they launch into a series of hilarious stories about their travels.

I didn't need to worry about them flirting with Mabel, though, because it quickly becomes obvious they're all gay, and two of them are together.

Wait, why was I worried about them flirting with Mabel?

Jesus.

She's not my girlfriend. Or even my date. She's my coach, ha ha. I should be paying attention to how easily she struck up a conversation with these men and learning from it.

After we eat, we're having so much fun we order another pitcher of beer and the conversation gets louder and more animated. Even I get involved in the discussion.

"Where in Australia are you from?" I ask. "I've always wanted to go there."

"We're from Sydney," Jeff says.

"Nice." I nod. "Have you always lived there?"

"Yeah, mate. Born and raised."

These guys are nice and funny as hell. They tell us about having to get used to tipping, leading to a discussion about tipping culture and their belief that people should be paid enough that they don't need tips, which Mabel and I don't argue with. They criticize our coffee and the fact that the price tag on items is not what they end up paying.

"I felt like I was in a movie the whole time we were here," one guy says with a laugh. "It's so familiar in some ways, and then in other ways so foreign."

Somehow, we end up doing shots of tequila because the Aussies think it's American, and I guess it sort of is?

They're fascinated when they learn I'm a hockey player. An *ice* hockey player. Apparently, hockey is getting more popular in Aus. We drink more as they quiz me about hockey.

Much later, as we all rise unsteadily from our stools, Oliver says, "I can't believe we got fuckin' maggotted our last day here."

Mabel and I crack-up laughing at that.

"Is that Australian for drunk?" I ask.

"Yeah, mate." He grins loosely.

"I'm fucking cactus," Jeff says.

"You are," Scott confirms. "Gone tits up."

"I'm feeling no pain myself," I admit. "Oh, shit. I can't drive home." This is so not like me.

Mabel waves a loose hand. "We'll Uber home."

"What about my vehicle? All your stuff is in it."

She makes a face.

"I'll drive you home," Scott says.

We all gape at him.

"I had one beer," he offers. "Someone has to stay sober for these dags."

I assume he's referring to his friends.

"Oh, that would be great!" Mabel says.

I frown. I'm supposed to let a stranger drive my Lexus SUV home? Also, a stranger who drives on the wrong side of the road? "You have a drivers' license?" I ask him.

"Yeah, mate, no worries."

"How will *you* get home?" I ask.

"We'll Uber. Where do you live? Is it far?"

"Across the river. Hoboken."

"Hoboken!" They're all amused by this.

"You'll have to give me directions," Scott says confidently as we head out.

I'm not feeling so confident, but what the hell, I'm going with the flow. Also not like me.

During the ride home, Mabel exchanges numbers with these guys so they can keep in touch. Really?

There are a couple of near misses when Scott forgets he's supposed to be on the right side of the road, and then all three of them freak out when we enter the Lincoln Tunnel.

"We're not driving under the water?" Jeff shouts. "Fuck me."

"It's fine," Mabel assures him.

We park in the underground parking beneath our building and take them to the front entrance. Scott has his ride share app open on his phone and we wait with them for the car to arrive.

"Thanks for an entertaining afternoon," I tell them.

"Yes!" Mabel agrees. "It was so fun talking to you."

"You both come to Sydney and we'll show you all around," Oliver says. "You'll love it."

"I'd love to go to Sydney!" Mabel clasps her hands.

"Yeah, me too," I say.

We exchange hugs and back slaps when the car arrives, then they climb in and wave as they drive away.

I look down at Mabel. "I can't believe what just happened."

She grins. "It was fun!"

I have to smile. "Yeah. It was."

14

BEN

After our second loss following the All-Star break, the dressing room is like a dungeon. The guys are all grumbling and complaining, tossing equipment around, and generally acting like pouty children.

"If you hadn't missed that pass, we might've scored," Hakim says to Crusher.

My mouth drops open. I look at Crusher, who's scowling at his skates.

"Never mind me," he replies. "What about that too many men penalty? Jesus, man, can't you fucking count?"

I lose my shit.

"What the fuck?" I yell at both of them. Then I look around the room.

Everyone goes deathly silent, staring at me.

"You know what the fuck our problem is?" I stand up, agitation and adrenaline coursing through my veins. "We're too focused on all the things we do wrong."

"We do a lot wrong," Crusher mutters.

"Okay, yeah, sometimes we do. But what do we do about it? Whine and bitch. That's not going to fix anything."

Every guy's face wears an expression of wary confusion.

Okay, this is not like me. I'm the quiet one. I watch and observe and take everything in, but it's not very often I speak up. Especially not loudly. Heatedly.

I shove my hand into my sweaty hair. I can't hold back. "We need to learn from our mistakes," I bark. "Mistakes are made for learning, not repeating. Jesus Christ!" I take a few steps across the carpet, aware of the trainers and equipment guys also listening. I'm so wound up, I don't care. "I know I screwed up against Dallas when I gave up the puck in our own end. I was pissed at myself." I shake my head. "But I try to learn from my mistakes. We have to learn. Learn from our mistakes, the wins, the losses, everything."

Heads move slowly side to side.

"We all need to be accountable for our mistakes. We all make them. But if we don't learn from them, we're gonna keep doing the same stupid shit over and over. We're not gonna get any better." Frustration makes my voice louder. "Mack." I turn to our number two center. "How's your faceoff win percentage?"

"It's shit," he says glumly.

"Yeah. So let's think about how to work on that." I look at Dilly. "You need to stop shooting into the goalie's chest."

He narrows his eyes and his mouth tightens but he nods. "Yeah."

"Let's work on it. Come on, guys. I'm sick of this. I'm sick of losing. I'm sick of the same things going wrong night after night. We're better than this. We did some good things tonight, too. That goal in the second... that was phenomenal. What an angle! We need more of that." There are murmurs of agreement. I turn to Edouard Lafond, a big D-man. "Eddy, you were fantastic, great defensive stick in the lane on that power play."

This time the sounds of agreement are louder.

"Yeah, Eddy!" Crusher says.

I pull in a deep breath, suddenly back outside my comfort zone. I can't stop now, though. "Let's all think about it. Let's think about our mistakes and how we can learn from them. Let's talk about it more tomorrow." I sink back down onto the bench in front of my cubby.

Goddamn.

I bend over to unlace my skates. The room is quieter than it was, but I can feel the difference. Before it was heavy and gloomy. Now there's a buzz.

I head to a bike to cool down. Mostly I need my head to stop racing. Did I just act like a complete asshole?

Smitty climbs onto a bike next to me. "Good talk, man."

I slant him a look. "Really?"

"Really. You nailed it."

I drop my head forward. "Probably pissed everyone off."

"I don't think so. We need someone to call us on our shit."

He's right. I just wish I'd planned that better instead of losing my mind and yelling like that. I sigh and we ride in silence for a few minutes until I climb off and head for the showers.

* * *

In the morning, we gather for our team meeting before practice.

"Benny," Coach barks at me. "You have something you want to say?"

I blink. "Uh…"

"Finish what you started last night," he says.

My mind scrambles a bit. "Right." I rub my mouth. He heard that? Great. I pull in a breath through my nose. "I guess my whole point was that we need to spend less energy on complaining about our problems and more energy on finding solutions and things we can control. We need to build each other up. We need to be more cohesive."

"Cohesive?" Turks says. "How do we do that?"

"The way we do that is to do our jobs. And communicate. We need to communicate more. During every shift. Hell, before every shift. After every shift. Off the ice. Verbally and non-verbally."

I catch Coach's eye and he gives me an approving chin lift.

Okay. Maybe I didn't totally fuck up by blowing up last night.

* * *

"What is this? An intervention?" I look at my teammates who've sat me down on the couch at home with serious looks on their faces.

"Maybe?" Smitty shrugs.

"If you're going to be the next captain, you're gonna have to up your game," Archie says.

Archie now also knows about this possibility.

"A captain doesn't have to be well dressed." I frown.

"Yeah, he does. You're supposed to lead by example, remember?" Smitty shakes his head.

I sigh.

The team is doing a sharpest dresser contest. Every game they take photos of us walking into the arena and fans are voting for the best dressed. I don't give a shit about that.

Apparently, I'm supposed to, though.

"We're taking you shopping," Archie says.

"Oh hell, no."

"Yep. Come on, dude. Got your credit card?"

"Yeah. But I don't think I trust you guys to buy me new clothes. Especially you." I look pointedly at Archie's sweater – a cardigan with brown trim and a geometric pattern in orange and pink.

"Point taken," Smitty says. "We won't let him pick out stuff. Just give his opinion."

Mabel arrives home just then, carrying a paper bag smelling deliciously like a burger and greasy fries, and looking, as usual, like an absolute snack. "Hi, guys." She sets her bag on the kitchen counter, unwraps her scarf, and shrugs out of her furry jacket. "How was practice?"

"It was good. We're trying some new things." Smitty stands. "We're just heading out."

"Where are you going?" Mabel hops onto a stool and opens her bag.

"We're taking Benny shopping for new clothes."

Her head whips around. "Really?"

"Yeah. He needs a new wardrobe. Specifically, game-day suits."

I sigh gustily. "I have suits."

"You do," Mabel agrees. "Although they appear to be the same ones you wore when you got drafted."

I scrunch my face up. She could be right, actually.

"He needs a glow up," Archie says. "Especially if he's going to be captain."

"No."

We all look at Mabel.

She shakes her head. "No, he doesn't." She picks up a French fry and takes a bite.

"He does," Smitty insists. "You just said his suits are old."

"Yeah, but that doesn't really matter. It's not what's on the outside that counts, it's what's on the inside."

A smile tugs at my lips.

Smitty sinks back down onto the couch. "Seriously? You're taking his side?"

"I'm not taking sides. I'm just saying, there's nothing wrong with Ben the way he is."

Something is happening in my chest. It's like a snowstorm. Only warm.

I can't help but think of Kodi, the one girl I went out with for more than a couple of dates, who got so frustrated with me because her friends thought I hated them. I told her I didn't hate them, that I just didn't have much to say. *Can't you just make an effort to be friendly? Can't you just be normal?* She definitely thought there was something wrong with me the way I was.

But Mabel doesn't.

I stare at her, the rest of the apartment fading away, Smitty and Archie's voices turning to a dull rumble. She's casually eating a burger, dressed in brown leggings and a short dress patterned in shades of brown and rust and tan. Her shiny hair in similar colors of brown and rust and gold hangs in waves down her back. I think I fucking love her.

Jesus. No, wait. That's crazy.

But that hot swirling feeling in my chest is still there. I rub at it.

"You could come with us," I blurt out.

She looks up at me, a fry poised near her mouth. "Shopping?"

"Yeah. You probably know better than these guys."

She pushes out her lips. "Hmmm. I did help you buy stools."

"Yeah."

She meets my eyes. "Do you *want* new clothes?"

"I guess I should look like the leader of the team if I want to be the leader."

She nods. "Okay, then. I'll help."

Somehow, I know Mabel won't make me wear something I'm not comfortable in, like the super tight pants Crusher wears, and the wild colors Archie wears. I feel better about this.

"Let me finish my lunch." She holds up her half-eaten burger.

An hour later we're walking into a shop in Midtown Manhattan that Archie says comes highly recommended. They do custom tailoring, which I might need because my thighs and ass are, well, big. Lots of the guys have the same problem. Hockey butt is real. The place is cool, with a velvet-upholstered seating area and mirrors and funky lighting.

I start looking at charcoal gray and navy suits. Archie's looking at a burgundy suit and Smitty holds up a white suit.

"No," I say to the white. "And probably no to that, too." I nod at Archie.

"I like it." Archie frowns.

"Buy it yourself, then."

"Maybe I will."

Mabel and I exchange amused glances.

"These are our modern suits over here," says Dimitri, who introduced himself to us when we came in and took some measurements. Mabel follows him over to another area and starts looking. I hear her and Dimitri talking animatedly as I look at a nice light gray Italian wool suit. I pull a jacket off the hanger and try it on. Seems okay.

I walk over to one of the mirrors to check it out.

"That's nice," Mabel says.

I look up. "Yeah?"

"Very classic," Dimitri says.

"Try the pants," Mabel says. "And I found a couple of other suits for you to try." She holds up two suits that look okay – another shade of gray and a navy.

I head into a dressing room which is as big as Smitty's living room and try on the gray suit Mabel found. Eeesh. These pants are tight.

I step out of the room into the seating area. "These pants won't work." I tug at the leg of one. "They're cheap hotel pants."

Dimitri cracks up laughing and the others give me puzzled looks.

"Cheap hotel pants?" Mabel repeats.

"Yeah. They have no ballroom."

After a beat, Mabel bursts out laughing too.

"I've heard that before." Dimitri wipes his eyes. "Yes, you do have some junk in the trunk. Let's look at more relaxed fits. If you like that fabric, we can mix and match the relaxed fit pant with the tailored jacket."

"I do like it." The wool is silky smooth.

"How about this one?" Archie holds up a burnt orange suit.

"No." I turn and go back to the dressing room. The other suit Mabel picked is great. The quality fabric makes a basic suit look nice, and when I go out to show her, she has a selection of shirts and ties lined up.

"How out there are you willing to go with shirts and ties?" she asks. "It's an easy way to jazz up a plain suit."

"Yeah." I peer at one shirt. "*A hundred and fifty bucks?*" I should be used to having money, but I guess I'm not.

She bites her lip. "I figured you can afford it."

"Bruh," Archie says. "We're not at H&M."

"It's 100 per cent Pima cotton," Mabel whispers.

"I do like the color." It's a light blue and there are a few ties I like in shades of blue.

"How about this striped one?" She holds it up.

"Yeah... I guess."

"Look... with this tie..." She lays the tie over it.

"That's nice."

Dimitri returns with the other pants and a couple more suits that are a bit more adventurous. What the hell. I try them on.

A few hours later my credit card is squealing as I pay for my purchases – three new suits, a sports jacket, two pairs of pants, six dress shirts and ties, a pair of shoes, a pair of jeans that fit my butt amazingly well, plus a couple of casual shirts and a sweater. Dimitri has given me suggestions for mixing and matching the jacket and pants. Oh, and a bunch of new socks.

As I pay, Mabel is helping Archie with tie selection to match the orange suit he's decided to buy for himself. We wait for him to finish up before stepping out onto Madison Avenue. It's started snowing since we went in, and the temperature has dropped about fifty degrees. "We'd better get home. Traffic could be nuts with this snow."

"Traffic is always nuts here." Mabel looks up at the sky.

"That is no lie."

Then Smitty and Archie decide they want to go to the Lego store.

Mabel makes a face. "I don't want to go to the Lego store."

I wouldn't mind going to the Lego store, but if Mabel doesn't want to, I can skip it.

"You go home." Smitty waves at us. "We'll Uber back later. Or take a train."

I shrug. "Okay."

"Will you be home for dinner?" Mabel asks him.

"You sound like a wife," Smitty says.

She rolls her eyes. "Just asking. Should I make dinner?"

"Nah, we might grab something. Or I'll make myself something when I get home."

We came in my vehicle, so we find it in the parking garage and load the purchases in the back, and Mabel and I head home through congested Manhattan streets toward the Lincoln Tunnel.

"That was fun!" Mabel says. "You looked so good in all those things. You have a really hot body."

I immediately sense that those words slipped out as the air in the car goes electric. I stare straight ahead out the windshield, my skin heating. I clear my throat. "Thanks. I guess they are a bit more modern than what I've been wearing."

Silence crackles around us.

She thinks I'm hot.

I think she's hot, too. No, wait. Hot doesn't even begin to describe her, with her messy hair and high tits and tight ass. Her kissable lips and bedroom eyes. I've thought way too many times about her underwear and about her sleeping in skimpy clothes on the couch and about inviting her to share my bed so she'd be more comfortable – except she wouldn't be comfortable because I'd be on top of her with my dick buried in her sweet pussy in seconds.

Oh, Jesus. Sweat trickles down my back. The guy downstairs reacts predictably and I force myself not to shift in the driver's seat as my jeans become uncomfortable.

We come to a stop at a red light. "Uh. Listen. That... what you said—"

"That you're hot? I'm sorry. That was—"

"No. When you said that I'm fine the way I am."

She turns and meets my eyes. Heat shimmers around us.

"That meant a lot to me. That you'd say that."

Her smile is slow and sweet and sexy as fuck. "You *are* fine the way you are. Just because we're trying to teach you to be more outgoing doesn't mean there's anything wrong with you."

In a world made for extroverts, I've spent most of my life thinking there is something wrong with me. I study her beautiful face with her big brown eyes and small nose and tempting mouth. And that warm fullness returns to my chest. Also to my groin. Dammit.

I need to talk about something else.

"I screwed up something last night."

Her eyes widen. "What? How?"

The light turns green and I return my focus to the road. "Okay, not really a screw-up. After the game. I got so frustrated with how down the guys were on everyone else. All we do is talk about how bad we are. And I kind of lost my shit." I tell her what I said.

She sits back and listens again. When I finish, she says, "Good for you. You were showing leadership."

"Maybe. But not in the way I want to."

"It's understandable that when you bottle things up, they come bursting out. You've probably been feeling like that for a while."

I rub my beard. "Oh, yeah."

"And maybe it would have been better to plan what you wanted to say and do it calmly. On the other hand, passion is good. I bet your coach isn't always cool, calm, and collected."

I snort. "Hell, no."

"You got their attention. And it sounds like it worked, if everyone was still talking about it this morning."

"Yeah. And everyone's willing to work harder: staying after practice to work on some things, putting a little more enthusiasm into things."

"That's great." Her tone is soft and warm. "Good job, captain. You seem really driven to win."

"Well, yeah. That's always the goal."

She nods. "The Stanley Cup."

"Yeah. Maybe it's a distant goal for us, but I remember what it was like, and I want it again."

"You won the Stanley Cup? When?"

"A few years ago. When I played for the Aces."

"Ohhhh. Right." She purses her lips. "So you know you have it in you."

"Well..." I flex my hands on the steering wheel.

"You doubt that?" she asks.

I debate blowing off her questions. But she's so easy to talk to. "Sometimes I do, yeah," I say slowly. "We won the cup my first full season in the league. It was the third time for the Aces. I was a rookie. I didn't play as many minutes as some of the other guys. I didn't score as many goals. I always felt like maybe I didn't really deserve it."

I glance sideways at her. With pursed lips, she nods. "I get that. But of course you did deserve it. Hockey's a team sport. You win as a team. You lose as a team."

I nod. "I know that. Everyone contributes in their own way. But it was more like, I was still a rookie, I hadn't put my time in, I didn't deserve to win the ultimate prize so soon. I should have had to work harder for it."

"So you're doing that now," she says.

"Yeah."

"I admire that."

How is she so open and honest about everything? I admire her, too.

15

MABEL

"He called us again."

"Seriously?" I let my head fall back and stare at the ceiling of Marek's condo. I'm on the phone with my mom. Julian is still harassing them about me. "Why?"

"He's worried about you."

"He's not worried about me," I mutter. I'm pretty sure he's only worried about himself. "I don't really know why he wants me back, since I was never good enough for him."

"Mabel, clearly that's not true. He cares about you."

Does he? If he's still calling Mom and Dad, maybe he does care about me. I feel those doubts rising up again.

"He says he'll forgive you for leaving him."

He'll forgive *me*? "Mom..." I stop. He'll forgive me... because it was my fault. I'm the one who ruined everything. I screwed up and that's what made him be so controlling. He was just trying to help me. Because I wasn't good enough. I wore the wrong clothes and I didn't look good enough. I didn't work on my "professional image" and so I didn't get promoted. I didn't make dinner, so I was lazy. I valued my friendship with Bellamy too much to abandon her on her birthday and made her a priority over our relationship.

Those self-doubts are taking over my thoughts again. I've been feeling stronger, like I've left all that behind, but my mom's blame is bringing them all back.

I'll never find a man who accepts me for who I am, because I'm too much. Too chatty. Too messy. Too unconcerned with appearances.

"I left because he wanted to change me," I finally say to Mom.

"But honey, when you're in a relationship, you *do* change. You grow and evolve. That's normal. It's important."

"What if I'm the only one changing, though?"

"Well…" She pauses. "You were growing up."

I know exactly what she's thinking. I *needed* to grow up. I was the one who *needed* to change.

"You had a good job. A nice home. You were really settling into a mature life. You seemed happy, and we were happy *for* you."

I remember how I felt when I was with Julian. Always on edge. Drained. Depressed. Wondering if I was crazy. I felt like nothing about me mattered – my identity, my thoughts, my feelings, interests, opinions, hopes for the future… it was all about him.

And they were happy for me.

My throat constricts painfully, and I close my eyes. "I have to go, Mom. I have an interview this afternoon and I need to get ready for it."

"Oh, good! I was going to ask how the job hunt is going."

"It's going." I swallow thickly. "I'll let you know how the interview goes."

"Okay! Good luck, honey!"

I end the call and slide down into the couch cushions. My lungs seem tight, like it's hard to get air into them, and my arms and legs feel heavy. I want to wrap the blankets around me and stay here on the couch, instead of going to my interview at Brockman University. It's another in-person interview, but it's a library assistant position, and the lowest paying of all the jobs I've applied for. Even if I get the job, I might not take it. Why bother going?

* * *

I'm lying on the couch when Marek and Ben get home from practice.

"What are you doing here?" Marek asks. "I thought you had a job interview."

I don't lift my head from the cushion or move my gaze from my phone screen where I'm watching a TikTok of someone making a disgusting pasta recipe. "What is it with these people not cooking the pasta? I don't get it." I watch the woman add a block of Velveeta cheese to the dry macaroni in the foil dish. Bleh.

Both guys go to the kitchen.

"Did your interview get canceled?" Ben asks.

"No. They need some liquid in there to cook the pasta. Oh, nooo... frozen peas? That's fucked up."

"Aaaaah! Jesus Christ!"

My head lifts.

Marek is standing in front of the open fridge. "What the fuck is this?" He recoils.

Ben laughs and pulls the head out.

I burst out laughing, too. I forgot I put my drama llama head in there earlier.

"Are you drunk?" Marek demands of me.

I roll my lips in. "I had a gummie a while ago."

"What? Jesus Christ."

I'd passed by a dispensary the other day so this morning I popped out to pick up a pick-me-up. I feel a lot happier. I turn my attention back to TikTok. "Butter! Perfect. So much butter. Now the liquid."

"What are you watching?" Marek asks.

"TikTok. Yes! Milk." The woman pours milk over the chunks of butter in the pan. "Holy crap, that's a lot of garlic." My eyes widen as several large spoonsful of minced garlic from a jar are added to the dish.

"Cooking videos?" Marek says.

"Yeah. Among others. Oooh... mustard! I did not see that coming." The cook squeezes yellow mustard onto the block of cheese with several loud farting noises. I giggle like a ten-year-old boy. These cooking videos are extra funny after the edible.

Ben walks over to stand behind the couch with an apple in his hand.

"You know they make these videos to play into our psychological need to watch train wrecks, right?"

I lower my chin and give him a look. "That sounds impressive."

His lips twitch. "We're all attracted to something crashing and burning."

"Huh." Maybe this is distracting me from the train wreck of my own life. I turn back to the video. "Ahhh! She's dumping frozen chicken tenders onto it all." I show my phone to Ben.

He doesn't even look at it, eyes fixed on my face. "You said you wouldn't be home until around two after your interview."

I shrug. The cook adds a bag of shredded cheese on top of the chicken fingers. "Oh, yeah. More cheese. I should make this for you guys some time." I cackle. "So healthy."

"What happened?" Ben asks quietly, a crinkle between his eyebrows.

"Nothing." I close TikTok and sit up. "We can start your next coaching session early!"

Ben makes a "yikes" face, no doubt at my somewhat baked state.

I run a hand through my tangled hair.

"What did you do, Mabel?" Marek joins us, frowning. "Did you not go to your interview?"

"No. I did not. It wasn't worth it."

"What does that mean?" Marek stares at me. "You need a job."

"I probably wouldn't have gotten the job. And even if I did, I probably wouldn't take it. It was only an assistant position and it didn't pay much."

"It's better than nothing, though, right?"

"Is it, though?"

Ben is watching me closely. I'm too high to care.

"Jesus, Mabel." Marek shakes his head.

Ben turns and gives Marek a long look.

Marek exhales. "You can't do shit like that."

"I can do whatever I want. You all assume I'm the one who ruined everything."

"Wait, what?" Marek frowns. "Who is you all?"

"Mom phoned earlier. She still thinks I should get back together with Julian. You all assume it's my fault. You all assume I'm a cornflake who makes bad decisions." I'd be angry if I wasn't so mellow. I stand up, ready for a good flounce. "Well, I don't care what you think of me." I strut down the hall.

Except I don't have anywhere to go. My "bedroom" is the living room. Fuck.

I duck into the bathroom and close the door. How long can I stay here? A long time.

I sit on the closed toilet, elbows on my knees, chin in my hands.

I did just act like a flake who makes bad decisions.

I exhale a long sigh.

Yes, I do sometimes make decisions based on emotion. More when I was younger. I have a tattoo on my left hip that attests to that. But I managed to go through college, get a master's degree and a good job. Find a boyfriend. Although, look how that turned out. That was my worst decision... and my family doesn't even realize it. I roll my eyes.

I was hurt after my conversation with Mom. My reaction wasn't exactly... stable.

And I did it in front of Ben. I may not care what my family thinks... but I do care what Ben thinks.

I've been sitting here for a while, I don't know how long but my butt is starting to hurt, when there's a soft knock on the door.

I roll my eyes. "What?"

After a short pause, Ben calls, "Are you okay in there?"

I nod. Which is stupid because he can't see me. "Yeah."

"Are you going to come out?"

"No."

I hear a low chuckle. "Mabel."

"Fine. I'll come out." I drag myself up and open the door. "Where's Marek?"

"He went out."

"Okay." I try to be businesslike. "Let's get to work." I walk past him to the dining table and take a seat, my spine straight.

He joins me.

"What do we need to work on next?" I ask him.

After a long pause, he says, "The gala for Keeping Kids Safe is coming up in a couple of weeks."

"Okay. What is it about the gala you don't like?"

"The usual. Making small talk with people I don't know."

"How fancy is this?"

"I'm not sure."

We do some sleuthing online and find the website. The event is being held at a restaurant on the edge of Liberty Park in Jersey City. We look at some past events photos.

"Okay, it doesn't look super glam," I say. "But very nice. Do you have to wear a tux?"

"No, thank God. Just a suit."

"And you have several nice ones to choose from." I grin.

"Yeah."

"Do you know who'll be there?"

"Not really. People who work for Keeping Kids Safe. Probably some politicians, like the mayor? I don't know. Team management. Me."

"Okay, so let's work on some small talk ideas that you can keep in your back pocket."

"I always forget that stuff. Then I'm standing there trying to think of what to say and it takes too long and gets so awkward."

I tilt my head. "Can you bring a plus one?"

He shrugs. "Probably."

"I could come with you."

His eyes flicker and his mouth twitches. "Would you do that?"

"Sure. I'll be there as moral support. I'll mingle with you. I can help you out, but only if you get really stuck."

"That would be great."

"Okay! I don't think you need me. You've totally got this! But if it helps, why not?"

"Yeah." He gives me a crooked smile. "Why not?"

A while later, I close my laptop. He's got notes on his phone and we've practiced making small talk.

He glances at me a few times, then says, "Do you want to talk about it?"

I grit my teeth, but I've calmed down from earlier. "About what?"

He makes a face like he's trying to find words, casting about in his mind, his lips pursing. He's clearly uncomfortable.

Of course he is. I want to smack myself. "I'm sorry. I don't know. I don't need to dump on you."

"It's okay. I may not know what to say, but I can listen."

My face softens and some of the tension eases out of my body. Yeah. That's him. Quiet. Stable. Supportive.

"I'm supposed to be helping *you*," I murmur.

"We have lots of time."

I nod. I stand and move over to the couch to sit, sliding down into the cushions. "My ex-boyfriend is still trying to find me." I look up at Ben.

His shoulders tense and his eyes narrowed, he follows me into the living room. "He wants to get back together."

"Yes." I press my fingertips to my upper lip. "But I don't want to. And I don't want him to find me."

"He did hurt you." His voice is grim as he sits next to me, his hands curled into fists that he rests on his thighs.

"Not physically. But yeah." I blow out a stream of air. "Not all at once. It happened gradually. I was sucked in by how charming he was. Successful. Smart. He's a university professor," I explain. "He's sophisticated and mature. He was really into me, and... I liked it. Most guys always think I'm a little too... nutty." I'm sure he gets that, but he doesn't say it. "It made me feel... I don't know, flattered and proud that he liked me." God this is embarrassing. I want to slide right off the couch and make myself thin enough to hide under it. "That someone like him could be interested in someone like me. Things moved pretty fast but it was nice. I moved in with him. And then things started changing."

"Fuck." He drags a hand across his mouth.

I tell him more. "He told me the reason I didn't get the promotion at work was because I dress too hippy-ish. That I needed to dress and act more professional if I wanted to be taken seriously. One time he said my outfit made me look dumpy. When I got upset, he'd say I was too sensitive. When I told him he hurt my feelings, he'd say he was just trying to give me constructive feedback. He made me feel stupid and inferior and degraded. Then he would apologize and act like he was sorry. After he would treat me shitty, he'd be nice again. And I kept hoping he would stay nice. But... he never did." I draw in a breath. "He didn't hit me or anything," I assure Ben, although I don't add that I worried about that after one of the last times I tried to tell Julian how I felt and he got so mad he picked up my favorite candle and threw it at the wall, then told me it was my fault because I got him so upset. "But he belittled me. Manipulated me and controlled me." I stop, once again so ashamed to admit that I got sucked into this. I don't want Ben to think less of me because I was so gullible. But I want him to understand.

"I felt guilty," I tell him. "For not being good enough for him. I tried harder."

He makes a sound in his throat that sounds like a growl.

"I felt like I couldn't make good decisions, because everything I did was wrong. I tried to talk to my parents about it, but they liked Julian. They still do," I add bitterly. I huff out another sigh and drop my head forward. "Julian is still calling them and trying to find out where I am."

"Fuck," Ben mutters. "Why didn't you leave him?"

"You mean sooner?" I give him a wry smile. "I was afraid."

Ben closes his eyes briefly, a muscle in his jaw jumping.

"I questioned myself. Maybe Julian was right. Maybe I wasn't smart enough. I felt ashamed. I didn't know what he'd do if I left. How he'd react. It's hard to explain the panic and depression, and how it stopped me from acting. I kept trying to do better, but then... one day he made me choose between him and my best friend. And I realized I was slowly giving up my whole life for him. My friends, my agency, my whole identity. I didn't know who I was anymore and what I did know of myself, I hated for being so weak and f-foolish."

"You're not," he says firmly. "You are not weak. The fact that you're here shows how strong you are."

"I felt weak today, after my mom called." I sigh. "I lost it and went back to feeling like it was all my fault, that I wasn't good enough for him, that I should have tr-tried harder."

I hate the way my voice quivers and I bow my head.

"Jesus." With a low noise, Ben slides an arm around my shoulders and gives me a gentle one-armed hug. I turn into him. He's strong and warm and solid. I press my cheek against his shoulder and lay my hand on his chest, trying not to cry. "I'm glad you're here. I want to hurt that guy."

His other arm comes around me, his big hand cupping the back of my head, pressing me closer. It's so comforting and reassuring. And also... seductive.

Because strong and warm and solid can be comforting, but also arousing. I want to press my breasts to his hard chest. I want to kiss him in the opening of his shirt. I want to feel his skin and breathe in his scent and taste his mouth.

Oh, God. I'm getting turned on.

The vibe around us is shifting. He probably knows I'm hot for him. He's probably embarrassed and trying to figure out how to get out of this. I squeeze my eyes shut and draw back from him.

But he doesn't release me. He's gentle though, loosening his embrace, then using his fingers to lift my chin so I have to look at him. And his eyes are dark and blazing. His mouth is soft, lips parted, and he looks at my mouth like he wants to taste me, too.

My breath catches and a heavy ache pulses between my legs.

It has to happen. Our faces move closer, drawn by an invisible cord, and our mouths meet. His is warm and firm on mine, pressing, then opening on me, opening my mouth to his. For a shy guy, he doesn't hesitate. But he's not aggressive... he's hungry and insistent, but gentle and seeking, and I'm willing and eager. His tongue pushes into my mouth and I love it; I love his taste, the sense of him consuming me. I want more.

I slide my hand into his hair, that thick, silky hair, tangling in it, giving my mouth up to his, pressing closer. His arms around me are strong, sheltering, making me feel... oh, God, I feel so much. My heart beats frantically and my skin burns with arousal.

We keep kissing, again and again, mouths wet and sliding, tongues gliding, licking, and sucking and devouring each other. His beard teases my lips and that heaviness low down inside me tightens and coils. Our hands move over each other, exploring, squeezing, caressing. He's all solid bone and firm muscle and as I get closer still, yes, he's hard. I let out a low moan and my head falls back as his mouth tastes my throat.

His body strains toward mine as much as mine does toward him. Sharp need spirals inside me.

Then he pulls back. I swallow a whimper and stare at him with wide eyes. He watches me, his mouth wet and swollen, his eyes bright with lust, but also steady and serious. I give a tiny nod and he smiles, his eyes close, and he moves in again to kiss me even deeper, turning my face for the best angle, slanting his mouth across mine, licking inside.

Now I do whimper, the need inside me reaching an unbearable peak. "Ben," I whisper.

"Mmm." He brushes his lips and beard over my jaw.

"Marek could come home."

He goes still, his nose pressed to my throat. He breathes in. "Yeah." I feel heat pulsing off him.

"We should..."

"Stop?"

"No." The word escapes me before I can filter it. I'm hot and melty, my head spinning. I'm aching for him and I don't want to stop. "We should... move."

I sense his relief as he presses his nose deeper against me and exhales. "Oh." He lifts his head and meets my eyes again. "Yeah. My room. Let's go."

16

BEN

I want to carry her into my room.

The place that's mine. Just mine. It's where I go to hide out, to be alone, to get my energy back. I don't have a home right now and it's been so fucking hard. This room is all I have, the only place that's just mine.

And I want her in there.

I separate myself from her clinging arms and legs and stand, grasping her hands and pulling her up too.

I almost cried when I thought she wanted to stop. Like, sobbed literal tears. I'm so hard for her I'm dying. But she has a solid point. We don't want Smitty walking in on us.

Being reminded of my buddy gives me an anxious twitch. I'll think about him later.

I pick her up and she squeals, hands grabbing my neck. "I knew you were strong."

I smile as I stride toward my room. I take her straight to the bed and I sit on it, her on my lap, then I shift us over so I'm stretched out on my back and she's on top. Her soft curves press into me as we kiss more.

Her loose dress rides up on her hips and I lay my hands on her ass. Her leggings are so soft, her flesh so firm beneath them, filling my palms, and I squeeze and mold her shape as our mouths move together.

I sit up and she's still straddling me and the buttons of her dress are right in front of my face. I look up at her eyes, her huge pupils making her eyes so dark, and she smiles as I begin to open the buttons, one by one. I lean in to press my mouth to her chest, between her tits, then I part the opening of the dress to reveal lace that cups those sweet tits perfectly. The roundness of her cleavage makes lust pulse in my balls.

She lifts the dress over her head and tosses it somewhere.

I tug her bra aside and reveal perfection – creamy skin, a perfect pink nipple, and I groan. Banding my arms around her, I move in and kiss her there, licking, fondling her breast, then pulling her nipple into my mouth.

"Oh, God."

I open her bra at her back and get rid of it, then sit back to admire this view, gorgeous curves right there. "So fucking beautiful."

Her smile is glorious and bewitching. I'm desperate for the taste of her again and I latch onto a nipple with more force this time, wrapping my arms around her slender body to hold her in place. Her head falls back, she leans into her hands on my thighs, and she rides me, grinding against me. My jeans and her leggings are in the way but it's not stopping her from seeking her pleasure and that's so fucking hot I nearly combust. I suck the other nipple, drawing hard, and she makes a low noise of delight.

"You like that."

"I do. Oh, God, I do."

I lick and suck and nip, and then I roll down to my back, watching her, filling my hands with her tits, massaging and squeezing. She gathers her hair in one hand and leans toward me, shifting so she's on her hands and knees over me, and she kisses me. I cup her face and meet her mouth and open hers in deep, dirty kisses.

Then I groan again as she finds my aching cock through my jeans and grips it. My skin tightens. Heat and pressure spiral low in my belly.

"Feel how hard my cock is," I growl.

"It's so hard." She rubs me and electric heat rushes through my body, and when her fingers open the button of my jeans and slide down the zipper, I help her eagerly by shoving the denim and my boxer briefs down my hips and thighs and then kicking them off. I sit up to get rid of my socks but she's already got my cock in her hand and I'm losing my goddam mind.

I make a noise that's embarrassingly needy and she hums a return sound, seeming enthralled by my dick.

I fucking love that.

"Need you out of these," I rasp, and she lifts her ass in the air so I can get the snug leggings off her. It takes a moment of acrobatics, with her on her hands and knees, and I move behind her to peel them down her legs and tug them over her feet. I take note of the pretty tattoo on her ankle, a delicate open book.

I pause for another moment of rapture to study her ass in front of me, more creamy smoothness and roundness. "Jesus. Can I..."

"Yes."

Well, that could give me permission for a lot of things, but I'll take it one step at a time. First, I get rid of my shirt, yanking it off over my head, then leaning into kiss her there, pressing my mouth to each cheek.

Oh, sweet Jesus.

I need to eat her. Devour her. I breathe in her scent and my dick goes impossibly harder. I open my mouth wide and dive in to lick her softness, to lap at her wetness, her taste sweet and zesty on my tongue. I can't get enough of her and I groan as I eat at her.

She falls to one side, looking over her shoulder at me. I glance up at her and her face is bliss, lips parted, eyes heavy-lidded. I follow her down to the bed and keep lapping and sucking, squeezing one butt cheek, then I lift her leg up and over so she's on her back, legs parted.

"Pretty." I trace a finger down one plump fold, so soft and pink. Then I bury my face between her thighs again. Making soft sounds of pleasure, she closes her eyes, lifts her chin, and clasps her breasts. Another groan climbs in my chest.

I tease her with my tongue and fingers, pull silky flesh into my mouth and suck. She reaches out for me, gentle fingers curving around the back of my neck as I savor her. I find her clit with my index finger and circle it, so gently, and she pulls in a breath, her hips lifting. "Yes."

I watch my finger on her, slick and wet.

Her breathing quickens and her abs contract. Her fingers tighten in my hair.

"Close?" I murmur. "I wanna make you come."

"Yes," she pants. "Close..."

I use my tongue, rubbing it there, and fuck yeah, she comes against my mouth, yanking at my hair, hips lifting to my face, crying out. I fucking love it.

"Yeah. Oh, yeah." I suck her clit until her thighs grip my head and she tries to push my face away. "I wanna do it again," I mumble, kissing the neat patch of russet curls.

"No. God. I can't. You don't have to."

"Fuck, I'd do this forever. Please."

"Oh my God. I want it to be good for you, too."

"This is so fucking good for me my brain has melted into my feet. I'm broken."

I hear her huff of laughter. "I want you inside me."

"I will be. I promise. I will, if that's what you want. Let me lick you more."

She moans and her thighs fall open again. "I don't know..."

"Yeah. It's good. It'll be good. I'll make it so good."

And I do it again, this time fingers inside her, finding the spot that makes her wail, pressing on it from the outside with the palm of my other hand on her lower belly, my lips and tongue working on her until she's nearly sobbing and writhing and coming apart on my mouth again.

I lift my face to look up at her. She's flushed, a little sweaty, and so gorgeous I can't breathe. I wipe my mouth. "We need a condom."

"Mmm." Her eyelashes flutter. "D'you..."

"Yeah." Thank Christ. I haven't had much action lately, but I'm still prepared. I move and yank open the drawer of the nightstand and pull out a box. I fumble in it for one then tear it open. My hands are shaking so much I'm afraid I'll rip it, so I slow down, fighting for breath, and then I'm afraid I'll come in my own hand before I get it on and get inside her.

Breathe. In. Out.

My heart is hammering, my blood sizzling. I can't even think, except for, *holy shit, Mabel is here, I'm fucking Mabel, and she is gorgeous.*

My eyes fastened on her face, my knees spread wide, I slowly push into her. She just came twice and she's juicy but she's tight and I don't want to hurt her. "Okay?"

She nods, watching me, too, her lips curved into a smile that seems both horny and awestruck. "Do it."

"You want me to fill that tight little pussy?"

"Yesssss."

Her channel is so warm and snug. I keep easing in, further and further, until I can't go any deeper. I pause, pressing right to her, as close as we can be, joined right there. "Oh, Jesus. Fuck. Look at that gorgeous pussy taking my cock."

She whimpers.

I grip her hips. "Don't move," I bite out. I pulse inside her and we both take shallow breaths, staring at each other. The eye contact is mesmerizing, almost too much, but I can't look away.

I've had enough sex that this isn't new. I'm not a virgin or even a rookie when it comes to sex. But this is... different. Maybe because I'm with someone who actually likes me. Who knows me. As we stare into each other's eyes I feel something twist in my chest, like it's wrapping around my heart.

I have to kiss her, so I stretch out over her on my elbows and hold her head in my hands as I find her mouth with mine. It's messy and urgent and I start moving, I have to, I can't stop myself. I want to pound into her and fuck her so hard.

I roll my hips, sliding in and out, and she meets me and matches the rhythm, hooking her ankles at my ass. Her hands glide up and down my back as we kiss and fuck and kiss and it's not going to take much. My balls are tight and hot pressure builds at the base of my spine.

Her eyelashes flutter. "I think... oh, God..."

Satisfaction fills my chest. "Yeah. Come for me again, baby. I'm almost there, sorry..."

"Don't say sorry. It's... good..." She's gasping. "Ohhhhh..." She lets out a low wail and squeezes me.

"Jesus!" I put my whole body into it, rocking against her. I press my face into the side of her neck, my blood pounding in my ears, my breath harsh. Every pull and slide increases the tension inside me. She's luscious and soft and hot and perfect. My balls squeeze, electricity shoots up my spine, and I growl as wave after wave of pleasure slams into me.

Sweaty and panting, we lie wrapped up in each other, joined together. I think my heart's going to pound right out of my chest.

How the hell did this happen? We were sitting on the couch and she was telling me about her asshole ex and I got all these feelings. I hate that motherfucker for what he did to her. I hate that she's still damaged from what he did. I hate that she was nearly crying and I wanted her to feel better and so I hugged her, and... and... well, there's been some kind of heat or spark between us for a while and I guess I shouldn't be surprised, but holy shit, that was a fucking forest fire.

17

MABEL

I am ashes. Incinerated, burned up cinders.

Ben eases his weight off me, at least partially, and collapses beside me. His skin is hot and damp, his breathing choppy.

"Did you know that orgasms make women more creative?" I mumble.

He huffs. "No. I did not know that."

"I'm going to be *so* creative."

He chuckles, his fingers brushing over my shoulder. "You're welcome. Be right back." He rolls out of bed and grabs some tissues off the dresser to remove the condom.

I smile. That was amazing. He's amazing. Not just his body, which is tight and lean and strong. Not to mention inked. I'll explore his tattoos in a few minutes. But his mind – his generosity, his genuine enjoyment of making me come, his filthy mouth – holy shit. I might have just fallen in love.

No. I'm kidding. I'm not falling in love again. I'm done with that. Done with men. However, sex is not something I want to do without. And wow. I lucked into some damn good sex.

It strikes me then that Ben is not shy in bed.

I shift and roll to face him as he rejoins me, laying my hand on his chest, studying his face. He lies back, eyes closed, his mouth wearing a satisfied curve.

"What?" He doesn't open his eyes.

"You were talking a lot."

A faint crease appears between his eyebrows. "When?"

"Just now. While we were..."

"Fucking."

I grin. "Yeah."

"Is that a problem?"

"No! Not at all. It was hot. But usually you're quiet."

"Oh."

After a moment of silence, I laugh. "Okay, back to normal."

One corner of his mouth kicks up and he opens his eyes. "I was trying to think of what to say. So yeah... back to normal. I guess things slip out when I'm..."

"Fucking."

He laughs. "Yeah."

Our eyes meet and we smile at each other.

"I wanted to take you to Rupert's for dinner," he says.

I blink at that non sequitur. "Oh."

"Because at Uncle Ernie's you wanted to order some fancy truffle thing and nobody else wanted it and I wanted you to have the fancy truffle thing or Wagyu beef or oysters on the half shell or whatever."

Something soft and hot unfurls in my chest, sending warmth through my body, and emotion swells in my throat. I touch his cheek with my fingertips, then brush them over his bearded jaw and down to his shoulder. I drop my gaze there to study the wolf in black ink as I regain control of my voice, then trace over it. "I like this."

"Thanks. One of the teams I played for was the Wolves."

"And... is this a sloth?" I touch more ink.

"Yeah. I like sloths."

"That doesn't seem appropriate. You're an athlete."

"They keep to themselves," he explains.

"Ahhh. Who knew?" I nod. "Actually, I did. Did you know that sloths can hold their breath even longer than dolphins?"

"I did not know that." His lips twitch.

"It's true."

"How about this?" He touches the tattoo on my hip.

"Oh, God." I close my eyes.

"'Girl almighty'?" he reads.

"Yes." I sigh. "My friend Bellamy and I got matching tattoos when we turned eighteen. We were big One Direction fans." At his blank look, I add, "That's one of their songs. We thought it was very badass at the time."

"Ah."

"Now it seems cringy."

"It could be worse."

"Yes, I guess it could."

"One time when we were on a road trip – this was with my last team – one of the guys got drunk and passed out so we drew a fake tattoo on him."

"Uh oh."

He grins. "Yeah. It was on his nipple. We used a black Sharpie and made it into a little face with a sombrero on it."

I choke on my laugh and bury my face against his chest as my shoulders shake.

"When he woke up and saw it, we told him he wanted to stop at a tattoo parlor and insisted on getting it done. We had him convinced it was real for a good few hours."

"Was he mad at you?"

"Naw. He was mad at himself when he saw it in the bathroom mirror. He was ready to flip tables."

I grin.

"I like this." He touches my ribs where I have a smallish tattoo of a stack of books with a trail of unfurling pages. "This fits."

"Yeah. I have one on my ankle, too."

"I noticed it earlier." He flips me onto my back and moves down my body, lifting my leg to peer at my ankle. "Very nice." And then he kisses it, a slow, gentle press of his lips. Cradling my foot in his hands, he kisses his way up my calf, and I'm melting all over again. It's so erotic, him sitting naked, kissing me, stroking my leg, looking completely absorbed. As he nears the apex of my thighs, my muscles tighten.

He looks up at me.

I lick my tender lips. "Um..."

"Too soon?"

He apparently has no issue with stamina, his cock thick and hard. It's handsomely shaped, with heavy veins, a flushed crown, full testicles, and thick dark hair surrounding the root.

"Maybe I should do... this..." I trace over a vein with a fingertip, then rub my thumb over the tight head.

His tongue swipes over his bottom lip and he looks down at my hand on him.

I stroke him, loving the feel, rubbing my thumb over the head. "Lie down."

He makes a strangled noise and rolls down to his back while I rise to my knees and move between his legs. "Fuuuck."

I smile and slide my other hand beneath his balls. "Ohhhhh." It's a sigh of pleasure. His balls are heavy and round and fit perfectly in my palm. I caress and squeeze them gently as I pump my other hand up and down. My lips part hungrily. I want to taste him, too.

I bend and kiss the tip.

He sucks in a breath. "Damn, baby." His hands slide into my hair, stroking it back from my face and holding it at my nape.

I curl my fingers tenderly around his cock and stroke, then flick my tongue out to lick, sliding wetly over him then circling the head. His body jolts and I love his rough groan. I want this for me, but I want to give it him, too. I breathe in his singular male scent, rubbing the tip of his cock over my wet lips.

"Oh yeah, baby." His fingers tighten in my hair. "That's so good. Lick me... open up and suck me."

I lick all up and down the shaft over velvety skin, then finally open my mouth and take him in, letting the wet flesh glide over my lips and deep inside.

"Holy fuck, Mabel. Oh, yeah."

I slide my lips up and down, loving the weight of him on my tongue, the salty taste of him filling my mouth. I lose myself in the smell of him, the taste of him, his hoarse sounds of pleasure filling my head.

"Work that hot little tongue on me. Yeah, just like that. Jesus."

His praise fills me with pleasure.

"Your mouth is so hot," he moaned. "Hot and greedy. I love it."

I love it too, the velvety texture of his skin, the throbbing hardness beneath.

"Yeah, yeah, that's good." His hips thrust into my mouth as if he can't help it. I find a rhythm, coordinating it with my hand because I can't take all of him. His hips pick up my cadence, gently pushing toward me. I open my eyes to look at him and he's watching me, his lips parted, eyes glittering. Something stretches out between us, something hot and intense.

"Love that," he whispers, his fingers twisting in my hair. "Suck me with that hot little mouth."

More heat rises inside me. I can't believe how excited I am by this.

"You love it, don't you? I love that."

I attempt a nod and then his cock swells even more and he shouts. His balls tighten against my fingers, his taste fills my mouth, and his body goes still, his hands tangled in my hair. Slowly, I let him slide out of my mouth and he releases my hair. He cups my jaw and gently massages it. "So goddamn beautiful."

I draw the back of my hand across my mouth and smile into his eyes.

* * *

"Tell me more about your friend with the matching tattoo."

I smile, later, still in his bed. "Bellamy. Don't you remember her?"

"Nope."

"I think you met her. We've been friends since eighth grade. She's my ride or die." I sigh. "We talk on video chats, but I miss her. Especially now. She never liked Julian."

"She has good judgment."

"Better than mine," I say morosely.

"Hey." His head snaps up. "Don't do that. You can't blame yourself for him being a shit weasel."

I choke on a laugh. "But I do."

"I heard that, earlier, when you were telling me about him." His voice roughens and his hands tighten on me. "I want to hurt that motherfucker."

I lift my head in alarm. "No!"

He looks back at me, eyes narrowed, and I'm reminded that while Ben is reserved and quiet, he's big, tough, and protective. I've seen him protect his teammates. I've seen him with his siblings.

And now I see him with me.

After all that time with Julian, thinking I deserved being treated like that, thinking that was the best I could have, that I wasn't worth anyone's protection... I have a sensation like the bed is dropping, like I'm falling, slowly, weightless and wafting. My heart thuds in heavy beats and I feel it all the way to my toes.

"No," I say more quietly. "Don't hurt him. We're done and I'm moving on. But..." I bite my lip. "Please don't tell Marek about it."

He gazes back at me with that stern expression that's making my heart dissolve and my lower belly flutter. "Why?"

I don't answer for a long moment. Finally, I say, "When I was in college, one of the girls who lived in my dorm was sexually assaulted."

He gives a slow nod, listening intently.

"We all felt terrible for her, but... some of the other girls started talking about it and saying things like, why did she drink so much that night, and why did she go back to his place. How hard did she try to stop it." I pause, remembering with shame that I didn't quash that talk.

"They blamed her," Ben says quietly.

"Yeah. It happens all the time. And I can only imagine what people would say about me. 'Why did she stay with him?' Like, I think I'm pretty smart. How could someone like me be so stupid?"

"Jesus," he mutters, and swipes a hand down his face.

"I'm afraid of what people will say. Even my family. It's just the reality... everyone has a tendency to blame the victim. It's a weird way of making us feel safer. *I* even blame myself."

His jaw clenches so tightly a muscle tics.

I suck on my bottom lip briefly. "Then there's the fact that Julian still wants to get back together. He's still calling my parents, Marek, he even called Bellamy." I meet Ben's eyes. "If I tell people about him – well, I told

Bellamy, but she knows not to say anything to him – but if my dad or Marek find out... if they say something to Julian... he could come after me. I'm afraid of him."

"Fuck." Ben closes his eyes.

"I don't want to be seen as weak and helpless."

"You are not." He cups my face in both hands and stares into my eyes. "You are incredibly strong. You're a fighter. A survivor. You got out and you're amazing. And if anyone blames you for what happened, I'll..."

Softness fills my chest. I lean forward and kiss him. "Thank you." Then I draw back. "So please don't say anything. I will tell my family. I want to get my life back on track first, so they know I'm dealing with it. With everything. So they know I'm really okay."

I can see the conflict on his face in the way his eyes shift and his mouth tightens. "Okay. But I want to go find that guy and fuck him up."

I don't need him to do that. I'm dealing with this on my own. But I love that he wants to do that for me. I love having someone on my side, who doesn't blame me, who believes me. I love...

Well. Ben is a great guy. But I'm just out of a toxic relationship, still rebuilding my life. The last thing I need is to get involved with another man. I should probably tell Ben that so he knows what this is...

The sound of the door to the apartment opening has both of us jerking our heads up.

Our eyes meet.

"Marek," I whisper.

"Fuck."

Well, this is awkward.

"He told us all to stay away from you."

I frown. "What? Told who?"

"The guys."

"Oh my God." I roll my eyes. "He doesn't control who I sleep with."

"I know, but... doing it right under his nose is not cool."

"He won't know. He won't come in here." Thank God Ben closed the door.

"He'll wonder where you are."

"Maybe." I elevate one shoulder. "I'll go sleep on the couch once he's asleep. I'll tell him..." Wait. I'm going to lie to my brother? I nibble my bottom lip as I weigh our options. I could just tell him what happened. I play that out and imagine him giving me shit for screwing around with another man when I've just broken up with my boyfriend.

It feels like it's been a year since I left Julian. In some ways, anyway.

But Marek's going to judge me. I know it. And I'm pretty sick of being judged by him.

"I'll tell him I was out," I finally conclude.

Ben's mouth turns down at the corners, but he nods. "Okay. But..."

I know what the but means. But... what are we doing here? But... is it going to happen again? And a million other questions I don't want to think about right now. I lean forward and kiss him. "It's okay," I whisper. "We'll figure it out."

18

BEN

"So how's the baby doing?"

I'm in the workout room at the practice facility and I'm undertaking my next assignment from Mabel – to strike up a conversation with one of my teammates that's not about hockey.

Alfie smiles. "He's doing great."

Alfie and his wife, Ayla, had a baby about six months ago, a little guy named Kane.

"Growing like crazy," he adds. "Even sleeps through the night."

I grin. "I don't know much about babies, but I know that's a good thing."

"Yeah. It's hard because Ayla's still nursing and she's the one who has to get up to feed him. We're gonna start giving him a bottle so I can do it sometimes, but she didn't want any nipple confusion."

Oh, boy. "That would be bad," I say. I don't even know what that is.

"Yeah, we had a hard time getting him to latch on at first."

This conversation is not going any way I anticipated. I'm sweating even more than I was as I pedal on the bike.

"But breast is best!" he says cheerfully. "Ayla was upset about it because she thought it was something she was doing wrong, and she was determined to breastfeed. But we met with a lactation consultant, and she said it wasn't Ayla, it was Kane, the lazy little bum. He was too lazy to suck."

I want to jump off this bike and get the hell out of here. I swipe my forehead.

"Anyway, we got through that and the little guy loves the boob now."

"Great." I search for another topic. Anything. *Anything.*

"I still can't believe I'm a dad," he says.

"Yeah, that must be quite a life change."

"No shit. Projectile vomiting, poop exploding out of the diaper, endless crying..." He laughs. "Keeping a small human alive is kind of terrifying. But also... wow. It really changes your perspective on a lot of things. Like, so much stupid shit doesn't really matter."

"I can see that. That small human must become the most important thing in your life."

"Yeah, exactly. Sometimes it's hard adjusting to that, but other times it's..." He pauses, staring across the workout room. "It just is. Because I love him more than anything."

I've always thought I'll have kids... someday. But seeing Alfie head over hockey skates with his little guy tugs at something in my chest.

"Well, I'm done." Alfie climbs off the bike.

"Yeah, me too." I grab a towel and mop my face, ready to hit the shower.

Okay, I did it. Now to report back to Mabel.

Just thinking about her makes my blood run faster.

Since that night we ended up in my bed, we've been banging every chance we get. Which is a challenge because Smitty's around all the damn time. I know, I know, it's his apartment. Now I'm more eager than ever to move into my own place. Only a few more weeks.

After the All-Star break we lost three games in a row. But since then, we've been playing better and it gives me hope that we can turn things around. Since I went off the deep end that night, we've been working on different things, and it feels like everyone's trying harder. I'm trying harder, too. Since losing my shit didn't seem to hurt anything, I've been speaking out more. I'm trying to be positive when I see good stuff. And I'm trying to be encouraging when I see other things we need to be better at. I'm trying to walk the talk, to lift the other guys up instead of being down on them, to help them when I can, and to work my ass off, too.

We also had a one-game trip to Charleston to play our nemesis. This was one game I really wanted to play well. In the room before the game, I channeled Super Duper Marc Dupuis and called out some of the guys with what we need from them tonight. Chopper... Alfie... Archie... Turks.

And we won, goddammit.

A few wins can change a lot. Our confidence is higher, our motivation stronger. It feels good.

Smitty and I came to practice together today, so we go home together, which means he's there when Mabel arrives home from another job interview. She's been called back for a couple of second interviews, but so far no actual job offers. It'll happen. She's definitely working at it and I admire how confident and composed she is. I've never seen her at work, but somehow I know she's a great librarian.

"Hi," I greet her. "How did it go?"

"It was good." She sighs. "But the job's not exactly what I want."

"You can't be so picky," Smitty tells her.

"I know, I know." She drops her purse on the dining table. "I was excited because it's the New York Public Library, but it's at their business resource center."

"Which means...?" I lift an eyebrow.

"It's resources about personal finance, investing, small business stuff." She makes a face. "It would be okay and I wouldn't turn it down, but I like working with kids. At least some of the time."

"Right."

"So, we'll see." She shrugs. "I'm starving." She walks to the fridge and opens it.

She's dressed in an interview outfit, which for her is slightly less, uh, funky than her usual style. Long flowy pants pool on the floor as she bends over to peer in the fridge, which makes the pants tighten over her round ass. She straightens with a container of yogurt in her hand, turns and catches me ogling her. She smirks.

I glance right away at Smitty, but he's looking at his phone. I need to be careful about looking at Mabel when he's around. I have a hard time keeping my eyes off her, though. Also my hands.

She grabs a spoon and leans on the counter. The fitted shirt she wears hugs her tits and a leather belt emphasizes her narrow waist. Her hair is in a neat librarian ponytail. "Did you do your homework?" she asks me, dipping the spoon into the yogurt.

"I did. I talked to Alfie." I pause. "About breastfeeding."

She grins and Smitty even looks up. "Breastfeeding?"

I shrug. "That's what new parents talk about, apparently. Also projectile vomiting and poopy diapers."

"That's great." Mabel nods approvingly. "Good work. What should we work on next?"

"Well. The fundraiser is coming up in a couple of weeks."

"Lots of time for that. I think you should keep having those one-on-one conversations with your teammates."

It went okay today, so I agree.

"You've been talking more in the dressing room," Smitty notes.

Mabel perks up. "You have?"

"Yeah."

"It's making a difference," Smitty adds.

"That is great!" I love her pleased smile.

"Also, your new wardrobe is getting big ups on the socials." He holds up his phone. "People are noticing."

"Oh. Good?"

Mabel laughs. "Yeah, that's good. Show me." She bends over Smitty to peer at his phone. "'Nothing wild, but stylish, classy, and tasteful,'" she reads. "Um... oh! 'This blue checked sports jacket is outstanding, a bit more casual but still elegant. It's nice seeing Antonov try different things.' Woop!" She turns around and blinds me with a smile. "There you go!"

I grin. "I guess I'll take it."

"Yeah, you will." She saunters back toward me. "Hey, you should organize a get-together for the guys. Like a team-building event, but informal. Just hanging out."

"Like axe throwing?" I ask dryly.

"Sure! Or an escape room. Or that bar with the pinball machines. You could have a pinball tournament."

I rub my beard. "That could be fun."

"I'll help. I mean, a bit. Behind the scenes. Let's look at your schedule and see what would work."

I'm not a guy who throws parties. I can be social when I have to, but hosting a party scares me. What if nobody comes? Or... even worse... one or two people come? But this is definitely something a captain would do. So I man up and do it. I'll tell everyone about it tomorrow and send a text with details to the group chat for the team.

Smitty disappears while we're working on this, then comes back to announce he has an appointment for a haircut.

"It's about time," Mabel says, but her smile is teasing.

When he's gone, we look at each other.

"How long do you think we have?" she asks.

"An hour?"

"That's not long."

"We better be quick then."

She laughs, a delighted musical sound that I'm coming to love, grabs my hand, and drags me to my bedroom.

* * *

"You have so many books," she says a while later as she gets dressed. She studies the pile on the dresser.

"This isn't even all of them. Most are in storage until I move in."

She nods. "Me, too. I couldn't bring all my books. They're at my parents' place." She moves to inspect the titles. "You must like David Aaldenberg."

"Yeah." He writes historical stuff. I have a few of his books. "That one's about the Cold War."

"I know." She smiles at me. "I've read it. What else do you like? Oooh, thrillers. Is this good?" She holds up a paperback.

"Yeah, I liked it. It has a really tricky plot."

"Cool." She sighs. "I can't wait to have my own place and all my things."

"Oh yeah, same."

I hear Smitty coming home. "Ah, shit," I mutter.

Pursing her lips, Mabel grabs a book and walks out with it. "Thanks, I'll return this to you when I'm done!" she calls to me over her shoulder. "Oh, hey, Marek. Your hair looks good."

I close my eyes and shake my head. We're playing with fire here. I'm starting to think I should just come clean with my buddy. *Hey, I'm fucking your sister. Just thought you should know.* The thought makes me cringe. I don't know what else to tell him, though. It feels like more than just fucking. But I made that mistake once, the first time I slept with a girl. I told her I loved her and then never saw her again. I can have casual relationships with a woman; I've done that lots. But calling whatever this is between me and Mabel "casual" doesn't feel quite right. It feels... disrespectful.

And yet Mabel's not serious about this. She's been clear that she's not interested in a relationship and who can blame her after what she went through with Julian the super prick? Only I'm not Julian and I'm not a super prick... would it be so bad to get involved with me?

Fuck, I can't think like that.

19

MABEL

Ben is a good guy. If I was going to fall in love again, it should be with someone like him. But I thought Julian was a good guy, too, and look how that turned out. Maybe I'm rebounding. Or reverting back to my teenage self and the crush I had on Ben. Or maybe... I really don't want to be alone despite telling myself I don't want or need to be in another relationship. Will any man really accept me for who I am?

Although I never feel Ben is judging me. And I like that about him. If anything, he's making me feel comfortable in my own skin again. More confident that I'm not a big loser.

So... we're sleeping together. And it's amazing. Seriously, the best sex of my life.

We're both on the same page. Neither of us want a relationship.

I get why I don't. Obviously. But why doesn't Ben?

I try to draw that out of him one night when Marek goes out and we're alone. Of course we end up in bed, because it's basically impossible not to. But after, I snuggle into him, and ask, "Have you ever been in love?"

Probably a loaded question that will make him freeze up.

"No."

I smile against his chest. Typical him with his lack of verbosity.

But then he surprises me. "The first time I ever had sex with a girl, I told her immediately after that I loved her."

"Ohhhh. How did that go?"

"Not well. I never saw her again." He sighs. "I was a stupid kid."

"How old were you?"

"Sixteen."

"Yikes."

"Yeah. I got all... emo about it. It was dumb. I never did that again."

"She didn't talk to you about it?"

"No." He snorts softly. "She was sixteen, too. We were both too young for that kind of conversation. Too young for sex, probably."

"Still. That must have hurt, a little at least. That she disappeared."

"Yeah. It was humiliating."

"But you've had other relationships."

"Eh... Nothing serious. Things never worked out."

I remember what he said, once, that the women he met weren't interested in long-term relationships. "What happened?"

I know I'm pushing it with the personal questions, but I've been open and honest with him about what happened with Julian, so I think it's fair.

"Well. There was this one girl – Kodi. We went out together for a while, but... her friends thought I hated them."

"Why would they think that? Ohhhh, wait." I give him a searching look. "It was because you were quiet, wasn't it?"

"I guess, yeah. They were always partying and going out. I went along, but that's not me. Kodi wanted me to make more effort with them. I think her exact words were, 'Why can't you just be normal?'"

Ohhhh. I close my eyes as a sharp object gets stuck in my throat. I remember Jenny saying he was the most boring date ever. I get why she'd say that. And why his girlfriend's friends would say that. But they're wrong. "That was because they didn't know you. Not because there's anything wrong with you."

He says nothing, his mouth tight.

"For real, Ben. When someone takes the time to get to know the real you, they don't think that. It was their loss."

His face softens and he reaches over to stroke my hair. "You said I was fine the way I was."

I did say that. I look into his eyes. "And I meant it." I want him to know that.

"I know." He smiles. "And it meant a lot to me."

Emotion brews in my chest. I'm starting to understand why he's hesitant about relationships. It's hard to trust someone after you've been hurt.

I know that myself. After I ended things with Julian, I couldn't imagine ever trusting a man with my honesty and vulnerability. But with Ben, I feel... safe.

Yet also scared.

"I'm sorry those women were such bitches. That was a terrible thing to say to you."

He chuckles. "Thanks."

"I need to pee." I roll away from him and out of bed and pad naked across the rug. I open his bedroom door and come face to face with Marek.

He freezes, his face almost laughably shocked. Probably similar to mine.

I slam the door shut.

"Aw, fuck," I hear from the bed.

I bash my forehead against the door, my eyes squeezed shut. Did I really just encounter my brother while I'm bare ass naked in his friend's bedroom?

"What the fuck is going on?" Marek shouts from the hall.

I hear rustling from the bed. I peek over my shoulder to see Ben standing there pulling on a pair of gray sweatpants. He shoves a hand into his hair and strides toward me, his jaw set. His steady eyes and straight posture reassure me.

"I got this," he says quietly.

I pull my bottom lip between my teeth. "Let me grab something." I dart across the room and grab my jeans.

Marek pounds on the door. "Mabel! Get out here."

Dealing with a confrontation like this is not something Ben enjoys. And yet there he is, stepping up, brave, unflinching. He opens the door and squeezes out, shutting it behind him. "Easy, man," I hear him say as I try to dress with fumbling hands.

"Where is she?"

"She's getting dressed. Give her a minute."

I pull in a breath and let it out. Ben's got this.

I almost want to cry. He's got this.

I can handle it. I'm a big girl. But the fact that he's handling this makes my heart inflate.

Their voices move away from the door. I run my hands through my hair then follow them out to the living room.

Marek levels a forbidding look at Ben. "I cannot believe this."

I walk up to Ben and grab his hand with both of mine. "It's okay, Marek."

His eyebrows launch up into his hairline. "It's *okay*?"

I glance at Ben, then lift my chin. "We're adults. We're both consenting. It's fine."

"I'm sorry, man," Ben says.

"Sorry for what, exactly?" Marek snaps.

"I'm sorry you found out like this."

"So you're not sorry for banging my sister?"

Ben's answer is immediate. "No."

I exhale softy. I didn't realize how much his answer meant to me.

Marek narrows his eyes at Ben. "What the fuck, man? You know there's a rule about a teammate's sister."

"Why? Why is that a rule?"

"I don't know! It just is."

Ben looks at the ceiling.

"Things get messy when you break up," Marek adds.

Ben slides a glance down at me, then says quietly, "We're adults. Whatever happens, we'll deal with it like adults."

I nod quickly. "Yes."

"How long has this been going on?" Marek demands.

"Not long. A couple of weeks," Ben answers.

"She's only been here for a month!"

"This is your home and we're guests here and I apologize, too, for sneaking around behind your back and for not telling you about... us. The thing is..." Ben rubs his mouth. "I wasn't sure exactly what to tell you."

I nod. "Me either. It's..." I can't say it. I can't say it's just casual. It's just sex. It's not *just*... anything. It's more than that. But I haven't even said that to Ben yet.

"Jesus Christ."

"Why are you home so early?" I ask.

"Taylor wasn't feeling well."

I'm dying to know who Taylor is, but this isn't the time. I nod.

"I'm so fucking pissed," he mutters.

"I see that."

"You were lying to me."

"Well..." I catch Ben's eyes again. Yeah, I'm not going to play that "well, technically" card. "Yeah."

Marek exhales sharply. "This is fucked up." And he turns and stalks down the hall to his room.

"Shit." Ben turns to me. "Are you okay?"

His concern for me makes my insides soften. "I feel terrible."

"I know." He reaches for me and pulls me into his arms.

His hug is exactly what I need right now. I lean into him and slide my arms around his waist. Guilt burns its way up my throat. And I'm not even sure if it's guilt about fooling around with Ben, or guilt about hiding it from Marek. Or guilt about getting caught.

I love my brother. We're different, but we've always been close. I don't like it that he's mad at me. And I bet Ben feels the same. I lean my head back to look up at him. "I'm sorry."

He closes his eyes and shakes his head. "Don't apologize to me. We got into this together."

Yeah, we did. And weirdly, that makes me feel better. To have a partner in crime. Or just a partner. Someone who accepts responsibility for his actions and doesn't try to blame me. Someone who has my back. My eyes sting and my heart is doing weird jumpy things in my chest. This man...

* * *

"Hey."

I look up as Marek comes into the living room the next morning. His face is set and his lack of a ridiculous greeting like "What's the deal, banana peel?" makes me sad.

"Hey." I worry my bottom lip between my teeth. Then I jump off the couch. "Don't be mad at me, Marek!"

He turns his back on me in the kitchen. "I'm not mad."

"Yes, you are! Geez, Marek." I walk over to the counter. "I'm sorry you found out about me and Ben like that. We... it just happened, and I'm not sure what it all means right now and..." I stop. "What exactly is the problem with Ben and me hooking up?"

His shoulders are up around his ears as he makes a smoothie. "Someone's going to get hurt."

My eyebrows shoot up. "And who are you worried about?"

After a few seconds of sticky silence, I say, "You're worried about Ben, aren't you?"

He sighs. "I'm worried about both of you. Ben's not exactly experienced in relationships. And you..." He faces me and meets my eyes. "You've just ended one. I still don't know what happened with you and Julian, but I care about you and I worry about you. This is not a good idea."

I lift my chin. "I know it's not good timing, but it happened. We're adults. If it's a mistake, we'll deal with it."

He shakes his head, still clearly unhappy.

Which makes me unhappy, too.

20

BEN

When my phone rings with an actual phone call, I assume the worst. Nobody ever calls me. My friends and family know better. I hate talking on the phone.

It's Marc Miller.

Christ. I'm being traded. It's only a few weeks until the trade deadline. Yeah, so what if they said they want me to be captain? They can trade anybody, anytime. I'm done.

"Hello?"

"Ben. Hi."

"Hi, Mr. Miller."

Mabel's with me, sitting across from me in a coffee shop. She watches me, eyes wide.

There's a brief pause and I close my eyes and try not to feel nauseous.

"I have some bad news," he says.

I nod, my heart squeezing into my throat.

"There's been an accident."

My eyes open. I frown. "An accident?"

Mabel straightens.

"Yeah." His voice is heavy. "A car crash. Carson and his wife and baby."

My gut spasms. "Are they okay?"

Mabel's forehead creases and she presses her fingers to her mouth.

"No." He breathes out noisily. "Carson and Ayla are in the hospital."

"Oh, Jesus." I drop my head forward.

"Their baby... didn't make it."

My face changes. I feel it – a tightening, my head drawing back, my mouth going slack. My thoughts go murky. Did I really hear him right?

Mabel scoots over and sets her hand on my back, her expression worried.

I swallow thickly. "Oh my God."

"Yes." Mr. Miller's voice chokes up.

My head is spinning. My gut is roiling.

"Who is it?" Mabel mouths.

I hold up a finger to her, afraid I'm going to puke.

"Carson's going to be okay. Ayla too. But..." He stops. I sense him fighting for control. "But this is obviously going to be difficult for them."

"Jesus." I can't even imagine. I shake my head, trying to clear it, but it doesn't work. I grab Mabel's hand and hold on. She squeezes tight.

"I called you first," Mr. Miller says. "I hope you can let your teammates know. I've talked to Gord." He's referring to Coach, Gord Bastien.

"What else can I do?"

"I... uh... we'll need to support Carson, obviously."

"Yeah. How long will he be in the hospital? Which hospital?"

"I don't know how long. He's at St. Matthews."

"Okay." I don't know what I'm doing. But I know I need to sound like I do. "I'll take care of it. We'll figure out a plan."

A plan? For what? Their baby is dead. Jesus fucking Christ.

"Thanks, Ben. We'll talk again. I'll let you know if I hear anything more."

"Yeah. Thanks."

I end the call and stare at Mabel's distressed face. "Alfie," I croak. "Him and Ayla. They were in an accident. Car accident. Their..." I can't say it. My throat closes up.

"What?" she whispers, squeezing my hand again. She waits.

I fight for control, my eyes burning. "Their baby died."

"Oh, no." She rears back, eyes wide, lips parted. "Oh my God."

I nod, head bowed, blinking back tears.

"Oh, that's so terrible." She moves in closer and slides her arms around my waist, hugging me, leaning into me.

I just saw Alfie last night at the pinball tournament Mabel helped me arrange. We all had so much fun. Then I remember that conversation I had with him in the workout room. How in love with his baby boy he was. How it changed him. Holy. Fuck.

A baby. He's dead.

What is *wrong* with the universe that something like this could happen?

I press the heels of my hands to my wet eyes. I've never experienced something like this, but I feel it like a knife in my chest. How will they survive this?

I absorb Mabel's presence, her comfort, glad I'm not alone right now. When she sniffles, I realize she's crying, too. "I don't know them well, but that's so tragic."

"Yeah." I choke out the word and hug her back, holding her tight. "I can't believe it. It can't be real. How could something that terrible happen?"

"I know. I know." She strokes my hair, kisses my jaw.

"I have to let the other guys know."

"Oh."

"I don't know how to do that. I can't do it. Right now." I clear my throat.

"It's okay. Take some time. This is hard."

"Fuck." I dash away more tears.

"Can I help? What can I do?"

"I... don't know. Just be here."

"I'm here." She meets my wet eyes. Hers are shiny, too. "I'm here. Let's go home. You can handle it there."

"Yeah. Okay." I have to do it before someone hears about this from the wrong source. But I honestly don't know if I can.

Back at the condo, I say, "I think I'll send a group text. Only because it's faster."

"Yeah. Then you can talk to everyone."

"Okay." Through a blur of tears, I compose my message. Before I hit send, I have the presence of mind to delete Alfie's name. He doesn't need to see that.

My phone blows up immediately, with texts and calls. I can't even handle them all. While I talk on the phone with my earbuds, Mabel takes my phone and texts guys back. We end one call and answer another.

Everyone's in shock. Nobody knows what to say or do. I have to take control even though I'm floundering in my own disbelief and grief.

"I need to call the hospital," I tell Mabel. "I should go visit him."

She bites her lip and nods, finds the number for St. Matthews, places the call and hands me the phone. I confirm Alfie's still there and he's in satisfactory condition. He can have visitors.

"Okay." I exhale long and slow. "I have to go."

She nods, bent over my phone again. "I'm telling everyone that."

"Thanks."

"Do you want me to come?"

I hesitate a fraction of a second. "Yeah."

"I will."

We both stand. She grabs her purse and coat, hands me my jacket. I probably would have left without one.

I have a vague idea of where the hospital is, but Mabel brings up the directions on her phone and guides me there. We find a place to park and enter the hospital.

I hate hospitals.

I visited a bunch of kids in the hospital at Christmas. I hated it then, but I could handle it. I don't know if I can handle this.

"You can do it," Mabel whispers in the elevator, clasping my hand. Her smile is sad but reassuring. Her faith in me strengthens me.

Alfie's in a private room. I don't know where Ayla is. I should visit her, too, if I can.

"I'll wait here," Mabel says outside the door of his room. "But I'm here." She holds my gaze.

"Thanks." I kiss her cheek, close my eyes, briefly, then enter.

Alfie's in bed. His face is bruised and cut and his left arm is in a sling. His eyes are closed.

I slowly approach the bed. If he's asleep, maybe I shouldn't wake him up? But his eyes flicker open hearing my footsteps. I stop beside the bed. We look at each other.

"I'm so fucking sorry," I whisper, my eyes stinging again. I grab his hand. "So sorry."

He nods, his mouth tightening, and he closes his eyes again.

For once, I don't need words. For once, I know my presence is enough. I know there's nothing I can say. There's nothing anyone can say.

I pull up a chair and sit in silence for a few minutes. Then I talk.

"I've let all the guys know," I say, my voice low. "They're all in shock. We're here for you, man. Anything you need. We'll do anything."

He nods again. "Ayla?"

What does he mean? "I think she's still here," I say. "Want me to find out?"

"She's here. I… I need to know she's okay."

"Hang on." I jog to the door. Mabel's leaning against the wall and snaps up straight when she sees me. "Can you find out about Ayla? Can he see her?"

"I'll see what I can do." She hustles over to the nursing station.

I go back to Alfie. "Have you seen her at all?"

"No. They told me she had soft tissue injuries but… but she was in shock."

I nod, trying to put things together.

Mabel comes in. She gives Alfie a warm sympathetic smile and I stand and walk closer to her to talk. We step outside the room. "She's just down the hall. She's okay. But she's kind of… out of it." She sucks on her bottom lip. "Um. They said she's on a lot of medication. They're going to bring her here."

"Okay."

I go back and tell Alfie that. I sit again. The smell of this place is making my stomach roll, not to mention the thought of Ayla being heavily medicated because her baby died. And Alfie's not exactly in great shape either.

"Is your arm broken?" I ask.

"Yeah." His voice is husky. "They need to wait for the swelling to go down to cast it."

He won't be playing for a while.

But who cares about that? I remember our conversation, how he talked about priorities changing. And I get it. Hockey? Who gives a shit when your child is dead? It doesn't even matter a little bit right now.

"Yeah," I finally say. "They'll get you fixed up."

I turn at a sound at the door and see Ayla in a wheelchair, dressed in a hospital gown, a nurse pushing it. Ayla's face is... I don't know how to describe it. I've never seen anyone so pale and so blank. Her eyes are empty. Her lips are nearly white. She looks vacantly at me, then at Alfie as the wheelchair nears the bed.

"Ayla." He lifts his head and reaches out a hand.

I stand and move away.

Ayla doesn't take his hand.

Something in my chest cracks painfully.

I can't fucking bear this. I look helplessly at the nurse, who is much more composed than I am. She leans down to Ayla. "Talk to your husband, Mrs. Alford. He needs to see you."

Ayla's gaze drifts away. "Yes." She doesn't move.

I pull in a long, slow breath, inflating my chest, pushing down the sick feeling. Fuck.

"Okay, buddy." I move back to the bedside. "I'm gonna go now. But I'll be back. Okay? We're all with you."

He meets my eyes and the agony there nearly takes my knees out. He swallows and nods. "Thanks, man."

I swipe at my nose and trudge out of the room.

In the hallway I go straight to Mabel and fold her into my arms.

She hugs me back. "It's okay. I got you. You've got this."

"No. This is so fucked up I can't even..." My throat squeezes painfully. I stand silently, then collect myself and draw back. "Let's go."

* * *

The next day, everyone comes over to Smitty's place.

I wanted to do something, but I'm fucking homeless right now, so I asked Smitty if I could invite the guys over. Luckily he agreed. He's wrecked about this, too, which has distracted him from being pissed at me about Mabel.

The team did a press release and tomorrow's game will have a minute of silence. But I felt I needed to get everyone together to talk about what's happened. It's a lot to process and I think we need to do it together. Mabel steps up like a champ and helps me with food and beverages, although a lot of the guys show up with a case of beer or a bottle of something. At least we have lots of chips and dip and other snacks.

Smitty's living room is crowded, with all the seating filled including the stools at the counter, so some guys are sitting on the floor leaning against the windows or cross-legged. Everyone wants to talk, and there's a lot of "what ifs" and predictions, some dire, some optimistic. Some guys get emotional – Turks has two kids of his own and Shawzy has three, and they're both really shook.

I mostly just have to listen, and I do, taking in their emotions. It gets heavy. I have to admit, I was sad before this, but hearing everyone else's grief devastates me. It's like I'm taking it all on myself. It's like I can feel their feelings.

I've noticed this before, like when my dad died. It was hard enough on me but dealing with the feelings of everyone in my family dragged me down into a really dark place for a while. That's scary. But the thing that makes me know I'm going to be okay is having Mabel here.

It's a late night and when everyone has eventually cleared out, I feel both good and totally fucking exhausted. Good, because we're all here for each other. Comforting each other even though we're all hurting. Exhausted because I spent every single one of my energy spoons on talking and listening and empathizing.

Mabel and Smitty are cleaning up the kitchen when I close the door on the last guest. I trudge toward them and collapse onto a stool.

"Are you okay?" Mabel asks, wiping the counter.

"Yeah. It's… a lot."

Smitty closes the fridge. "Thanks for doing that, man. I think it was needed."

"Yeah." I nod. I prop my elbows onto the counter and rest my head in my hands. "This sucks."

"It does." He shakes his head. "Okay, I'm going to bed. G'night."

"Night, Marek." Mabel runs a cloth under the water in the sink.

We're quiet when he's gone. She wrings out the dish cloth and hangs it on the sink, then turns to me. Her face is troubled. She glances down the hall where Smitty just walked, then moves toward me. She smooths her hand over my forehead, then my face. "You were amazing tonight."

"I was?"

She nods, holding my gaze, draping her arms over my shoulders. She presses her soft lips to my temple. "You were. And I know it was hard for you."

She does?

"You take on other people's emotions," she says softly, fingers in my hair. "It's part of who you are. And it can be hard, when it's something like this."

I nod. "It's a lot." I lean my head on her shoulder. "I fucking hate this."

"I know. It's awful." She lets out a slow exhalation. "I wish it never happened."

"Me too."

"I'm glad you were there for your teammates. I just..." She stops.

"What?" I look up at her.

Her pretty mouth pouts a little. "I just want you to know that I'm here for you. Because you need someone, too."

Jesus.

21

MABEL

As if things aren't bad enough, the next day I get a DM on Instagram... from Julian. I blocked him everywhere else but not Instagram because he was never on Instagram. But he is now. I should have known.

> **JULIAN**
>
> Mabel we need to talk. You're acting like a child.

I have no intention of replying.
Another message follows:

> **JULIAN**
>
> This isn't over between us and if you don't talk to me you'll be sorry.

I stare at my phone and read that message again. And again. My heart bumps against my breastbone.

I'm alone here in the condo. I don't think Julian knows where I am. He just found me on social media. The building has good security. But still, adrenaline spikes through my veins.

"You fucking asshole," I whisper. I read the threat in his words.

How hard would it be for him to find me? I don't think my parents or Marek have told him where I am, but staying with Marek has to be something he's considered. He doesn't know Marek's address; we never visited Marek here. All he knows is New Jersey. But Marek is somewhat famous and if he wanted to, Julian could probably find him.

That can't happen.

I have to leave.

How the hell am I supposed to do that? I need a job to get an apartment. The process is frustratingly slow but I've been feeling positive that eventually I'm going to get the job I want. But Julian can't find me here. The tone of his message is unmistakably threatening. I never feared him physically... but maybe I should. And I definitely don't want Marek and Ben caught up this. This is my problem, not theirs.

I need to move farther away.

Gah. It's been hard enough doing this, never mind moving to Alaska or something. Alaska would be a good place, though.

No.

I don't know.

I rub the spot between my eyebrows where it throbs. I'm not thinking straight. I don't know what to do.

* * *

I have an interview at Newark Public Library. The job is at one of the smaller branches as branch manager and children's librarian. That sounds like an enticing combination of responsibilities. I don't have a ton of experience to move into a managerial position, but for the salary they're offering, they're not going to get people with a lot of experience.

I may not even be staying here, but I don't want to bail on an opportunity, so I go in optimistic and enthusiastic.

After, I go to the Hargrave Center where the Storm are having their morning skate. Ben said I could get a ride home with him and Marek.

Security allows me into the arena and the team is still on the ice so I make my way to behind the benches. There are a bunch of media guys sitting a few rows up and on the other side a group of kids watch.

I immediately seek out Ben.

Before my own brother.

It's like I'm back in high school.

I shake my head as I watch the guys shoot the puck at Ford in net. Then I squint as I watch Ben behind the net. Ford's knees are bent, feet wide as he watches Marek skate in on him with the puck, but I clap a hand to my mouth as Ben dislodges the net and moves it to the side. Marek shoots the puck into the net easily since Ford's not even in front of it. I can't stop the giggles as Ford realizes what's happening and smacks his stick on the ice. But I can see his grin behind his mask.

"Nice move, Benny," Cale Skinner calls. A bunch of guys skate around Ben and pat him on the helmet and I hear more laughter. Ben's smile flashes and he taps Ford's pads with his stick.

I didn't know Ben was such a jokester. And the guys are all laughing and easy with him.

I love it.

They get back to more serious work, flying up the ice and rifling the puck at the net one after the other. One of the coaches blows his whistle and beckons for them to join him at the boards. I can't hear what's being said, but they're all listening intently.

The last few games have been a big improvement over earlier in the season. Even over last month. Since that day that Ben blew up at the team, they've won seven out of nine games, and one loss was in overtime. Even after the accident involving Carson and his family, they went on to win their next game. In fact, they crushed the Bears, apparently taking out their emotions on the other team. Ben told me after that he talked to the guys before the game in the dressing room about winning it for Alfie. And they did.

Tonight the Golden Eagles are in town and I'm coming to the game.

I watch the rest of the morning skate and smile as the guys leave the ice, joking around and laughing. It's good to see them happy and relaxed. Ben and Marek were both pretty down about how things were going a month ago.

Ben sees me and lifts a gloved hand. I wave back. Some of the other guys wave at me, too. I feel like these guys are my friends. I like that.

I don't want to leave here.

22

BEN

I got the keys to my new place on the first of March, but we had a game that night, so I couldn't do much. My furniture and stuff from storage is delivered the next day, though, and Mabel helps me pack up the things I have at Marek's place and take them up to my condo on the nineteenth floor. My condo is pretty much directly above Smitty's, so it has the same view, and Mabel goes straight to the window to admire it, even though it's a cold, overcast day with threats of either rain or snow.

"So nice," she says with a sigh, then turns and looks around. "Same layout as Marek's place."

"Yeah, pretty much."

"But your walls are not white."

"They are not. Actually, I like that beige color. It'll go with my furniture."

"It's not beige, it's taupe."

One corner of my mouth lifts. "Okay."

We're there when the movers arrive and start lugging stuff in. It's nice to have help. Well, it's nice to have Mabel. Some of the guys offered to help, but I'd rather do it on my own. She unpacks boxes of kitchen stuff and puts it away, then gives her opinion on how to arrange the furniture in the living room. I wouldn't have thought to put the couch with its back to the kitchen, but it works and that way you look out the windows at the view.

"You need more pictures for the walls," she says.

"You don't like my hockey pictures?"

She grins. "I love them. And all the trophies! But you have lots of room here for more."

She has a point. This place is bigger than the last apartment I rented.

"I am so fucking happy to have my own place," I say.

Her smile is warm. "I bet. I know you like your own space."

It's nice having privacy and not worrying about Smitty. He's still pissed about what's going on. And I hate it. He's my best buddy on the team, well, pretty much anywhere. My other good friend Boosh (Julien Boucher) is back in Chicago.

Mabel hates it too and I feel bad that there's a coolness between her and her brother. He needs to see that this is what Mabel wants. We're both adults. I still feel guilty, about it, though.

I tried to talk to him about it. He told me that Mabel just got out of a relationship. I know that. He thinks she's on the "rebound." I try not to be offended that that's the only reason she'd be interested in me. He also reminds me that her life is a mess right now, and I'm aware of that too, but she's working on it.

"I do." I move closer to her. "But just so you know... you're always welcome here."

"Aw." She gazes up at me as I set my hands on her waist. "Thank you."

"But you'll have a room of your own now at Smitty's place."

"Yes. That'll be great. I'm tired of everyone seeing all my clothes. I still need to find my own place, though. I've been looking but it kind of depends on where I end up working."

I frown. "So if you got that job in Brooklyn, you'd move there?"

"Maybe?"

"It doesn't take long to get from here to Brooklyn. You could stay in this neighborhood. Close to your brother."

"I guess. Actually, I think I might go to Los Angeles."

"I'm sorry, what?" I don't think I heard her right.

She shrugs, and her smile is strained. "I've been thinking maybe a fresh start would be better somewhere else."

Somewhere away from me? Or her brother? Or her dickface ex-boyfriend?

My heart drops to my feet, leaving my chest cavity hollow. I try to breathe. I don't know what to say.

"Los Angeles would be nice," she adds. "It's warm there. Sunny."

Outside the apartment window, snow is fluttering down and melting on the ground. New Jersey's not always sunny and warm, and there may not be palm trees here, but it's not that bad.

"Why?"

"Why is it warm there?"

I make a noise. "No. Why would you go there?"

"I just told you. It's nice there."

I have questions. If it was anyone else, I'd shut up and mind my own business. But it's Mabel and... I can't stop myself from asking. "What is going on? Is this because of Julian?"

"Of course it is!" she says lightly with a small laugh. "That's why I'm here!"

I narrow my eyes at her.

"The farther away from him the better," she adds. "And I've always liked the Pacific Ocean."

I've never heard her say that, but what do I know.

I want to put an end to that crazy thinking right fucking now.

But do I have that right?

We're banging. A lot. But... that doesn't give me the right to tell her what to do. Much as I want to.

Maybe I should tell her how I feel. Yeah, I've caught feelings. If I'm honest and tell her that, maybe she won't leave.

Christ. I can't do that. Put myself out there and confess my feelings? Holy shit, I have a hard time talking about the weather.

Not with Mabel, though. Still. The fear of telling someone you love them and them not feeling the same is massive, and not just because of what happened when I was sixteen. Telling a woman I love her is one of the most terrifying things I can imagine.

I'm breaking out in a sweat just thinking about it. The room seems to be rolling around me. Am I hyperventilating?

At some level I recognize that not only am I afraid of making myself vulnerable, I'm petrified of losing Mabel. And I don't know whether telling her how I feel about her will keep her from leaving – or send her running.

Maybe this is just a knee-jerk reaction on her part. Maybe she'll think about it and change her mind. Maybe I can show her that she's safe with me before that actually happens.

"How's your bedroom?" she asks.

Change of subject. Okay. Good. Whew. "You definitely need to see my bedroom." I take her hand and tug her along behind me.

She laughs and doesn't resist.

* * *

"I need help."

We're at Uncle Ernie's – Archie, Crusher, Dilly, Skinny, and me. Smitty's not here because he's still pissed at me.

We've all given Uncle Ernie hugs. He lost his great-grandson in the accident and he's wrecked by it. He's still worried about Ayla, and Alfie. He brought us pizza and beers with a wan smile. It's hard seeing the usually cheery guy so heartbroken.

"What kind of help?" Crusher lifts a piece of ham to his mouth.

"Woman help."

"Whoa." They all give me shocked looks.

"Didn't know you had a woman," Skinny says.

"Fair."

"Have you tried a dick pic?" Dilly asks.

Everyone glares at him.

"I'm kidding." He lifts his hands in the air.

"It's Mabel," I say.

Their eyes all go round.

"Mabel Smits? As in, Smitty's sister?" Dilly gapes at me.

"Yeah, that Mabel." I sigh. "I like her."

"Oh, man." Skinny winces. "Does Smitty know about this?"

"He does," I say glumly. "He's not happy about it."

"Could be worse," Dilly says. "I mean, he's friends with you. What if it was someone he hated?"

I don't know what to say to that.

"So you're going to ask her out?" Archie says.

I hesitate. "Like, on a date?"

They all exchange worried glances.

"I thought you had more game than this," Skinny says. "You've dated before, right?"

"Yes. Jesus. It's... we've been..."

"Ohhhh." Dilly grins. "I get it. You've been doing the dipsy doodle with her but now you want more."

"Dipsy doodle?" I rub the twitch in my left eye. "Oh my God."

"Ha. No wonder Smitty's pissed." Archie nods knowingly.

"Okay." Dilly leans forward. "Yeah, you have to take her on a date."

"Okay. She's coming with me to the Keeping Kids Safe fundraiser."

"No." Archie shakes his head. "That is not a romantic date."

"I'll make it romantic."

"Why don't you tell her?" Crusher says. "Just tell her you love her. Then she'll know you're serious."

"No!" Dilly gapes at him. "You can't say that on the first date. You can't even say you love tacos on the first date. Keep that word out of your mouth."

"It's not exactly like a first date, though," Skinny points out. "They've been boinking."

I roll my lips in and close my eyes. I knew this was a bad idea. I thought making myself a little vulnerable to my teammates would help me be closer to them, but it's just showing me how weird they are.

"Seriously." Dilly nods. "Get her flowers. Compliment her. A lot. But not just on her looks, also her personality."

"Okay."

"Flowers and chocolate," Crusher adds. "Maybe even wine."

"Or something she really likes," Dilly says. "That shows you're thoughtful."

"You could write her a poem," Archie says. "That's a romantic way to show your feelings."

The guys all look uncertain, like they're not sure if they should laugh.

"Here are some things that rhyme with 'I love you,'" he adds. "Blue, glue, shampoo, beef stew, and kung fu."

"I should write those down," I say with an eye roll.

"Manners are important," Skinny adds. "Like opening the door for her, helping her with her coat, holding her chair for her."

I nod. That actually makes sense.

"Don't forget to start with the basics." Dilly grins. "Have a shower."

I give him a disgusted look.

"That's what my mom told me when I was fifteen. It's solid advice."

"Wear nice cologne," Crusher says. "And take care of the manscaping."

"It's a little late for that," Dilly points out. "She's already seen his manscaping."

I cough.

"And dress nicely," Archie says. "That shows respect for her."

"I'll wear one of my new suits."

"Then pay attention to her. Listen to her and nod a lot, and make eye contact."

This is sounding like Mabel's extrovert lessons.

"Definitely don't check out other chicks while you're with her," Dilly advises.

They all nod.

As if I'd do that. I'm not interested in checking out anyone but her.

"Also, make her laugh," Skinny says. "Chicks love guys who make them laugh."

I make a note to find some jokes. "Okay, I think I've got it."

"Let us know how it goes."

Now I'm more terrified about the fundraiser than I was before. Now I don't have to impress only the people from Keeping Kids Safe and the team, but also Mabel. But it'll be worth it.

23

MABEL

I have a new dress for the fundraising event. I know this isn't a date; I'm going as Ben's extrovert coach. Also, I really shouldn't have spent money on a dress when I have dresses and it doesn't matter what I wear. But I still want to look nice for him and for the people he wants to make a good impression on.

I went shopping, thinking I would buy myself a little black dress. Something tasteful and sophisticated and discreet. Every woman is supposed to have one, right? But I don't. Little black dresses are boring. I love color and patterns and sparkles.

I went shopping on Washington Street where there are a few women's clothing stores. The first shop appeared perfect – an elegant black and white striped awning over the door and understated, classic clothing in the window. I left empty handed half an hour later. Then I spied an Anthropologie store across the street. I love Anthropologie. In the window, several dresses caught my attention. I had a faint hope that maybe there would be an LBD that's more... me. But my attention was snagged by a chiffon dress in my colors: shades of bronze, spice, and amber, with a bit of gold metallic thread. I didn't even care what the style was, I had to have it.

So now I'm wearing this beautiful dress with a halter neck and long ruffled skirt. The skirt is shorter at the front so it shows a little leg. I've done my make-up in bronze shades and my hair is in long, loose waves. I bought a pair of sandals, too, strappy ones with a pencil-thin heel. I love them, too.

I go up to Ben's apartment. We decided that was less awkward than him picking me up and dealing with Marek's displeasure. I carry my coat so Ben can get the effect of the dress. His reaction when he opens the door does not disappoint.

His gaze sweeps down, then up. I strike a pose, thrusting one leg out through the skirt opening à la Angelina Jolie, planting a hand on my hip.

"Wow." He meets my eyes. "You look incredible."

"Thank you." My breath leaves me and my skin tingles everywhere as he continues to study me with hot eyes. "You look amazing, too." I step toward him to tweak the knot of his tie. His new suit fits perfectly across his shoulders, the dark gray fabric smooth and expensive looking. He opted for a crisp white shirt, which is classic, but added a more colorful tie, one with a charcoal background and a whimsical bird and plant pattern in blues and spice colors. "Your tie matches my dress."

He looks down. "It does."

I lean in closer, nearly pressing my nose against his neck. "You smell amazing, too."

"Thanks."

"I have something for you." He turns away and picks up a package from an end table.

It's a bouquet of flowers.

"Ohhhh." My eyes widen. I take them and study the colors: deep red, peach, and orange roses, ranunculus, and lilies, with dusty green eucalyptus mixed in. "I love it." I lift my gaze to him. "The colors are so beautiful."

"It reminded me of you."

Who is this sweet-talking man? I go up on my toes to kiss his cheek. "Thank you. I guess I'll leave these here."

"Sure. We'll come back here later. Also, I have these." He hands over a small box of hand-crafted chocolates and a bottle of red wine.

"What is all this for?" I look at them in wonder, then back at him.

"I want to show you my appreciation for you coming with me. And for how you've helped me."

I grin. "You rehearsed that, didn't you?"

He grins back. "Yeah. But I mean it."

"Aw. That's so sweet."

"Also, I want you to know that I don't just think you're beautiful, but also smart and fun and kind."

I think I'm going to cry. What is happening here? My chest fills with so much effervescence I might float away. "Thank you." I touch his cheek. "I also think you are smart and kind. And thoughtful."

We share a long, gooey smile.

"We should go," Ben says in a husky tone. "Yep. Our car service is waiting."

"Right." I blink a few times, then lift my coat. Ben takes it from me, holding it up. With a smile, I turn to push my arms into it and he settles it gently on my shoulders. He opens the door for me and lets me precede him into the hallway, and does the same at the elevator and the front entrance of the building. A town car waits for us in the driveway and he opens the back door for me to slide in first.

Such a gentleman. Although I think he always opens doors for me? For some reason I'm noticing it tonight.

We make the drive to the venue where the event is being held in Jersey City. It's right on the edge of Liberty State Park, on the water of the Morris Canal Basin. As we alight from the car, I take in the potted cedars with little white lights strung through them and the golden glow of the front doors. Other people are walking up the front steps to enter, and Ben takes my arm to join them, which I appreciate in my skinny heels.

We follow the other guests into the large room where the party is being held and I take it in with wonder. The ceilings are two stories high, and strings of more white lights cascade down from beams. Candles glow on round tables, and the two-story-high wall of windows looks out over a long lawn, with the river and the Manhattan skyline glittering in the distance. "Wow. This is beautiful."

Ben nods, looking around.

Is he nervous? This is what we've been preparing for. I can't get side-tracked by flowers and wine and twinkle lights. I'm here for him.

"There's Sue." He nods, then sets his hand on my lower back to guide me toward her.

He introduces me to Sue, an elegant Black woman with long braids in a stylish updo. She shakes my hand and smiles. "You know Maya, of course, Ben."

Ben says hello to her, too, and introduces me to Maya Pérez. We're joined by a couple of men who greet Ben warmly. More introductions have me shaking hands with Marc Miller, the general manager of the team, and an elderly man named Gunnar Hayes, who is the owner of the Storm. Their wives stand behind them, holding drinks, and I reach out to them as well, with smiles. "Hi. I'm Mabel."

The evening turns into a whirl of people, drinks, and delicious food. Hors d'oeuvres and glasses of bubbly wine are passed around by servers. There's a silent auction with amazing prizes that we of course enter. Ben buys about a thousand dollars' worth of tickets. We meet the mayor of Jersey City, a few city council members, and a bunch of businessmen and women. We pose for pictures, both formal ones by the professional photographer working the event, and informal ones for other guests. I stick by Ben's side as he talks to people and I'm probably the only one who notices subtle signs of nerves when he searches for something to say or tries to remember a name. I'm good with names, luckily, and I covertly give him clues.

There's a briefly awkward moment when Ben's GM asks about his new place and when he's moving in, and the GM's wife asks if he bought a house. "No, I bought a condom," Ben answers.

Silence drops over the small group. I pull my bottom lip between my teeth, madly trying to figure out how to rescue him.

Then Ben laughs. "Well, that was awkward. It's a *condo*."

Everyone else laughs, too. Whew.

"Good recovery," I whisper to him a bit later.

He closes his eyes and shakes his head. "I couldn't decide whether to say condo or condominium and that's what came out. I can't believe I said that."

"Forget it. You handled it great."

I spend some time talking to Maya Pérez. She's about my age and we discover a few things in common. She's been to a full moon circle! We laugh about our experiences and I tell her that Cami and Tala and I want to go back to that spa to go to the salt cave.

"Oh, I want to do that, too!" she says.

We exchange numbers and I promise I'll let her know when we plan it.

After an amazing dinner of local sea scallops and braised short ribs with a delicious mystery sauce we later learn is made from hard-boiled egg yolks, mustard, pickles and capers, the tables are moved for dancing to the music of a string quartet who play popular songs à la *Bridgerton*, which delights me.

I love dancing. I don't know if me helping Ben tonight includes dancing with him. I remind myself of my purpose here. But then I think of the flowers and the chocolate and the wine, and how attentive Ben is being to me, and this really does feel more like a date than being his extrovert tutor.

There's a break in socializing where we're alone for a moment. Ben smiles at me. "Would you like to dance?"

I smile back. "I would love to."

We set our glasses down on the table and join a few other couples on the dance floor. It takes me a minute to recognize the song "Cheap Thrills." "This is so fun."

Ben exhales. "It's okay."

"You're doing great."

"It's going fine. It's a lot of work, though."

I have to remember that for him. For me, it's easy and fun. I love meeting people and learning more about them. For him, it's effort. "Nobody would know," I assure him. "And we don't have to stay late if you're running out of spoons."

"Spoons." His lips quirk.

His hand tightens on mine, strong and warm, his other hand on my hip as we move together to the music. Dancing with him is easy, too, and I love gazing up at his handsome face, my heels putting me closer to his height but still six inches shorter. I move my fingers on the soft fabric of his suit, his shoulder strong beneath it.

Warmth curls through me. I've had some wine, but I'm not drunk... so this floaty feeling isn't from the alcohol. "Could you stop being so attractive? It's distracting me."

He laughs. "Sorry. I'll do better." His eyes crinkle up. "You're pretty distracting yourself."

We eye each other as heat builds between us.

"If I said I'd like to score on you tonight, would you think I was being too forward?"

I burst out laughing, throwing my head back. "Oh my God. A hockey line."

"I made you laugh." He looks oddly proud.

"Yes, you did."

"I'm really hoping to score the game-winning goal with you tonight."

I giggle again. "Where are you getting these?"

"I'm a hockey player. We all know those lines. Just be glad I didn't use: is your name Gretzky? Because you're the only one who can make my stick rise."

I groan.

"Right? Some of 'em are so bad."

I'm still smiling. "You don't have to use those lines on me since I'm pretty much a sure thing."

"Oh, yeah?" He turns me with a little pressure from the hand on my hip. "Good to know. You are so naked in my head right now."

I lean my forehead on his chest, laughing again.

God, this is so much fun.

I lift my head. "I know this isn't your idea of a great time, but I'm having fun."

"You know what? I'm having fun, too."

"Good."

Later in the evening, Ben is surrounded by apparent hockey fans wanting to say hello and take selfies, and he handles it all mostly smoothly, with a couple of semi-awkward exchanges about whose phone to use and an attempt to sign a glossy card when his pen won't work.

When Marc Miller and the owner of the team both leave, Ben looks at me. "I think we can escape now."

"Okay." I'm amazed he's lasted this long. And seems to be doing okay.

We collect my coat and head outside. The cold air carries the scent of the river and it's lovely to climb into the warm, dark car when it arrives. It whisks us over to Marin Drive and we stay on that street most of the way home, snuggled in the back seat.

"Thanks again for coming with me," Ben says. "You made it so much better."

"Aw, thanks. But I think you would have handled it fine by yourself."

"I'm glad I didn't have to. I have fun with you, Mabel."

I smile at him. "I have fun with you, too."

He gazes back at me searchingly, as if he wants to say something.

"What?"

He swallows. "I... I want to give you a penalty. For stealing my heart."

It's another cheesy joke, and I laugh at it, but his expression is earnest, not smiling. "Oh." I blink at him. For once, I'm not sure what to say. Is that a joke? Or is he serious?

"I wrote something for you."

"Okay." My eyebrows pull together in puzzlement.

Ben pulls out his phone, unlocks it and finds what he wants. He hands it to me. I read the screen.

> Roses are red, like my face when I see you,
> Violets are blue, like the time I had the flu.
> Your smile is bright, like my phone at night,
> And your eyes are shiny, like a spoon in the light.
>
> I know this is awkward, and probably weird,
> But I like you a lot, even more than my beard.
> So here's my bad poem, it's the best I can do,
> Just know that I'm awkwardly falling for you.

When I've finished reading it, I read it again. My stomach tightens. I stare at the phone while I try to collect my thoughts, which are suddenly all over the place.

Is this another joke? But again, he's not smiling. He's waiting for me to respond, and I sense his anxiety.

The poem is objectively bad. But it makes my heart go all soft and squishy. It makes my trembling lips want to smile and small wings flap in my stomach.

It also scares the shit out of me.

All these things he's done tonight... the flowers, the wine, the chocolates... those are romantic, date things. He's been so chivalrous and attentive. He danced with me, and complimented me, and flirted with me. He made me feel admired. Wanted. Even... loved.

And that's exactly how I felt when I started seeing Julian. When he showered me with expensive gifts and thoughtful gestures and compliments. When he love-bombed me.

I was fooled, then. I was swept off my feet and enjoyed the attention. I thought Julian really cared about me. But it was all about inflating his ego and controlling me. It was manipulation.

I was duped before. Since I ended things with Julian, I've questioned myself so many times. Questioned my judgment – how could I have been fooled by him? How could I let that go on? How can I ever trust a man again?

My shoulders have tightened up around my ears and I'm staring blankly at Ben's phone. My hands start to tremble and my heart develops a tachycardia. Memories flood back, along with the feelings of being both admired and precious, and being manipulated. Weak. Foolish. Ashamed.

A sick feeling sweeps through me and I swallow down a sour taste.

We're pulling into the entrance of our building. I shove Ben's phone back at him and as soon as the car comes to a stop, I wrench open the door and scramble out onto the sidewalk, nearly tripping in my heels.

"Mabel." Ben follows me, tossing a thank you over his shoulder to the driver. "What?"

My legs are so unsteady, I'm stumbling over the concrete toward the door. Ben hurries after me to yank the door open.

"You don't need to open the door for me!" I cry, recognizing in the far recesses of my flustered brain how rude and stupid that is.

"Uh... sorry?" He follows me into the lobby and over to the elevators. "What's wrong, Mabel? I know the poem wasn't good, but I'm trying to tell you... I love you."

Oh, God.

I pause and stare at him for a moment.

"I wanted to tell you sooner. But I... well. Then you said you were thinking of going to LA. I wanted you to know I have feelings for you."

Shaking my head, I step into the elevator and push the button for Marek's floor. I cover my eyes with my hand, head bent. "I can't." Terror claws at my insides and I gulp for air. "I can't do this."

"Mabel." He touches my shoulder, so gently, but I shrug his hand off. I can't look at him. "I need... to take a step... back."

"Okay." His voice is low but steady, solid like a rock. "A step back. Okay."

"I need time. To... think." The elevator slows at the seventeenth floor and the doors glide open. I leap out. "Thank you. I mean..." I'm more lost for words than Ben has ever been. I don't know what to say. Thank you... or fuck you? Goodnight? Or goodbye? My chest burns. "I can't..." I swallow thickly. "Goodnight, Ben."

And I flee into Marek's apartment.

24

BEN

I'm in a foul mood.

After what happened the other night on the way home from the fundraiser, I haven't seen or talked to Mabel.

I don't know what happened. We were having so much fun. It was a great night. Things got sexy on the dance floor and horny in the back of the car on the way home. Until I showed her that poem.

I fucked up and I'm pretty sure it's not because she's offended by bad poetry.

No. I told her I love her. That was what did it. I should have known better! I can't fucking believe I was that stupid again. I came on too strong, too soon, and probably scared her.

I send her one text message telling her I'm sorry and to take whatever time she needs. I don't want to harass her. I know how important boundaries are, especially for her. I'll give her the time she needs. I just hope that she'll talk to me again one day. I hope I haven't fucked everything up totally.

This is probably exactly what Smitty was afraid of and I kind of hate myself.

I drove to the arena by myself for practice today since I'm shit for company right now. There I try to set aside my grumpiness and pay attention to the guys. I'm learning that practices aren't just for me. Yeah, I want to work hard and do better, and set a good example, but they're also a great chance for me to connect with the guys. I've always noticed what other players are doing, but now I make it a point to comment or help if I can. The other day, Skinny came and asked me to work on stick handling with him.

And it's all paying off. We're playing a lot more cohesively. The vibe in the room is better too. Even though we're all devastated about Alfie's accident, we're winning games. It's almost like this devastating tragedy has made us stronger. Brought us together.

We're heading into the home stretch of the season. We're three points out of wildcard spot. We're actually feeling like we can do this.

But when I leave the arena, my gloom returns. I get to go home to my empty condo. Yay.

All I wanted for months was to go home to my empty condo all by myself. It's so fucking weird that now I feel kind of lonely when Mabel's not around. She brings so much brightness and energy. I could probably handle going home alone if I knew it was for a few hours and I was going to see her later. But I'm not. And I'm pissed. And depressed.

Today I walk through the empty concourse of the hockey complex to leave through the front doors. There are a few people hanging around the lobby area and as I stride toward the doors, I hear my name.

"Ben Antonov."

I turn my head to look. A guy about my age is standing there. He's average height, lean, sandy haired, and wearing a double-breasted overcoat in an ugly brown plaid. I give him an inquiring look, not really in the mood for fan bullshit.

He walks toward me. "Ben Antonov?" This time it's a question.

"Yeah." I stop. "That's me."

"Where's Mabel?"

My chin jerks down and my eyebrows pull together. "What?"

He glares at me. "My girlfriend. Mabel Smits. I saw pictures of you two together at some party, so don't try to pretend you don't know her or where she is. I need to know."

Ooookay. In the space of two seconds, a thousand thoughts wheel through my head. I know what he's talking about and I know who he is.

Julian motherfucking Clark.

And he's looking for Mabel.

"I don't think so, pal," I snarl. And I turn to leave.

He grabs my arm.

I'm aware of the attention we're attracting from the other people in the lobby. Christ on a cracker.

I'm also salty for a variety of reasons other than him, and this definitely doesn't help.

"Tell me where she is," he demands.

I look down at his hand holding my jacket sleeve. I look back at his face. This bastard hurt Mabel.

Heat burns through me and my muscles tense.

In the very back of my mind, I'm cognizant of the fact that what I'm about to do is not sportsmanlike. It's not exemplary, captain-like behavior.

I don't give a shit. He hurt Mabel.

Just to be completely fair, I say, "I'm gonna hit you."

My right foot drops back, my right hand curls into a fist, and I lift my arm and drive my knuckles into his face.

He lets go of my arm and yells. Light on my feet, I raise both arms so my left is guarding my face, and prepare to jab my fist into his face again.

He doesn't hit me back, just yells again. "What the fuck!"

An intense bloodthirsty urge to pummel him rises up inside me.

People converge around us, but I ignore them, focused on Julian. I grab his jacket in both hands and give him a rough shake. Then I shove him away from me, hard. Oh fuck, his nose is bleeding. "You leave her the fuck alone," I bark. "Don't call her. Don't text her. Don't even *think* about her, asshole."

"Jesus." His hands go to his face and he yawps at me.

"I mean it." I narrow my eyes and take a step closer, hands up in case he's not getting the message. "I will fuck you up if you ever try to talk to her again."

Julian glances at the people watching us, all with shocked looks on their faces. "You hit me," he says incredulously. "I'm bleeding."

"Yeah, you are." I lift my chin contemptuously.

"I'm calling the cops!"

"Phhht. Go right ahead." Fuck. That might not be so good.

"And I'll sue your ass," he whines.

"Oh, fuck off." I shake my head, push past him, and walk out.

Okay. Adrenaline buzzes through my veins, making my arms and legs tingle. My breath comes quicker as I stride onto the plaza outside the building, my hands still in fists.

That fucking asswipe. How dare he come here and try to find her? How fucking *dare* he?

Also, goddammit, he found her because of me. Because of the pictures from the Keeping Kids Safe fundraiser. I shouldn't have taken her to such a public event, knowing she's trying to hide from him. *Fuck*. I berate myself all the way to my car.

As I open the door, I glance behind me to make sure dickface isn't following me. The last thing we want is him following me home, which is the same building Mabel's staying in.

Nope. No sign of him. Good.

No sign of the cops, either. He legit could get me in trouble for assault. Fuck.

I climb in, grip the steering wheel, and take a few breaths.

He better have gotten the message.

My phone is blowing up before I even get home. Mostly texts. But then a call comes from Coach. I'd rather staple my scrotum to the ceiling than answer it. But I accept the call. "Hello."

"Benjamin."

Fuck me. I'm in trouble. "Yes, sir."

"What the fuck happened?" he bellows.

I grit my teeth and stare at the road. I haven't had time to prepare myself for what to say. What not to say. As always, my default is to say as little as possible. In this case – nothing.

Coach has no patience for the time I need to respond. "Apparently there was an altercation in the lobby at the arena. And you were involved."

"Yes, sir." I can't deny it. "That's right. There was a guy there looking for me. He hurt... someone I care about." I probably shouldn't be having this conversation while driving. I grip the steering wheel and swallow.

"So you decided to chuck some knucks?" he yells incredulously.

I wince. "Yeah."

He sighs heavily enough to blow my eardrum out. "We've been watching you develop this year. Your hockey skills. Your leaderships skills. You know we hoped to make you team captain."

"I know." I've fucked that up. I know it. "I'm sorry."

"We can't have players going around assaulting people off the ice!" He gets worked up again.

I can only nod slowly with grim acceptance as I listen. This is not unexpected. I knew before I even hit Julian what this could mean. And I did it anyway.

Because... Mabel.

"I know, sir."

"Communications is working on this to try to kill it but there were people there who took pictures."

"Yeah." My throat tightens.

"We especially can't have our *captain* assaulting people off the ice. Jesus Christ." He exhales again. "We'll meet tomorrow and talk more about this."

"Yes, sir."

I end the call and take a few breaths, replaying everything he said as I finish my drive home.

When I'm holed up in my condo, I check my messages. Wow, it's impressive how fast this news travels. I have texts from a bunch of guys. Now I can send a message to the group chat.

A hammering on my door startles me.

It has to be one of the guys. I haul ass to the door and fling it open. "What?"

Okay, it's not *one* of the guys. It's Smitty, Crusher, Dilly, and Archie.

Smitty rolls his eyes and stalks in, followed by the others. "What the hell happened?"

"Come in," I say sarcastically, and let the door fall shut behind them. "I punched a guy, okay?"

"I heard that." Smitty looks askance at me. "Why?"

"It was Julian."

His jaw goes loose. "Julian? Mabel's Julian?"

The other guys look at us with perplexed expressions.

"He's not *her* Julian," I grit out. "And she's not his. I made that clear to him."

"I don't... how..."

"What the hell is going on?" Archie asks.

I walk over to the couch and drop my butt back onto it. I rest my elbows on my knees. "Julian Clark. He's Mabel's ex-boyfriend. She broke up with him just after New Year's. He's been trying to find her because he's an abusive asshole."

"What?" They all look shocked and file in to take seats.

Smitty slowly sits on a chair facing me, staring.

"What's with the dead roses?" Archie waves a hand at the wilting bouquet on the counter that Mabel never got to enjoy.

"Never mind. Julian saw pictures of me with Mabel at the fundraiser," I continue. "He wanted to know where she is."

Smitty's eyes narrow. "That's... creepy."

"No shit." I exhale a long gust of air. "I'm sorry. I know Mabel hasn't told you what was happening with them. She plans to. But at this point, you need to know. She doesn't want you to tell him where she is for a reason."

"Oh, Jesus."

"He abused her." I meet his eyes, my jaw set. "It hadn't gotten to physical abuse, but I'd bet my Stanley Cup ring that it would have, if she hadn't left him. He's a narcissistic asshole who manipulated her and destroyed her confidence. He made her feel like... like she'd lost herself."

His face collapses.

Shit. I shouldn't be telling him this. Mabel made me promise not to tell her brother. She didn't mention the other guys, but somehow I don't think she'd appreciate them knowing either.

She also made me promise not to rough up Julian. Ah, well. I'm already fucked.

Smitty shakes his head. "Are you serious?"

"Fuck, yeah. As serious as a penalty shot for the other team in game seven."

"She... what did he do?"

I sigh. "You should talk to her about it. There were lots of things." I tell him some of the stuff she told me, about criticizing her clothes, her career, her friends, how he'd blow up at her and blame her for upsetting him, then apologize and promise it would never happen again.

"I... why didn't she tell us that?"

"Because... well, lots of reasons." I explain it to him, like Mabel told me. "It's easy for us to say she should have left sooner, or she should have done this or that. But she was living in that situation. She was scared. She was convinced it was all her fault because of his gaslighting."

Smitty rubs his face. The other guys all sit slack-jawed and wide-eyed.

"She was ashamed," I add quietly. "That she got into a situation like that, even though it wasn't her fault. She didn't want you and your parents to think less of her because she screwed up."

"Let's go." Crusher stands.

We all look at him.

"Go where?" I ask.

"Let's go find that guy. We'll get the rest of the team, too. How many times did you hit him? Whatever it was, it wasn't enough."

Dilly and Archie stand, too, clearly ready to rumble.

"Guys, guys." I pat the air in a settle-down gesture. "We can't do that."

"Why not?" Dilly folds his arms and scowls. "I'm ready."

"Much as I'd like to destroy him, I'm already in trouble." I tell them about my phone call with Coach without being specific about what I've just fucked up.

"Oh, shit." Smitty grimaces. He knows what this means.

"Yeah. Whatever. Also, we need Mabel to be okay. We don't need to get ourselves arrested. She just wants to be done with him."

Smitty groans.

The guys reluctantly sit again.

"Just say the word and I'm there," Crusher says. "Mabel's too sweet to put up with that bullshit."

"That guy deserves to hurt," Dilly adds.

Smitty looks around at them and their hardened expressions. He drops his head forward. "I wish I'd known."

"I know." I hesitate. "She wanted to get her life back together before she told you and your folks, so you wouldn't think less of her."

He lifts his head and meets my eyes. He exhales sharply. "We all thought Julian was a good guy. But I did notice that she was different with him. More subdued. You know what she was like as a kid. Off the wall. Impulsive."

I lift an eyebrow. "Fun-loving. Energetic. Genuine."

Smitty frowns.

"Unpredictable," I add. "Exciting." I pause. "Irresistible."

"Jesus." Smitty holds up his hands. "Okay, okay."

"I've already apologized for not telling you about us," I say. "But we *are* adults and don't really owe you an explanation. The fact is, I'm in love with Mabel."

The guys all nod.

Crusher looks at Smitty. "Sorry, man. We gave him advice to help him."

"Help him what?" Smitty frowns.

"Help him romance Mabel."

"Yeah, well, the advice didn't exactly work how I hoped," I say glumly. "She freaked out."

"Huh? Over what?" Archie tilts his head.

"I guess I came on too strong."

"What happened?" Smitty asks.

I shift uncomfortably. "She said she needs some time."

"Ohhhh." Smitty's eyes widen, then close, his head falling back. "Is that why she went to Philadelphia?"

My head snaps up. "She went to Philadelphia?"

"Yeah. To visit her friend, Bellamy."

"Fuck." My stomach plunges to my toes. I squeeze my eyes shut. What if she doesn't come back? She already said she might go to California. "When did she leave?"

"The day after the fundraiser." Smitty pauses. "She didn't take all her stuff, for what that's worth."

He apparently knows what I'm thinking.

"Okay." I squeeze my forehead between thumb and fingers. "I guess she doesn't know about Julian being here."

"No."

"If she's on social media, she will," Crusher says. "People took pictures of her ex with a bloody nose."

Smitty bites back a grin. "Darn."

Our eyes meet.

He lifts his shoulders. "I think she really likes you, man. From what she was saying to me. I think she'll be back. And..." He gives a wry smile. "I forgive you both for lying to me."

"Gee, thanks." I smile back, just as sardonically. We share a moment of understanding.

"I'm okay with you two dating," he says. "I guess. You're a good guy. She deserves that."

"She does." She definitely deserves a good guy. I don't know if I'm that guy. But if I have the chance, I'll do everything I possibly can to be good enough for her.

25

MABEL

"I don't really know if that was love-bombing."

I'm at Bistro Bliss with Bellamy, near her Philadelphia apartment, along with our friends Nori and Shantae. We've just finished brunch but we're still drinking mimosas. I like how the bubbly wine is making me a little tipsy.

I look at Nori and bite my lip. "It felt like it."

She nods. "I get that."

"It reminded me of when Julian and I started dating. He showered me with attention. All these sweet text messages and compliments and gifts. He took me to my favorite restaurants. He even took me to a bookstore on one of our dates." I make a face.

"But it wasn't sincere," Shantae says.

"Apparently not. Things changed."

"It's to trick you," Nori says. "You think it's real and he's crazy about you, but he's really doing it for selfish reasons. Setting you up for manipulation and abuse."

"Yeah." I know this. "One time he gave me a Coach bag and I was so thrilled, and then when I annoyed him, he asked for it back."

Bellamy closes her eyes, looking like she's going to cry. "That asshole."

"Punishing you, for whatever it was you did," Nori says softly. "Trying to devalue you."

"It worked," I reply glumly. "Anyway, all the stuff Ben did reminded me of that. The flowers, the chocolate, all the thoughtful gestures."

The cute waiter approaches. "Another round?"

"Yes, please!"

He smiles and disappears.

"Do you really think Ben had selfish reasons for doing that?" Shantae asks.

"I don't know. It seemed very... fake. Like, he wrote me a *poem*."

"Aw. That's sweet."

"It was." I sigh. "It was really bad. But it was sweet. It's not like him. He's a hockey player, not a poet."

"Hmmm." Bellamy frowns.

"He wrote it for *me*. That was so thoughtful that he went to all that trouble. But then I think... am I stupid to think that? Is he trying to manipulate me?" I cover my face with my hands. "Fuck Julian. I'm so messed up."

"It's good to step back and think about it," Bellamy says slowly. "And talk to us about it. We're here for you."

"That's exactly why I'm here. I knew I needed some distance. Some perspective."

"Apparently narcissists do that stuff so they can get the love and affection they need, because their self-worth is so low. Did it seem like that?" Nori cocks her head.

"No. Definitely not. He *is* hard on himself because of his introversion but not like that. He knows who he is. Like, he knows he's a good hockey player. He knows he can make the team better."

"Were there any other red flags?" Shantae asks.

I think back.

"Not respecting your boundaries," she offers.

"No."

"Checking in with you all the time?"

"No." I shake my head and sip my drink. "Not an excessive amount. He's very good at text messaging." I give them a wistful look. "He's kind of shy about talking, but when he has time to think about what he wants to say, he's really good at it."

"Was he jealous of other men?"

"I don't think so..." I think back to that night at Uncle Ernie's when the other guys were being kind of inappropriate, and I caught a look on Ben's face that was... unhappy. But it wasn't exactly jealous. Maybe a little possessive but not in a creepy way that set off alarm bells for me. More like he was worried that the guys were offending me, or not respecting me.

Our fresh drinks arrive and I push aside my empty glass and pick up the new one.

When the waiter has left, Shantae asks, "Does he have friends? Because guys with no friends are a red flag."

"He's... quiet," I say. "He likes to be alone. He does have friends, though. He really cares about his teammates. And they love him."

"Has he tried to contact you since that night?"

I look down. "He sent one text message saying he's sorry he upset me, and to take the time I need. Nothing else." He could have blown up my phone, demanding I answer him and see him. But he didn't.

"Ohhhh," they all say on a long exhale.

"You need to talk to him," Shantae concludes. "Tell him how you were feeling. That'll be the test, because if he's a narcissistic love-bomber he'll lose his shit when you confront him about it."

I consider that. It's true. But I already know. I already know Ben will not lose his shit when I tell him I freaked out because of things Julian did in the past. I already know he didn't lose his shit because I told him I need space.

"Whoa." Nori looks up from her phone. "I just googled him."

I lift my eyebrows.

"Have you seen this?" She holds her phone up to me.

I lean over to look at the screen.

At first I can't make sense of what I'm seeing. It's Julian, with his hands over his face. Bleeding. And Ben. Looking... fierce.

I frown and grab the phone to read what it says on the post. My eyebrows shoot up and I look at my friends, bug-eyed. "Ben punched Julian in the face."

"Whaaaaat!"

I read the post which ends with "no charges have been laid." I lower the phone. "Oh my God."

Shantae takes the phone and peers at it. "Wow. This is giving... knight in shining armor."

"Are you sure?" Nori asks with a worried look. "It could be giving psycho with anger management issues."

"He was defending Mabel. He punched the guy who abused her."

I blink. "I'm confused. Julian was in Newark, at the Hargrave Center? That's... weird."

"He was looking for you," Bellamy guesses.

"You think? But... I still don't get it." I shake my head. "Hang on, I'll text Marek."

I pull out my own phone and send off a message to my brother. "Thanks for being here, you guys."

"Of course. You are amazing, Mabel. Julian was a total jerk and anyone who doesn't see how amazing you are can suck rocks."

I laugh. "Thank you."

"And that includes your parents," she adds. "They should be on your side. Not Julian's."

"Yeah. Thank you. I kept telling myself I didn't care what they thought, but truthfully it kind of hurt that they thought I was better off with Julian."

"I'm sure that's not true," Shantae says gently. "I'm sure they wanted you to be happy."

"*Their* idea of happy. Mature and settled down."

"It's not like you're stoned or day drinking every day."

"Just today," I say with a laugh. "Oh wait, there was also the day Ben and I went shopping. We spent the rest of the afternoon doing tequila shots with some Australian guys in a pub... and I did blow off an interview because I was high on a gummy... oh, shit." I look at them all in dismay. "I *am* a cornflake!"

They all chuckle.

"No, you're not," Bellamy says. "You don't do that every day." She pauses. "Do you?"

"No. Of course not. I've been working hard to find a job. But you have to have fun sometimes, right?"

"Right."

"You have a degree, you had a good job, you're responsible and mostly mature," Nori says with a grin. "You are not a cornflake."

My phone pings and I read the message from Marek. "Julian *was* looking for me," I tell my friends slowly. "He saw pictures of me with Ben at the fundraiser, so he went to the arena. He was demanding Ben tell him where I am."

"Oh, God." Bellamy winces.

"Ben punched Julian and told him to never talk to me again."

"Go Ben!" Shantae cheers.

The others laugh.

My heart does some kind of complicated gymnastics move in my chest. "But it's not all good. Now he's in trouble with team management. And he was working so hard to be made captain." I close my eyes, my throat squeezing. "I hope he didn't mess that up by sticking up for me."

When I open my eyes my friends all look worried and sympathetic.

"I hope not, too," Bellamy says. "But I'm impressed with this guy."

"I don't know if punching people is a good idea," I protest. "I mean, he does it on the ice. But off the ice it can get you arrested."

"True," Shantae says. "But I still like him for it. Because Julian's a jerk."

I sit quietly for a few minutes, thinking. Then I say, "I appreciate Ben sticking up for me. But I really need to stick up for myself."

"You did," Bellamy says. "You left Julian."

"But he hasn't given up. He's basically stalking me. I need to put an end to that." I raise my chin. "I have to go talk to Julian."

"Ooooh." They all make identical noises of concern.

"Not alone, you're not," Bellamy declares. "I'm going with you."

"We'll all go with you." Nori nods.

"When and where?" Shantae says.

"Right now." I set down my mimosa.

"No, honey, we can't go right now. We've all been drinking."

"Right, right." I press my fingertips to one eyebrow. "We've had a butt-load of champagne."

"A buttload?" Nori looks at me skeptically.

"It's an actual wine measurement."

They all give me a look.

"It is! It's a hundred and twenty-six gallons of wine. Way back, seafaring merchants shipped wine and booze in big wooden casks, which came in different sizes. A rundlet was the smallest and a tun was the biggest, and a tun equals two butts."

"Your mind is a scary place," Shantae says.

I laugh. "Okay, we'll go tomorrow."

"I can take a day off," Shantae says.

"I don't work tomorrow," Nori adds.

"I'll drive," Bellamy says.

"Won't he be at work?" Shantae asks.

"Yes. And that is perfect."

* * *

"What do you need?" Bellamy asks the next morning. "What did you bring for clothes?"

"I'll wear what I always wear. That'll piss him off."

I do my makeup, curl my hair into messy waves, and change into ripped jeans, a cropped black sweater, and my Doc Martens.

"You look snatched," Bellamy says.

"Thank you."

"Okay, let's go."

I grab my purse. Bellamy picks up Shantae and Nori and then we set out on our two-hour-plus drive to Sherrinford.

Halfway there, my phone rings. Frowning, I check the call display. Ope! It's the Newark Public Library! I let out a little screech.

"What? What?" the others all demand.

"I have to take this call. Shhhh." I wave a frantic hand.

I speak to the woman who interviewed me and almost black out when she says they're offering me the job. Branch manager and adult and teen librarian. Full time. Dental and health insurance, paid time off, a retirement plan. I will have to work every other Saturday but that's not unexpected. They're going to courier the written job offer. I don't tell her I'm actually in Pennsylvania right now. I'll go back to Marek's place tomorrow.

When I end the call, I punch a fist in the air and yell, "Woooooohooooo!"

"What, what?" Bellamy asks. "Was that about a job?"

"Yes! Newark Public Library branch manager!"

They all cheer and my heart swells with their delight.

Now I'm even more eager to confront Julian. More confident. I'm no longer unemployed. In fact, I'll be *branch manager*. And soon I'll have a home of my own. I am moving *on*. And up!

On campus, I direct Bellamy to the parking garage in the red brick building that houses Julian's faculty. I've been here a few times. I know where his office is, although he could be teaching right now. Or having lunch. We stopped for food when we got to town, so it's nearly one in the afternoon.

"Damn." He's not in his office. I turn to my friends. "Let's check the faculty lounge."

They nod and follow me down the hall like a team of avenging angels, all of us striding with heads held high. I open the door of the lounge and walk in. The room is a little shabby, with old furniture and a worn rug on the floor.

All heads turn and look at me. I recognize a couple of faces, wearing expressions of surprise.

I don't care. I sweep the room with my gaze and it lands on Julian, standing over by the coffee machine. I march over to him in my black boots and stop in front of him. "How's your nose?"

He blinks. "Mabel. What are you doing here?"

He looks fine, other than a smudge of darkness beneath his right eye. "I'm here to tell you something."

"Uh..."

Stay calm. "I need you to listen to me."

His gaze flicks to my three friends standing behind me, basically blocking him in.

"I need you to stop trying to contact me," I say clearly. "You went to New Jersey looking for me when I've told you we are done and I don't want to see you again. That was inappropriate. In fact, that was stalking me. I will not let that happen." I hold his gaze. "You deserved what happened."

His face tightens and his lips thin. Once more he glances at the others in the room.

"You treated me like I was an object that belonged to you. But I'm *not* an object. And I *don't* belong to you. You are a narcissist and you hated that I left. That I rejected you. That I ignored you. That's the worst thing that can happen to you, isn't it?"

His mouth opens but he says nothing.

"You need people to admire you. You can't feel good about yourself on your own. But I am not going to do that. We are *done*. And I have a whole squad of pissed-off women behind me." I wave my arm in a dramatic gesture. "Not to mention a team of big, brawny hockey players who know how to fight."

His eyes flicker.

Wow. He's... speechless. I consider this a win.

I'm sure he's going to be absolutely furious about this, though. This is his worst nightmare – being called out, held accountable, embarrassed.

"Do not call my parents again," I warn him. "Do not call my brother again."

"And definitely don't call *me* again." Bellamy steps forward.

I turn to her. "He was calling you, too?"

"Until I blocked his number." She looks at him. "I've met a lot of pricks in my life, but you, Julian, are definitely a cactus."

I snort-laugh.

"If you ever contact her again," Nori says, looking scary despite her petite size and delicate features, "I will find you and shove a penny up your eyelid and tape it shut."

"Is that clear enough?" I ask him. "Don't make me bring the New Jersey Storm here to deliver the message. Or the police."

He doesn't answer, just stands there looking pissed, his face red, his lips thin.

"That also means you will leave Ben Antonov alone. No charges. No lawsuit. Got it?"

His jaw tightens.

"Say it, Julian." I hold his gaze steadily.

"No charges," he says in a low voice. "No lawsuit."

I want to cheer, but I keep my face neutral. "Okay. Let's go, girls."

I whirl around and whisk out of the room with them behind me. I turn in time to see Shantae giving Julian the middle finger salute as she leaves. "You, sir, are the reason God created the middle finger."

We make our way outside before we collapse into nervous yet relieved laughter.

"A cactus!" I chortle. "Oh my God, I love you, besties."

"We love you, too. Let's get out of here."

We hustle back into Bellamy's car and hit the road again. She starts a playlist and we sing along, belting out, "Karma is my boyfriend!" at the top of our lungs.

I have the drive home to think about everything. Everything that just happened. Everything we talked about yesterday. Things I talked to Ben about. Like, how the first girl he told he loved bailed on him right away. How humiliated he was by that. How I basically did the same thing.

Oh, God.

How that other girl wanted him to be different. And I worried that he thought *I* was trying to change him by helping him communicate better. But then he reminded me that I said he was fine the way he was. And I meant it.

I understand his guardedness when it comes to relationships. I know how hard it is to trust someone after you've been hurt. It's hard for everyone, but probably even more so for someone introverted who already has a hard time being vulnerable.

And I realize what a step that was for him to tell me he loves me. How brave he was. How much he must have trusted me to say that. And I didn't trust *him*.

But no... it's not Ben I didn't trust. Even when he went overboard with the gifts and compliments, it wasn't that I didn't trust him. I didn't trust *myself*.

I believed in Ben. I know in my heart and my soul that he's a good guy – a "straight arrow" who in high school everyone thought was boring but now I see is honorable and decent and hard-working.

Ben is not like Julian. Not at all. I've been afraid to trust my own judgment, but with a little distance and time, I know I can rely on my instincts. And I need to talk to Ben and tell him that. Like, right now.

I need to get back to him. I'm afraid I've ruined something great with a guy I like and admire and maybe even... love.

26

BEN

My meeting with Coach has my gut feeling like a giant hand is squeezing it.

I know I fucked up. I admit it. I'll face the consequences of my actions. If they no longer want me to be captain of the team, so be it. But I could not let that shit goblin get away with hurting Mabel. I'd do it again.

Mr. Miller is in Coach's office too when I arrive there. Great.

They gesture for me to take a seat, and Mr. Miller slides the door of the office closed, soundproofing us in.

I rub my palms on the knees of my dress pants but I hold their gazes when they talk.

"So do you want to tell us your version of what happened yesterday?" Coach says.

"You've already heard a version?"

"We heard from the security guard who was on duty yesterday. And a couple of other people."

I pull in a slow breath, nodding. "Okay. Here's my version. That guy is an abuser who hurt someone I care about. I admit I hit him. But he deserved it and I'd do it again."

They regard me silently.

"Is he... pressing charges?" I ask.

"No. We've talked to Legal about it, though. He still could."

"I'll deal with that if I have to. I'm sorry if I've put the team in a bad spot. It was totally my fault. And I understand if you're taking my name off the list of possible captains."

They exchange glances.

"We considered that," Mr. Miller says. "But we wanted to get all the facts."

"I understand."

"Marek came to talk to me earlier," Coach says. "He wanted to explain what happened."

My jaw loosens. "He did?"

"Yeah." One corner of Coach's mouth lifts.

"He told us that the man you punched is his sister's ex-boyfriend."

I nod, my mind racing.

"He said Mr. Clark is an abuser. He said she was lucky to leave the relationship before he actually physically hurt her."

I blink a few times, shocked to my core that Marek told them this.

"Marek also said that you and his sister are in a relationship. And you were defending her."

I gnaw briefly on my bottom lip. "Yes. She left that guy a couple of months ago, and he's been trying to get back with her ever since. Trying to find her. And it was my fault he did. He saw pictures of Mabel and me at the Keeping Kids Safe fundraiser, so he came here looking for me. And he found me." I lift my chin. "He demanded to know where Mabel is. I'd say I lost my cool, but the truth is, I knew exactly what I was doing."

"Marek said Mr. Clark is lucky *he* wasn't there or he would have hit him, too."

I huff a tiny laugh. "Oh, boy." This makes my breath tighten in my chest. Smitty was defending me. A sense of relief slides through me that I didn't permanently wreck our friendship by getting involved with his sister. And hiding it from him.

"Okay, yeah, that was a lapse in judgment," Mr. Miller says. "We wanted to talk to you and hear your explanation before making a decision."

I nod, keeping my mouth shut.

"You've taken responsibility," he continues. "And while we can't condone that kind of thing..." He glances again at Coach. "We understand the reasons for it."

Something loosens in my chest. A bit.

"So... we won't announce the decision until after the end of the season. Right now, we're focused on making the playoffs and seeing how far we can go. But you will be our next team captain."

My breath leaves me all at once. I try to keep my face stoic. I swallow. "Thank you, sir."

"We've been watching you step up," Coach adds. "You've really stepped into the leadership role we hoped for. We hear great things from Sue Milner about your interactions with the organization, how you've really embraced their mission."

"Thank you. It's all been... easier than I expected."

Because of Mabel.

They smile.

"Glad to hear that," Mr. Miller says.

"I'll work my hardest to be a good leader for this team," I tell them. "I care about these guys and I want them to feel that thrill of holding the Cup one day."

Mr. Miller rises and claps a hand on my shoulder. "As do I, Ben. As do I."

I leave Coach's office feeling somewhat better. Now I just have to deal with Mabel and what's going on with her. She's been in Philadelphia for a few days. I don't know for sure if she's coming back. Smitty says she left her stuff here but she'd talked about moving farther away so that doesn't make me feel optimistic.

I go to the locker room to get my bag for our trip to Charleston. The bus leaves for the airport in a few minutes.

I've been beating myself up about being too loose with the "L word". But over a few days some of my anger at myself has faded. I was honest with Mabel. If she doesn't feel the same, she should at least do me the courtesy of telling me. We're not sixteen, like I was with Hannah. We're both adults. If she's ghosting me, that is not cool.

I have a hard time seeing Mabel do something like that, though.

Ghosting is not her style; she's open and sincere and doesn't have any issues approaching people. Like I do.

So then I go back to wanting her to have the time she needs to deal with whatever she's dealing with. It's a fucking roller coaster of emotions and I don't like it.

But I have other things I need to focus on. We have a game tonight. A big game, since we're still battling Charleston in the standings.

27

MABEL

I'm sitting in the Philadelphia airport, waiting for a flight to Charleston.

I was going to take the train back to Hoboken but then I decided to check the Storm's schedule and discovered they're playing in Charleston tonight. And after that they have games in Tampa and Fort Lauderdale. They won't be home until Sunday night! I can't wait for that long to talk to Ben!

So I booked a flight to Charleston. Yes, it was impulsive. I've been trying so hard not to be reckless with my spending while I'm unemployed, but I had to do this. At least I have a job now!

My flight is delayed – gah! I need to get there before the game! Frustration creates a rising pressure inside me and I try to distract myself and make good use of the time to do some research. I look at the library branch where I'll be working and where the Path stations are. I check out apartments, then make arrangements to look at a few places in Harrison. I'm a little freaked out about the rents, but I think I can manage it on my salary.

My flight is delayed again. Deep breath.

I text Marek to find out what hotel the team is staying at in Charleston.

MAREK

Where are you and what are you doing?

MABEL

I'm at the airport waiting for a flight to Charleston. I need to talk to Ben.

MAREK

Oh hell yeah you do

I frown at my phone.

MABEL

What does that mean?

MAREK

The guy's crazy about you. He's worried. He thinks he screwed up

MABEL

I know, I know, but it was my fault! I want to tell him that

MAREK

Good. Do you care about him too?

I press my lips together, a rush of emotion nearly choking me.

MABEL

Yes

MAREK

Good

I chew my bottom lip, then tap in another message.

MABEL

So you're okay with that?

MAREK

Yeah. He's a good guy. He cares about you. You two are good together.

Now tears threaten, my sinuses stinging. I blink rapidly.

MABEL
Thank you.

MAREK

I need to call you. Texting is bugging me.

My phone rings.

"Hi?"

"I'm pissed at you." Marek's talking in a low voice, as if trying not to be overheard.

"About Julian?"

"Yeah."

"Will you listen to me if I explain things?"

"Yeah. Although Ben did a pretty good job of it."

Oh. "What did he tell you?"

"That you were embarrassed. Ashamed."

I swallow. "Yes. I felt so stupid for getting involved with someone who was such a jackass to me. I was going to tell you, really. I just wanted to get my life back together so you all would know I'm not a complete dumpster fire."

I tell him all the things, my fears, my humiliation.

"I wish I'd been there that day so I could've punched him, too," Marek says fiercely. "If he ever comes near you again, I'll cut off his balls with a skate blade and choke him with his own dick."

I splutter out a laugh. "Whoa! Easy, there."

"Not even kidding."

"I'm sorry that Ben and I didn't tell you about us. We were staying in your home, hiding stuff from you. I'm sorry."

"I get it." He sighs. "I'm sorry, too. I'm sorry I doubted you. I thought you were being your impulsive self and bailing on a good thing. I should have trusted you to know what you were doing."

"Yes. You should have. And that's what made it even harder to tell you... that I *did* screw up by getting involved with a guy like that."

"Fuck. I'm so sorry."

"I really care about Ben," I tell my brother. "You talked to him? Are you guys okay?"

"We're good."

"Good."

He gives me the deets on where they're staying and what time they leave for the arena.

"Oh! Gotta go! They're making an announcement about my flight."

"Okay. Love you."

The flight is delayed again.

Now they're saying our departure time is 1.10 p.m. It's about a two-hour flight. The team is leaving for the arena at four. I might make it? Gah!

I go up to talk to the gate agent. I don't want to be that person and I know there's nothing she can do, which is in fact the case, but I feel I have to try something. Short of sprouting wings, there's not much else I can do.

* * *

Once we land, I take a taxi from the airport to the Hyatt, embarrassingly asking the driver if she can "step on it."

"What's the rush, hon?" she asks, pulling out into traffic.

"I need to talk to the man I love. I have to get there before four o'clock."

"Ah. Okay, then. I gotchoo." She speeds up.

I fidget and bounce in the back seat of the car, compulsively checking the time and our location on my phone. It's going to be close. I only need a few minutes. But I don't want to do this in front of the whole team. Or... who cares? I'll do it any way I can. I just need to make sure he knows I love him and I figured out that I could trust my feelings.

Then we get stuck in traffic.

Of course we do.

"Busy here for the game tonight," my driver says cheerfully.

"Yeah." I sigh.

We pull up at the front of the hotel and a big bus is parked there. No doubt the bus taking the team to the arena. I pay the driver and jump out with my carry-on bag. I can't tell if anyone's on the bus because of the heavily tinted windows. Crap.

Maybe they're still inside? I start toward the hotel door... aaand the bus pulls away.

I let out a small scream, attracting the concerned attention of a few people around me.

I grab the door handle of the taxi I just exited and yank it open. "Follow that bus!"

"Hon, you really do think we're in a movie, don't you?"

"Can you do it?"

"I can do it."

I climb back in, dragging my suitcase with me.

I send a frantic message to Marek between distraught glances out the front window to make sure the bus is still in sight.

MABEL

I'm in a taxi behind your bus. Can you get Ben aside when you guys get off?

MAREK

WTF

MABEL

My flight was delayed. I need to talk to him!

MAREK

This is a lot of drama

MABEL

Can you do it

MAREK

I'll try

It's only a few blocks to the arena. You'd think they'd walk, these strapping athletes. Jeez. They're just pampered, spoiled rich boys.

The bus enters a loading dock to go into the arena.

"I can't follow it there, hon," the taxi driver says.

"Are you sure?" I shake my head. "No, no. It's okay. Let me out here." I pay her again and haul my suitcase out.

I start down the ramp but am immediately halted by security. "I'm Marek Smits' sister." I beam a smile. "He plays for the Storm? He knows I'm here. We need to talk."

The guy frowns and shakes his head.

Aaargh.

"Really. I'm supposed to be here." I muster every bit of fake confidence I can. "It's okay to let me in. It'll just be for a few minutes."

"I can't do that."

I consider flashing my boobs.

"Oh, watch out! The bus is backing up!" I point behind the guard's shoulder.

He turns to look.

I dart around him and sprint down the ramp, dragging my pink suitcase.

"Hey!"

Marek and Ben appear.

"Oh, thank God!" I run right up to them. "That guy wouldn't let me in!"

"Jesus, Mabel." Marek shakes his head. "Sorry, man. She's my sister."

"She can't be in here!"

"I know, I know, it's just for a minute."

"Okay. Fine."

I scowl at the security guy. "I just told you that! You couldn't listen to *me*? Jeez."

"You have one minute," Marek says, and backs away.

I turn to Ben.

"What is happening?" he mutters.

Holy crappleberries, he looks good. He's wearing his charcoal suit with a silvery gray shirt and tie in checkered shades of blue, fuchsia, orange, and gray. The jacket hugs his powerful shoulders and lean waist, and the pants are snug enough to see not only his thigh muscles but the outline of his... phone.

He looks so handsome and precious and my heart lodges in my throat. I clasp my hands together and stare at him as words back up behind the blockage in my esophagus. Have I lost my chance with this man? Am I too late?

"I'm sorry," I choke out. "I'm sorry I freaked out."

One corner of his mouth lifts.

"I had to talk to you." Now I grab his hands, well, one hand, he's got a coffee cup in the other. I squeeze. "I went to visit my friends and we talked and then I went to see Julian…"

His eyes widen, then narrow.

"And I told him off and told him to leave you alone, and well, me too, and then I wanted to see you, to tell you that I love you and it wasn't that I didn't trust you or believe you, it was that I didn't trust *myself*, because Julian made me doubt everything. I felt overwhelmed. Julian showered me with gifts and expensive dates and compliments when we first started dating. I didn't know at the time that it was love-bombing." I pause. "Have you heard of that?"

"No." He moves his head slowly side to side, eyes fastened on my face.

"It's what narcissists do to manipulate you and make you feel indebted to them. Dependent on them."

His eyes flash.

"At first it made me feel good. I felt wanted. For a girl who hadn't had much luck in the romance department, it boosted my ego."

His jaw tightens. And he listens. As always. My heart squeezes.

"But then he'd do shitty things like ask for the designer bag he bought me back, because I did something he didn't like. And he started doing other things. I've told you."

He nods tersely.

"Anyway, that night of the fundraiser, you were being so generous with the flowers and the chocolates and the compliments. At first, I thought it was sweet… I mean, I still do think it was sweet, but when you gave me that poem, which wasn't like you at all, and then you told me you loved me and oh, God, I feel so horrible for how I reacted because I know what happened to you before and how you must have felt, but I panicked because it felt like love-bombing again, like it was too much and too fast and I needed some space to process it and think about it."

His face changes as I talk, his eyes closing briefly, his mouth thinning.

"And you gave me that space." I squeeze his hand again. "You gave me what I needed even though I didn't handle it well and you were probably sorry that you said what you said because I'm such an idiot."

His fingers curl around mine. "You're not an idiot."

My throat constricts. "I ran away. But I needed to do that. I needed to think. I needed to talk to my friends. It helped. I could see that you are nothing like Julian. *Nothing.*" I hold his gaze. "And I am so, so sorry for over-reacting."

He steps closer and bends his head to me. "I was a little pissed that you took off like that," he admits, his voice low. "But I did recognize that I probably came on too strong. And I was pissed at myself for doing that. I should have known better."

"No! Don't ever be mad at yourself for being vulnerable. I know how hard it is. And I'm sorry I didn't react well. You were brave to do those things. To s-say that." I choke up a little. "I want to be the person you feel brave enough to be vulnerable and honest with."

His eyes warm and soften.

"And... I love you, too," I say, digging deep for my own courage.

"Oh. Mabel."

"This is the ugliest place in the world to tell you that." I let go with one hand and swipe at my wet eyes, standing at the bottom of a concrete loading dock leading into the bowels of the arena with HVAC equipment and machinery rumbling around us, people buzzing around getting ready for the game.

The corners of his mouth lift. "Not the most romantic place, no. But I'll take it."

We smile into each other's eyes.

"Benny!"

We both look to see Marek gesturing from down the hall.

"I gotta go."

"I know. I just wanted to tell you that. We can talk more later. If you want."

"Yeah." He bends and brushes his mouth over mine. "Are you coming to the game?"

"I... I don't have a ticket." I press the back of my hand to my nose. "But I can try to get one."

"Okay. Come back to the hotel after."

I nod. "I have your room number."

His eyebrows elevate.

I shrug. "I have connections. Will you get in trouble if I sneak into your room?"

"Yes." He pauses. "But only if we get caught."

"I'll be careful. I know you're already in trouble because of me."

"Benny! Get your ass in here!"

"Go." I let go of his hand and he takes a few steps backward, shaking his head as if he can't believe what just happened. "Good luck!" I punch a fist in the air. "Go Storm!"

28

MABEL

I find my way to the box office and purchase a single ticket right behind the Storm's bench. It's expensive as hell, but oh well. It's still a couple of hours until the doors open so I head outside and find a bar, where I pass the time with a couple of margaritas and a basket of chips.

My mind is a jumble of thoughts, my heart a tangle of emotions. I'm not sure I can even believe what just happened. That Ben loves me. And I love him. And it's going to be okay.

There are still things we need to talk about. But I feel like it's going to be okay.

I find my seat just as the warm-up starts. I see when Ben notices me and I smile.

I love watching him in his element, so confident and skilled and fearless. It makes me proud. And turns me on.

Oh my God. Only few minutes into the first period and Ben lays a brutal hit on one of the Cyclone. He did the same thing that first time I watched him play, and the Storm ended up winning that night.

Ben also got in a fight that game.

It seems like Ben is everywhere: hitting, passing, shooting the puck. He's playing with a different center right now since Carson is still recovering from the car accident, but he and Macklin Murray seem to have found a rhythm, along with their right winger, Chris Turkett. Ben sets up each of them for a goal and then scores himself, giving the team a three-nothing lead going into the second period.

It's so exciting to watch!

In the second period, the Cyclone seem to regroup. They score right away, and then score again near the end of the period, making it a one-goal game. Eeeek.

Along with the rest of the crowd, I'm on the edge of my seat for the third period. The Cyclone are fighting back, but the Storm are stopping them at every turn. I can't stop smiling. And gasping. And sighing.

Then the Cyclone score again to tie it up. Dammit! There's still lots of time for them to get the go-ahead goal. Except the Storm coach, Gord Bastien, challenges the goal on the basis of the player who scored being offside. Oooooh.

The crowd doesn't like this.

The game is on hold as the video is reviewed. And reviewed. And reviewed. We all watch the replays from different angles on the score clock screen, looking at the Cyclone player with the puck cross the blue line and also another Cyclone crossing the blue line.

I bite my lip as I watch the replays. It's so close it's hard to tell. The player without the puck looks like he's trying to hold up, but his skate blade seems to cross the blue line before the puck. I know it's the position of the player's skate and not his stick that's the determining factor. If both skates are over the blue line before the puck, the player is offside. And his back foot is so, so close...

Finally, the situation room makes their decision and the ref announces the decision. "After video review... the play is offside..."

"Yes!" I jump up to cheer, earning dirty looks from the Cyclone fans around me.

"There is no goal!" he finishes, to loud boos and jeers from the home-town crowd.

This seems to take the wind out of the Cyclone's sails, which is a couple of mixed metaphors right there, and this time Marek wins the faceoff, gets the puck to Dillon, heads to the net, and when Dillon shoots the puck, Marek tips it in for another goal.

"Yeah!"

Now we're up by two goals and it feels safer, but I'm still on edge as the Cyclone pull their goalie and swarm the Storm's net for the last few minutes. So many times I think they're going to score, and Ford makes some incredible saves and we hold them off until the horn blows to end the game.

We did it!

And Ben is named first star of the game.

* * *

Back at the hotel, I hang out in the bar, keeping an eye on the lobby to watch for the arrival of the team. When I see them throng into the lobby, all the big guys in suits and smiles, I turn my back in case anyone sees me. I give them time to go to their rooms before I stealthily make my way to the elevators and go up to the eighth floor. I peek both ways down the hall before I exit and scurry to Ben's room. I knock softly on the door.

He immediately opens it. And smiles.

He's gorgeous, still in his suit, now a little rough looking with ruddy cheeks and tousled hair from his shower.

"Come in." He jerks his head and I hustle in with my suitcase that I had to leave in a bag check area at the arena during the game. He, too, peers out into the hallway.

"The coast is clear," I say, pulling out another clichéd movie line.

He closes the door and turns back to me and I can't stop myself. I launch myself into his arms.

He catches me and laughs. I wrap myself around him like a koala and kiss him all over his beautiful face. "You played amazing tonight!"

He turns us in a circle. "Fuck, yeah." He kisses me back and stumbles toward the bed. He lowers my feet to the floor then cups my face in both hands and kisses me again, so tenderly, and emotion flows through me like hot honey.

We undress each other and ourselves in a commotion of hands, still trying to kiss, stumbling and grappling and pulling at clothes until finally we're both naked. He picks me up and tosses me onto the bed in a display of strength that I thoroughly enjoy, then climbs on and moves over me. His eyes meet mine and our gazes lock in a heated connection as the hotel room fades away around us and my blood zings through my veins. The curve of his lips is seductive and his hand drifts down my body as his eyelids lower, his face moves closer to mine, and our lips meet again.

I slide a hand around his neck, kissing him back with everything I have, every feeling, every word I can't say right now. When we're both out of breath, he moves his mouth from mine, his forehead against mine, his nose alongside my nose, staring into my eyes with so much emotion I feel it in my chest, in my soul.

"I love you," he murmurs.

"I love you, too."

We kiss and kiss, hungrily, mouths wet and sliding, tongues licking into each other's mouths while one of his hands roams over my body and the other curls around my head. I touch him, too, gliding my hand over his strong shoulder, down and up his arm. He shifts back to look at my body, tracking his hand gliding over my thigh, tickling me, lightly scraping with his fingernails, squeezing, then pushing my thigh to the side, opening me. His fingers brush over the curls on my mound, making me ache even more.

"So beautiful," he murmurs. "I missed you so much, Mabel."

"I missed you, too."

He shifts again, moving over me, kissing my mouth, his hand coming up to cup my face, then sliding into my hair. I bend and lift the leg he pushed open, pressing my thigh against his hip, my pelvis lifting needily. He kisses my throat, the side of my neck, sucks so gently on my skin there, licks over it.

"I missed these beauties." He kisses each nipple, then bends over me, pulling me closer so he can pull one nipple into his mouth.

"Oh, God." I grip his hair, sensation shooting through me to my center.

Taking his time, he brushes his mouth and his beard over my sensitive skin, kissing my nipple, licking it, then sucking again. Fever spreads over my skin, burning hot.

I lift my leg over his hip, trying to pull his lower body closer to mine because I need him there, so much. His hand moves to my butt, tickling and lightly scratching there as he sucks my nipple, making me insane with so much sensation. I can't help myself, I move against him, my body beginning to writhe with need.

He pushes my leg off him, hand on my inner thigh, pressing my leg to the bed, and then he touches me *there*, right where I need him, between my legs, his hand cupping my pussy in a possessive, tender hold. My aching clit pulses against his palm. He finds my mouth with his again in deep, devouring kisses and his fingers move on me, teasing me, brushing over my clit, finding the liquid heat between my folds.

"I need to taste you here," he murmurs. "I need to lick you. Eat you up." He shifts onto his hands and knees, and with his gaze fastened on my face, he moves over me, sliding his arms under my thighs, palms coming to my stomach. I can't stop moving, my hips lifting, my hands gripping his hair, and then he opens his mouth on me.

"Oh, God!"

Yes, he eats at me, with his lips, his tongue, his whole mouth, sucking and tonguing me with such worship I'm mindless and hot and frantic. He cups my breasts, flicks my nipples, and turns me into a melted mass of pleasure, soft, boneless, fluid.

My thighs are over his shoulders, his mouth buried between them, and my fingers tug on his hair. "I'm c-coming…"

Pleasure twists up inside me, tighter, higher, until it's almost unbearable. I'm shaking, my heart thudding, my ears roaring. Cries of relief and ecstasy spill from my lips as the pleasure peaks and wave after wave of heat flows through my body until I'm weak and slack.

He rises onto his knees and takes his cock in hand. Then stops. "Fuck. I don't have a condom."

"I guess I should be glad you don't go on road trips with condoms."

"Do you have one?"

"No."

His lips quirk. "I guess I should be glad you don't chase after hockey teams on the road with condoms."

"I didn't plan to do that when I left home."

We smile at each other.

"I'm on birth control," I tell him, which he already knows; we had that conversation ages ago. "I'm okay without a condom if you are."

He nods slowly. "Are you sure?"

"I trust you. Do you trust me?"

"More than anyone in the world." He bends down to kiss me again, his mouth hot and firm on mine as the head of his cock notches at my entrance.

I know that. I feel it. For both of us trust is huge. For him to trust me enough to make himself vulnerable – emotionally, physically, intimately – means so much to me. And for me to trust him the same way, after opening myself up to someone who saw my vulnerability as a weakness, who used it against me, is so freeing and empowering. I feel like me again. "I love you," I gasp.

He proceeds with agonizing slowness, drawing out the pleasure and the anticipation of having him inside me, moving the head of his cock lazily through my slickness. My arms are up on the pillow by my head, my chin lifted, my mouth open as I try to get air into my lungs, my body still vibrating with need. "Please. Push in. I need it."

He smiles, a little bit smug. "You need my cock?"

"I need you."

"I... *Christ*, Mabel... look at you taking me..." He gives me an inch. And withdraws. "I love watching this." Two inches. And out. And in... more.

"Fuck me, fill me, give it all to me..." I blink up at his face and from the tight expression I see he's torturing himself, too.

He teases me, slipping in and out. I'm empty and aching and greedy, ready to sob at how much I crave him. "Ben..."

"I can't stop looking at you... at us... but I'm so close..." A groan rumbles from his chest.

I'm barely conscious, floating, needing, wanting, trying to lift my hips and take him deeper.

And then he's in, pressing, gliding, filling me. I cry out with the beauty of it.

"So hot, baby. I love being bare inside your sweet pussy." His hands grip my inner thighs, holding them apart as he moves, thrusting in measured strokes. I can't stop the noises that cascade from my lips as he penetrates me so deeply, so lusciously. I grip his wrists and move his hands up, to my waist then my breasts, and he curves his fingers around me and gently squeezes. "I love having your wet all over me."

"That feels so good." I gulp in air. "You fill me up so good."

On his knees, he presses one hand flat between my breasts, his heavy cock sliding in and out of me. I watch his body, the perfect V shape of him between my legs, the tight abdomen and trail of hair over his lower belly to the thick nest of hair at the root of his cock. The lamp light gleams golden on his skin, gilding the hair on his burly thighs, highlighting the muscles of his shoulders, arms, and chest. "Ohhhhhh."

"Fuck, that feels good. Bare... skin to skin... Jesus, Mabel." When I contract my inner muscles, he lets out a low growl. "Oh, yeah."

Our eyes meet, his blazing with a golden flame, full of worship and devotion. With him, I feel safe. I feel beautiful and strong and safe. I'm so grateful to have this man in my life, when I thought I was done with men and relationships, when I thought I'd never find anyone who loved me for who I am. I want to give him so much – anything. Everything.

I watch his face, entranced as his eyes fall closed, his long eyelashes resting on his cheeks, and then he falls over me, taking his weight on his elbows, his arms sliding around my head, one hand coming to my forehead in a possessive, protective gesture that soothes my heart and makes me melt around him. I hook my ankles at the small of his back and wrap my arms around his neck as our mouths meet again. The press of his body against mine, skin to skin, is voluptuous and substantial, his body hot and solid against mine. Heaven. Home.

Our bodies push together, seeking more, finding a rhythm that matches our heartbeats, his breath a hot gust over the skin of my neck. Then he kisses me, a gentle kiss of such devotion, tears spring to my eyes.

Our mouths fuse together as the pace of his thrusts accelerates and I lift to him, ripples of pleasure coursing through my body. He goes rigid and tight against me, his cock pulsing. I squeeze him with my inner muscles and he shouts and fills me with liquid heat, his movements wetter, slicker. It's erotic and intimate. It's reverence and tenderness. It's trust and love.

He goes still against me, pressing his mouth to the side of my neck. I kiss his shoulder, both of us fighting for oxygen, our bodies damp and sticky and quivering. Then he moves, a long, slow glide out, back in, out, in.

"So sweet," he mumbles. "So gorgeous. Perfect."

Perfect.

29

BEN

"I had pregret." I stroke Mabel's hair back off her face where she lies on the pillow next to me in the hotel bed. We're talking about what happened when Julian showed up at the arena looking for her.

"Um... what?" She peers up at me with a puzzled notch between her brows.

I trail my fingers over her cheek. Christ, she's beautiful. "Pregret. I knew what I was about to do was wrong, but I also knew I was going to do it anyway."

She chokes on a giggle. "Oh my God. I love that so much."

I grin.

"I'm glad you didn't really get in trouble about it," she says more seriously.

"Me, too."

I tell her about my subsequent conversations with Coach and Mr. Miller. "Smitty stood up for me. Or maybe it was for you. I had to tell him about Julian. I know I said I wouldn't but..."

"I understand." She hitches one shoulder. "We talked on the phone earlier. I was going to tell him at some point. And my parents."

"He seems to have come around about us being together, though."

"I knew he would."

"You did, huh?"

"Of course. You're a good guy. If my family thought Julian was good for me, they're going to loooove you."

"I guess I'll take that." I kiss her shoulder.

"Why did you write me a poem?"

"Oh, Jesus." I close my eyes and flop my head down on the pillow. "I blame the guys for that."

"They wrote the poem?"

"No, I wrote it. But it was their idea. I asked them how I could show you that I like you. They said I should make you laugh and hold the door for you and give you gifts and write a poem for you."

She cackles. "Oh my God! Really? They told you to write a poem for me. Ahahaha!"

I open my eyes and grin at her. "It seemed like a good idea at the time. I don't have a lot of experience with that kind of thing."

"'I like you a lot, even more than my beard?'" She chortles again.

I rub my beard. "It's true."

She manages to control her giggles. "I actually love the poem. Now that I'm not freaking out."

"'Just know that I'm awkwardly falling for you.'"

"Yeah." She holds my gaze. "I love that part the most. I know it's been fast and I just came out of a horrible relationship but there's a connection between us. I was mad at you for rejecting me when we were teenagers and I wanted to keep that anger going but I couldn't because you still fascinated me with your quiet and your introspection and how you don't say much but when you do it's something worth listening to." She lays her hand on my cheek. "I don't want you to think your introversion is something that needs to be fixed. I love you for it. I love that you talk when you have something important to say. I love how you listen and observe. I love how much you care about your team and your teammates, so much that you're willing to do hard things for them. And I love that you've taught me that being alone is important."

I smile, my gaze moving over her beautiful face. "Thank you. I love you because you try to understand me. You *do* understand me. And I think you're fascinating, too, how your mind works, the things you keep in that brain of yours, and how brave and open you are." I lean in to kiss her, softly. "That's why there's such a strong connection between us – because I feel seen and heard when I'm with you." I search her eyes. "I don't always feel seen and heard."

"Yes. We both know what it's like to be judged and found wanting. We both value the people in our lives we care about. And you have both feet firmly on the ground and that makes it easier to stay balanced, which I need."

"I don't feel judged with you," I continue. "I feel stronger. Brave enough to be vulnerable. I think being vulnerable is the only way to have a real connection with someone. At first when I realized I'd caught feelings for you, I was afraid to tell you. But I had to do it."

She nods slowly.

"Same goes for you. Just be yourself – quirky, beautiful, imperfect, fascinating."

Her eyes shine. "I promise I will always respect your need for privacy and alone time and to not be the center of attention. And I promise I won't phone you unless it's absolutely necessary."

I laugh. "Thank you. I promise I will answer your phone calls when you do. But only yours."

"That is the nicest thing you could say to me."

We smile into each other's eyes.

I've always thought I'd be happier if I could just be like everyone else. The world is made for extroverts. I worried that I'd never meet someone I'd feel comfortable enough with to be my real self. That nobody would ever take the time to get to know the real me enough to love me.

But with Mabel, I feel safe to be my true self. I can be weird or quiet or alone. She makes me feel like my thoughts matter. My feelings matter. My voice matters. I have something to offer the world and maybe it's different – but it still matters.

I kiss her with everything I have, pulling her soft, sweet curves against me, tangling my hair in her hand.

Long, hot moments later, she says breathlessly, "I haven't told you my best news yet."

She's told me all about her visit with her friends and their trip to confront Julian. I'm glad she has friends who have her back. And I'm proud of her for doing that. I hope he got the message loud and clear. "There's more?"

"I got a job!"

"Oh, hey! Really? Where? Which one?"

She tells me about the job offer and that the written offer will be waiting for her when she gets home.

"That's fantastic!" Happiness for her bursts in my chest like a cork popping off a bottle of champagne.

"They were happy I didn't have to give notice to an employer and I can start the week after next," she says. "And I've already been looking into supervisory courses, since I don't have experience with that."

"Congratulations. I'm glad it's a job you wanted."

"It'll be great experience. I know I have a lot to learn but I love learning. And I'm going to look at apartments... uh, shit, I have an appointment set up for Saturday. I have to get back."

"We leave in the morning for Fort Lauderdale."

She nods. "Right. I should book a flight, too." She pushes up to sitting and reaches for her phone.

While she finds a flight home, I find the extra key to my condo. When she's done, I hand it to her.

"What's this?"

"A key to my condo. I want you to have it."

"Why?" She takes it slowly and closes her fingers around it like it's precious. "I know your own space is important to you."

"It is. But I want you to know you can come into my space any time. And I want you to be there when I get home Sunday night."

Holding my gaze, she nods. "Okay." Her smile is luminous. "I will be."

And she is. She's home.

EPILOGUE
MABEL

"And now I would like to introduce the captain of the New Jersey Storm. Ben has played for the Storm for three seasons and has demonstrated his leadership skills on the ice and off the ice. We're pleased to have him as an ambassador for Keeping Kids Safe. Having someone like Ben join us and let kids know he believes in them and supports them is so important. His voice will be reassurance for kids who are in the recovery process, and encouragement for those who haven't come forward yet. Please welcome Ben Antonov."

I watch Ben walk up to the dais and join Sue Milner. He shakes her hand with a smile, then turns to the crowd gathered in the large, bright multi-purpose room at the new Keeping Kids Safe Center.

I know how nervous he was about this event, but I don't think anyone else would guess from his demeanor as he steps up to the microphone. It's his first public event since being officially named captain of the Storm a couple of weeks ago in mid-August.

"Thank you, Sue. I'm thrilled to be a part of this group and to give back to the community. I'm proud to use my voice and platform to give kids who need it a voice of their own. Hockey is a team sport, and kids who've experienced abuse also need a team around them. Keeping Kids Safe knows the importance of a coordinated effort to protect children and youth. As a hockey team, we go through a lot in a season, but that's really nothing compared to what some of these young people go through, so I'm happy to lend my support to this endeavor and to be on their team."

I clap along with the others, my smile so wide it hurts.

Ben continues. "Keeping Kids Safe has been fundraising for the last five years with the goal of opening this beautiful new space and doesn't it meet expectations?"

There's another brief round of applause.

"This building gives the ability to see kids from the initial investigation and right through. It's a calm and welcoming space, meant to help the difficult experience of reporting abuse. All the critical services that a family needs to work with are all together here under one roof." He pauses. "Child abuse is really hard to talk about, but hopefully we can open the conversation and strengthen community support. This space is beautiful and functional and I know we'll be able to help so many kids here. Oh! Hey now."

A big dog bounds up to Ben and dances around him.

Maya Pérez rushes up, chasing the dog. "Sorry! Rocky! I let go of the leash! Sorry!"

"That's okay." Ben crouches and rubs the dog's head. "Hey, Rocky, did you escape?"

Rocky gives Ben's face several enthusiastic licks and Ben laughs.

"He loves you so much," Maya says, grabbing the leash. "Come on, Rocky."

Grinning, Ben gives Rocky a few more rubs, then straightens. Everyone watching is smiling and murmuring watching Ben interact with the golden retriever. My heart grows three sizes.

He could be thrown off by the unexpected interruption, but he looks at ease. I mean, it's a dog. He loves dogs. More than he loves people. Ha ha.

"Rocky wants to make his presence known," Ben says. "He's an important member of the team here." He turns. "And now I'll introduce my boss, Marc Miller, GM of the New Jersey Storm."

Marc Miller joins him at the microphone. "Thanks, Ben. The New Jersey Storm organization is also proud to be a part of the Keeping Kids Safe Team. Ben is the first guy to stand up for his teammates and now he's standing up for this team, as well. On behalf of the Storm Youth Foundation, Ben and I are thrilled to present this check for fifty thousand dollars."

The applause is huge this time as Ben and Marc hold up a big fake check, and Sue beams and shakes their hands.

The grand opening ceremony of this beautiful new center finishes up.

I turn to Marek, Ford, Dillon, and Nash, all here to support their teammate and friend. "He did great."

"Of course he did," Dillon says.

I smile. It'll never be something Ben enjoys, but all the practice and preparation made it *look* easy for him, at least.

Ben makes his way over to us eventually. "Thanks for coming, guys." He looks around. "Where's Alfie?"

Carson Alford, AKA Alfie, was with us for a while. It's been a tough summer for him and his wife, after losing their child. This is the first time Carson's come out, as training camp starts soon. He's recovered from his physical injuries, but it will take longer to recover emotionally. Mentally.

"He had to go," I say quietly. "I think this was hard for him."

"I'm sure anything to do with kids is hard for him," Ford says quietly.

"Yeah." Dillon nods with a sad smile. "I'm glad he came, though. Hopefully we'll see more of him."

"We have to make sure we invite him," Ben says. "Even if we're just hanging out."

"I'm afraid I'm going to say something stupid around him." Ford frowns and rubs his jaw.

"I think we all are," Ben says. "But if we say something stupid, we apologize. It's better than not saying anything or ignoring him."

I smile at how Ben is the one encouraging people to speak up.

"Yeah, for sure." Nash nods.

"I'll tell you this," Ford says. "I'm never having kids. After hearing about abused kids this morning, and Alfie losing his son, it's never happening."

"Oh." I purse my lips. "You shouldn't let that stop you."

"Well, that's only part of it. Can you imagine me as a dad? Ha! A kid would drive me nuts. And I'm probably not the best role model."

I bite back a smile. He is a little eccentric. I think that's why I like him. And maybe he has a point about having children. Now. "Who knows what the future holds?" I say. "Maybe someday you'll meet a woman and fall in love with her and want a family with her."

He snorts. "Not gonna happen. Okay. Where are we going for lunch?"

Ben takes my hand as we follow his friends out of the building and we share a smile.

Yes, being part of a team is important. The Storm grew as a team last season, thanks to Ben's leadership. Ben is a part of this community team. And Ben and I are a team. A big part of that is trust. Trust is what turns people into a team and Ben and I had to learn to trust ourselves first. I didn't trust myself to listen to my own feelings or spend time alone, but I've learned so much from Ben about that. And I think he's learned from me that he can trust that his voice is worth listening to; with his team, in the community, and with me. Trust is built over time. We're still working on it and sometimes it's hard and takes a lot of introspection, but it's absolutely, definitely worth it. He's worth it. We're worth it.

"I loved your speech," I say as we lag behind the others walking to our cars. "I loved the part about being a team."

He smiles down at me.

"I love that we're a team. I just... worry..."

"What?" He stops walking and faces me, still holding my hand.

"I'm learning to trust myself again. I'm working on figuring out who I am again. But it's a work in progress."

"I told you before – we're *all* a work in progress."

"Yeah. But I'm still kind of messed up. I let you down once because I was scared. It could happen again." I meet his eyes.

His are warm and steady. "Will you tell me if it does?"

"Yes."

"Then we'll get through it together. Because we're a team."

ACKNOWLEDGMENTS

I'm so thrilled to have my first Boldwood book out in the world and I have so many people to thank for this! First of all, thank you to Emily Kim for making this deal! And of course, thank you to the entire Boldwood team for taking me on, welcoming me, making this a better book, and getting it out into the world. Special thanks to Kate Willoughby for being such a supportive and encouraging writing partner and nudging me along. I also have to thank Cathy Yardley for your amazing coaching on this book. Your ability to pinpoint issues and to know exactly what I'm trying to do is extraordinary! As always, thanks to my own little team: my invaluable assistant Stacey; Heather Roberts who helps promote my books; my daughter who does my bookkeeping and assists me at book signings; the gang in my reader group who are always there for me, especially Elizabeth and Amy. Also thank you to reviewers, bloggers, and influencers who read and review my books – you are all so appreciated. And to my readers, a couple of notes: if you've read my book *Back Check*, you'll know I re-used a joke. I'm sorry! I just had to do it; it was too good not to! And to my Aussie readers – I hope this time I used the term "dag" correctly! IYKYK. Of course, the biggest of thanks to all my readers. I am honored to share my stories with you.

ABOUT THE AUTHOR

Kelly Jamieson is a USA Today bestselling author of over fifty romance novels.

Sign up to Kelly Jamieson's mailing list for news, competitions and updates on future books.

Visit Kelly's website: www.bit.ly/kellyjweb

Follow Kelly on social media here:

facebook.com/KellyJamiesonRomanceAuthor
x.com/KellyJamieson
instagram.com/authorkellyjamieson
bookbub.com/authors/kelly-jamieson

LOVE NOTES

LOVE IN EVERY CHAPTER

WHERE ALL YOUR ROMANCE
DREAMS COME TRUE!

THE HOME OF BESTSELLING
ROMANCE AND WOMEN'S
FICTION

WARNING:
MAY CONTAIN SPICE

SIGN UP TO OUR
NEWSLETTER

https://bit.ly/Lovenotesnews

Boldwood

Boldwood Books is an award-winning fiction publishing company seeking out the best stories from around the world.

Find out more at www.boldwoodbooks.com

Join our reader community for brilliant books, competitions and offers!

Follow us
@BoldwoodBooks
@TheBoldBookClub

Sign up to our weekly
deals newsletter

https://bit.ly/BoldwoodBNewsletter

www.ingramcontent.com/pod-product-compliance
Ingram Content Group UK Ltd.
Pitfield, Milton Keynes, MK11 3LW, UK
UKHW021137100125
453395UK00001B/15

9 781836 336815